P9-DEO-260

THE UTMOST ISLAND

By the same author:

OUR LIVES HAVE JUST BEGUN

Henry Myers

THE
Utmost
Island

"Six days' sailing north of Britain
lies the Utmost Island of the Sullen Sea."
—PYTHEAS THE MASSILLIAN

Crown Publishers, Inc., *New York*

ABIGAIL E. WEEKS MEMORIAL LIBRARY
UNION COLLEGE
BARBOURVILLE, KENTUCKY

813.52
M996u

COPYRIGHT, 1951, BY HENRY MYERS

PRINTED IN THE UNITED STATES OF AMERICA BY
KINGSPORT PRESS, INC., KINGSPORT, TENNESSEE

To
Marion and Virginia

Men like to call each other "my boy." It is more than a pretense that they are not growing old: it is a wistful echo of those very distant days, many centuries ago, when it was taken for granted that boyhood never ended and old age never began.

Boys could grow up then and still be happy, for they had no disquieting need to readjust themselves at maturity; all their new experiences would be merely new games with new names, such as Money or Women or Weapons or Death, but games for all that, to be played by the rules that games have.

"THE SKY RESTS ON THE SHOULDERS OF FOUR DWARFS. They stand at its corners, holding it up, and their names are Nordri, Sudri, Ostri and Westri—"

—a man told his little son, about nine hundred and seventy-five years ago, one morning in Iceland. Today you tell a child such a thing—or would, if it hadn't been so long forgotten—to make him eat his breakfast; but ten centuries ago, when we trusted our eyes, you told it to him because it was true and he would have to learn it sooner or later.

The year 977 was a good time in which to be six years old. People knew then that a mountain might really be a giant; they had not yet reluctantly concluded that a giant was only a mountain. The obvious, unquestioned wonders that you saw, or thought you saw, were told to rapt son by rapt father, which indeed still goes on, though the wonders today are less amazing because there is less amazement. You tell me that fire is combustion. I prefer to think that fire is the god Lok, who also takes the shape of a salmon. It is I who seem to be right, because a leaping salmon looks like a leaping flame, and if you had argued with me about it in 977, I would have turned into a bear and killed you.

That is to say, I would have gone berserk. I would have put on a bear's sark—oh, very well, his *skin,* but it was wrong of you to forget the old words—and with his sark I would acquire his nature, and bite and claw and rend and foam at the mouth until you were lying dead before me, whereupon my frenzy would pass and I would regain my human form.

Of course the little boy never doubted these things. They were exciting, which was always an excellent reason for believing, and they were told him by his father, which was another. When the fabulous words came out through the great, flaming, red beard, they were twice believed, by teller and hearer. Throughout his life, the boy thought the Gods had red beards.

None of it was denied by his mother, for the reason that he had none. Divorce was easy and childbirth difficult: mothers were often lost, one way or the other.

His father was guide and teacher enough, for he knew all about growing up, having just done it. Together, they visited the plain whereon the hero Hjalmar had been given his choice of fighting either Angantyr's eleven brothers or Angantyr himself, and chose the latter because he was the more terrible and there would be more honor in killing him.

"Come forth, Angantyr! Come forth and fight!" the boy shouted, at anything that might be Angantyr with a changed shape. But the shadow or bush or fox knew better than to accept the challenge. His father smiled approvingly to see his son thus prepare for manhood, and his small person hungered for more such esteem.

It was the last time and the last place, yesterday in the tenth century in Iceland, when we could be aware of that kind of world and have that kind of fun. There never was so right a spot for it, so by itself, so suited to be the final stronghold of wonder. The Giants had built a surrounding wall of mist, with

2

the sea for a moat, to keep the world away. A boy might think of what lay beyond only because of the name of a place called Norway, whence his and other great-grandfathers had come, or the bones of Irish Christians whom those same great-grandfathers had found here and slain.

Living at the tail-end of an epoch that was about to pass, it was yet inconceivable that their life could ever be different. Any change, however slight, of custom, belief or pleasure, seemed impossible, absurd, to be hooted at if any madman were to dream it.

There was no premonition, no fleeting or uneasy vision, of the mighty transformation which was creeping toward them along the edges of Europe. Fate had not the heart to tell them that their dear and ancient ways would end, that the Middle Ages lay in ambush back of the horizon. The exulting berserk Hero, singing mocking songs as he flung spears from his burning house upon the foes who ringed it, would be replaced by the Knight Errant, with his rules and niceties, his quest, his blessing, and his sword for hire. Their Gods were going to die.

He must learn to be a Bonder. Since his father was a Bonder, it followed that he would be one, too, and must know how to rule the farm he would inherit.

"If you can do that better than the other Bonders," said his father, bribing him with a glittering future, "they may choose you to be a King; and the kind of King they make you will depend on the kind of Bonder you make yourself. You may be chosen Folk-King, and rule certain districts; or Sea-King, and rule certain ships; or Host-King, and rule certain warriors." Then seeing a conceited King-look spread over the little face, he hastened to add, "But whatever kind of King you may become, you will be a chosen King and nothing more, and must ever vie with other Bonders to prove that you are still the ablest, with weapons, wits and words."

The boy considered these various kinds of Kings, liked each in turn for the picturesque things they could do, and in turn wished to be each of them. He made up his mind at last to be

3

a Sea-King, for the decisive reason that that was the kind of King his father was.

That led to their playing a new game in which a certain ledge of rock became a ship and he and his father the crew. They both voted that he should be the Sea-King and command the voyages which they imagined. He stood where the helm was said to be, managing a tiller of air and shouting orders which were obeyed without question, because a Sea-King knows what he is about and everyone on board defers to his judgment. He began to speak of himself as "The Sea-King," both when pretending he was at sea and when he was really at home. "Sea-King" became a nickname for him—or, as it was said then, an Eke-Name—until it seemed he had never had any other. He behaved so as to make it fit him. The household began to take it for granted that he would be a Sea-King indeed, exactly like his father in every respect, except that his hair and beard were going to be yellow and he was a little more thoughtful.

II

THE sea not only guarded the Icelanders, it helped them raid anyone else. The Sea-King sailed with his father, one delightful day, to make friends with wind and waves, and learn that ships are horses that you ride through water. It was frightening to see Iceland fading back of them in the mist, and the unstable water below, but he was among men, on a raiding-trip, so he sneered his fears away.

With sun and stars to guide them, they headed for a fat, lazy country that was not expecting them, waited just beyond sight of land for night and mist, then rowed in suddenly and attacked with fire and torch. The Sea-King, ordered to remain aboard away from the fight, heard the surprised foe screaming with terror as they realized who the raiders must be. Then, swiftly, before the alarm could be spread, his countrymen came wading back to the ship. Some were carrying gold and silver ornaments, and some herded their captives aboard. He joined in jeering at the wretches who would be slaves when they got back to Iceland, and in a mocking shout back through the darkness at those still left alive on shore. Then they put to sea again, and went on to another land and another, piling riches into the hold, with no cost but a captive thrown overboard for Odin, to ensure the God's lasting favor. And then at last they sailed back home, with a shipload of Swedish horses and Irish slaves and gold and silver and women to replace those dead or divorced, and a new song about their triumph.

> We fell upon them suddenly,
> With a shout,
> With a rush,
> With a sword,
> With a torch.
> Now we return in victory,
> But they are slaves, or dead.

He went on many such raids across the bosom of wise, gray-bearded Ocean, and each time, when he returned, he felt new love for his fierce, brave island, with its glaciers and volcanoes and geysers and gales and lakes of boiling tar and the mighty tales that must be true of those mighty places. Then the sea would close in again and shut out all the rest, even from memory. His land was alone and wonderful and its Gods were best.

On one of these sea-trips his father was reminded of a voyage he had taken ten years earlier and was moved to tell him about it. It had to do with yet one more game, called Revenge. As he remembered his way through the story, he smiled, indicating that Revenge was a pleasant game. He told it as man to man— or boy to boy—as he gazed across the water into the setting sun, which every evening at that time visits its friend, the past. His own fiery red beard caught the glint, so that all that redness, of beard, sun and flaming path that stretched between them across the water, burnt the story into the very bottom of his son's mind, where it rested for years, waiting till it should be called forth to fill a need.

"I lent the pillars of my High-Seat to Thorgest Drangar," he said. "They were carved with the image of Lok on them, who has always befriended me and helped me prosper. Thorgest had not done well and he thought that Lok might help him as he had helped me.

"As soon as he had the pillars in his house, Lok did indeed come to his aid. His farm yielded a good crop, his wife became pregnant and his worst enemy was poisoned, no one knew how. Then I asked to have my pillars back, but he refused. The reason was, as I learned later, he envied me my land, which was larger and better than his; he thought he might get it away from me by keeping my luck. When he went on refusing, my temper boiled up and the next thing our swords were out and I had killed him. Well, I was ready enough to pay the fine, according to law, for I had my pillars back and they were worth the price.

"But Thorgest's malice pursued me from his grave, and once at night my door slammed and I knew he was haunting my house. He had been planning and plotting with his kinsmen, who were law-men, how to get my land, and they were in control of the Thing when the case was tried. They must have seen Thorgest's ghost, too, and promised him to complete their scheme, for instead of being fined I was exiled for three years, in which time they reasoned that they could get my land and also find legal tricks by which to keep it. There was nothing I could do, because there were too many of them, so I set sail, with a few servants and slaves, for some land to the North, which had been seen by Ulf the Crow when he was blown off his course.

"We reached it, after a difficult voyage, and found that it was a desolate, sunless place, covered with ice and torn by a freezing wind. So we left it and sailed to a small, unpeopled island off the coast of Ireland, where we lived our three years, pleasantly enough.

"At the end of that time, we went back to Iceland. I told everyone precisely where I had been, but I said it in such a way as to make it seem a lie, as if I were trying to conceal something of great value. At last one night, when they thought they had me drunk, I let them drag a story out of me that I had been living on Ulf's land, which I had named Greenland because it was such a fertile and beautiful place, and that I meant to return there as soon as I had farm tools and other things I needed. The healthy look of my servants and myself bore out my story. They believed it."

His smile broadened. "A number of those land-hungry judges of mine who had condemned me at the Thing, hastily sold their farms and scurried off to Greenland, to be the first to settle and claim it. They came back two years later, such of them as were left alive, and there were several who had a hand or foot frozen off. I was in possession by then, on our farm, which I have clung to ever since. They cursed me and Greenland. They seemed to think I had named it badly."

His son gloated with him. "Was it *very* bad there?" he asked, hoping to increase his zest.

"Well," his father replied thoughtfully, "I would not urge any true friend to live there, unless he was desperate, and all the rest of the world had come to an end."

Then he threw back his head and roared with the loudest laughter his son had ever heard, so that he simply had to laugh, too, partly over the delicious taste of the revenge and partly at the sight of his father's beard bobbing up and down and seeming to be part of the sunset.

III

THE Sea-King grew up, further and further from the ground. At last his head was six feet toward the sky, where it ran into new, strange emotions that were waiting there. He dealt with these as with everything unfamiliar, that is, by the aid of magic. He sought for magical explanations about love. This had its legends and its Runes, as exciting as those concerning sorcerers or the sea, and therefore as believable. The Gods themselves went courting across their rainbow bridge and their mates were many and various. He knew a song which told how Niord was wedded to a fair Giantess, Odin to the forces of Nature, the Death-Maiden Svafa to a man as mortal as himself and his companions.

That is why, when he was twenty-two, he was willing to think he had married the Goddess Freya.

It was an easy mistake to make. Do you love your God? Well, he loved his Goddess. She was known to dwell in a vale near by, where the green things were her fine brocaded dress and the yellow flowers her hair. That was an artful disguise, which had hidden her from the Irish Christians. But he, who perceived that the beautiful divine woman and the beautiful divine place were the same, easily saw through the enchantment and went about saying softly: "Freya, I love you!"

He did not feel that he was speaking only to air, nor even to a bodiless ideal whom he never really hoped to see. Freya was completely real to him. She seemed to hover near, peering at him from amid the trees.

And in fact, she was. Be it said that he was a handsome young man; wherefore there was a shy, pretty girl who had been watching him for many days, observing him from a distance, terrified lest he see her, yet contriving that he should when it would be most propitious. She heard what he said to Freya and dared to profit by it. That was her right, for in one respect it might be said she was Freya: she was not too unlike the particular picture of female loveliness which he carried in his head and was ready to worship. So one day, when she let the rustle of her garments reveal her presence and he turned suddenly and saw her, a weakness possessed him, a spell enveloped him and he thought she was Freya indeed, come down from the mountain-top. His arms seemed to detach themselves from his body and encircle her of their own desire. He was held by an incantation which he himself spoke in the whispered names he called her, all of them Freya's names: Giver of Love, Most Gently Born of the Gods, Wearer of the Flaming Necklace. When she began to cry a little because she knew these were Freya's names and feared he was honoring her too highly for her safety, he called her Weeper of Gold, which name the Goddess also has because her shimmering tears float upon the Ocean at sunset as she mourns the death of a day.

"My name is Helga," she told him as soon as he would listen. This he took for part of her divine concealment. He pulled the hood of darkness down over his senses, asking no question and hearing no explanation about where she came from, nor about her family, nor her dowry, nor anything concerning her, but was willing and glad to have it all exactly as it was, so aptly had she stepped into his brain when it was readiest to receive Freya's image.

Her father and brothers came and saw to it that the marriage was formal and binding, and likewise the inheritance rights and the settlement, although they were in no position to do much bargaining, as Helga was marrying late in life, at the age of nineteen. The Sea-King surprised and somewhat confused them by forgoing the shrewd dickering that was expected of all men. In them and their ceremonials he saw only the completeness of Freya's conjuration, designed to mislead all but himself, who so devoutly believed in her and loved her. Considering the time and any signs by which he could judge, he was right. At the very least, it is too bad he was wrong. A heavenly reward for his deep and ardent faith would have seemed just.

When they had been married for a month and a month and a month and a month, the enchantment or the illusion or the love or the work of Trolls or whatever it was began to wear off. He tried stubbornly not to see, but his eyes did, and they fought with him until they made him admit they were right. She had small meannesses, small fears, small plans. Yes, and small beauty, sitting smugly in the great carven chair in which she liked to be the lady of the house. But disappointment and reality could not be accepted without one last struggle, so he made the forbidden test which we must never make if there is a likelihood that we are married to a heavenly being, that is, call her by her right name.

"Oh, Freya!" he said sorrowfully, looking at her with a rem-

9

nant of hope that dwindled to nothing even as he formed the sounds. As usual, she misunderstood him, thought he meant it for some sort of joke and simpered accordingly. With that he knew that the spell was gone forever. He turned and went walking alone, which there and then became a habit. Ahead of him and away, his lost Goddess danced across a hill.

IV

AYEAR went by. It tried to make its short life a just one by bringing him both a loss and a gain: his father died and his son was born.

Following the ancient custom, the infant was placed on the floor and the household waited for its father's decision: whether it was really his and should get his love and protection, or whether it should be left on a hill-top for the eagles or whoever wanted a foster son. Even if he had been capable of choosing the hill-top, he would not have done so in this case, for he saw with enormous satisfaction that the baby had the face and so perchance the nature, too, of its dead grandfather. So he gave him the same name: Eric. Whatever good fortune was in the name would remain in the family.

With an exact plan already in his mind for the kind of man his son should be, he picked him up from the floor, wrapped him in his cloak and sprinkled him with water. Helga and the other women gave a relieved sigh when they saw the infant's legitimacy thus established; it had rights now under the law and if anyone killed it after this, it would be murder.

Now he had a chance to gratify a wish that everybody has: to live all over again through the person of his son, with no mistakes this time. He waited eagerly as the baby grew to consciousness, to understanding, to speech. He waited to see what he would notice, and pounced upon it, to be the first to tell him what it really was, what to look for in it, how it should be thought about. And on the day when little Eric was four years old, he found himself telling him that the sky rests on the shoulders of four dwarfs, whose names are Nordri, Sudri, Ostri and Westri.

He did not always walk alone now. There were rambles together over the hills, when he told young Eric tales he had heard from old Eric: of the mountains that are really Giants, of the sea and raiding, and of Odin and Thor and Frey. Yes, and at last, one day, of Frey's beautiful sister Freya, Giver of Love, Most Gently Born of the Gods, Wearer of the Flaming Necklace, Weeper of Gold.

"She has six cats, has Freya, that draw the golden wagon in which she rides; it comes toward you suddenly, on a lonely road, and the man who sees it is so bemused that he cannot step aside, but lets the Goddess ride over him. He bears the marks of that forever, though he comes to think it was an illusion, a dream that led to nothing. But it was not for nothing. Oh, not for nothing!"—and he put his arm tightly about little Eric's shoulder, while with his other hand he showed him how to get a firm grip on a sword.

Sometimes he had to be away from Eric, at sea, raiding or trading, under the command of some great Sea-King. He was not yet a Sea-King himself, but hoped in his heart he still would be and that Eric would be, too. In the meantime he learned the things a Sea-King had to do, and the manner of their doing. On one of the trips he relearned something that was both necessary and dreadful.

It was a raiding trip, that took them along one of the great Russian rivers, as far as Hungary. There they captured a number of slaves, among them a man who became his property, and whom he called "Turker" because everything south of Sweden was known as Turkey. The thing that was necessary was slavery, for the Bonders knew no other way of getting the hard work of a farmstead done. The dreadful side of it was the way Turker was captured.

Turker did not see them as they approached. He was occupied in teaching a little boy—his own little boy, as could be seen by the likeness between them—to sail a boat in a stream. Eric's father was sent to engage him in talk while the others were to steal up behind them. He did as he was bid, since he was new to slave-catching and did not want to set his judgment against theirs, but he did not like the part of it that he was set to do. When he drew near to Turker, he saw that the man and his son were different from Icelanders and other Northern people he had seen. They were undersized, both of them, with keen little black eyes that reminded him of birds, and long black hair. But they were father and son, too, and that made them seem to have an unpleasant kinship with himself and Eric. He went ahead with what had been agreed upon, pretending to Turker that he was a trader. It was pitifully easy to do, because Turker really was a trader, and understood the Norse tongue.

"I have a son at home," said Eric's father, "about the same age as yours." He patted the little fellow on the head and cringed inwardly at the friendly smile he received. "His name is Eric," he added, in order to keep on speaking, and, for the same reason, asked, "What is your boy's name?"

"Atyl." The small owner of the name showed a smug pleasure in hearing it pronounced. "He is named," his father explained, "after our ancient hero, King Atyl the Great."

"A very fine name," the other father heard himself say admiringly, "and I am sure he will live up to it." This evoked an enthusiastic flood of anecdotes about young Atyl's attainments: how he could already ride a horse as well as most men, recite poetry so that the neighbors marveled, and do countless other wonders beyond his years. "Now he has set his heart on learning to sail a boat."

No man who dreamed of being a Sea-King could resist that. He plucked the little vessel out of the water, showed Atyl how to adjust its sail, set it afloat again, and then all three of them lay on their stomachs blowing at it, as if they were the wind.

All the while Eric's father felt as if he were in a nightmare, trapping himself, so much did he and Turker and their two sons

12

seem ghosts of each other. As his companions closed in, Turker had reached the point of inviting him to be their house-guest. He almost warned Turker of his danger, but could not bring himself to betray his own countrymen. Then it was too late: they had Turker, who was screaming to his little boy to run! run! run! The boy got away, but they dragged Turker to the ship and were away before the alarm spread.

Turker took his Thralldom to heart, seeming unable to accept it as other captives managed to do. It especially grieved him when they cut his long hair, cropping it close, as Thralls had to wear it to mark them off from their masters. He seemed to have been proud of it, and touched the short strands gingerly, as if in pain. When he was asked any questions, he refused to answer or to speak at all, although they knew he understood Norse from the way he had spoken with Eric's father. All the way to Iceland he was silent, evidently thinking of what he was leaving, and weeping like a woman. That was a great joke, because when you were captured you naturally abandoned your old ties and accepted those of the man who owned you. It was only after they were in Iceland and had come to the farmstead that he became less sad; his face even lighted up with a kind of desperate pleasure. That happened when he first saw Eric. Then he grew very excited and spoke in the Turkish tongue, which no one understood, but they could see that Eric reminded him of his own little son. He and Eric became friends at once, which was a great satisfaction to Eric's father, who felt the boy would be in sympathetic hands when he was away. The task which he assigned to Turker was to be Eric's companion and guard.

From then on, he felt safe in going away and leaving his son with Turker. It was like remaining with Eric himself, even when sailing a distant sea. For he never got over the notion that he and his Thrall were exactly alike, in everything that mattered. Each time he returned, he had an impulse to clasp Turker's hand in his own and hail him as a true, dear friend, but he never did. His hand refused to obey him and would not meet Turker's. Odin had told, once and forever, what the life of a Thrall should be, in the station in which it had pleased the Gods to place him, and an ancient Sybil wrote it down, clearly and to be observed.

13

His name shall be Thrall,
His work be hard,
His body bent,
His clothing poor.

He lives like a Thrall,
Lifts heavy loads,
Eats what is left,
Sleeps where he can.

His wife is a Thrall,
His children, too,
They tend the swine,
They are despised.

Turker would not have grasped his master's proffered hand, even if it could have moved itself toward him. The slave's pride was more terrible than the master's, since it was a sole remaining possession and therefore to be clung to the more fiercely. Turker would have bowed, smiling deprecatingly as if unworthy of such an honor, but he would not have extended his own hand, and any Bonder who saw it happen would have approved of how well he knew his place in the face of such generous condescension. Turker's hunger for the affection of the little boy who resembled his own was misleading to free men who had no way of understanding a Thrall: they mistook his submissive manner for resignation to his lot and knew nothing of his hatred for his captors, which was the more poisonous because it had to be hidden.

Four years more marched by and the world was marching with them, along a path that could not be barred. History was refusing to stand still, whether or not a man wanted to relive his past. Things were trying to turn into other things, news of it was trying to be heard. The guardian sea let an occasional ship steal in, which, amid an innocent cargo, carried rumors of a change, a change, a change. Despite what anyone could do, it was ever creeping nearer, on and on, now driven back, now advancing again, threatening to be upon them at last. King Harold Bluetooth had tried to bring Christian Bishops into

Norway, but Earl Haakon killed him and put everything back the way it was, for which he was affectionately called Haakon the Good. For a while the ancient ways resumed their comforting sway, then the evil came again. King Olaf, who was thought dead, unaccountably returned with an armed host, and with a Christian Priest beside him who carried a sword and used it, too; together they hunted the good Haakon to a filthy death in a pit beneath a pigsty where he was hiding. Now Olaf ruled Norway as a baptized Christian, followed to the font by men with neither shame nor honor. They said he ruled by a Divine Right. Divine, by the word of a strange Divinity, not chosen by Bonders equal to himself. There was to be no choosing ever again in Norway. Olaf was to be followed to the throne by his sons, Divine as himself, whatever they were like, and there they would sit forever and ever, while the past and its Heroes were forgotten.

Strangest of all was the readiness with which the coming change was being accepted. *It would change,* many said, and behaved as if it already had. They began neglecting the old Gods, or sacrificing before them because they thought it a harmless precaution, no longer because of a deep belief in their power. This weakening of fervor may have been the Gods' own fault, for they were no longer sustaining Iceland as they should. The land was too poor to bear all that was needed, and living by sea-raids was too uncertain, too perilous, too difficult. A new way to get things done had to be found, and the old Gods were keeping the old ways going. Therefore, men knew in their hearts that the old Gods must go, though habit made them put off saying so.

Some stood to gain by the change and some to lose, which is the greatest difference of interest that is possible. Long before these two factions saw that they were heading toward open conflict, or even that they were two, the need to describe them caused two old words to take on new meanings. One of these words, "Christian," had long meant a follower of Christ; now it was beginning to mean one who lived in the new walled towns of Europe that were built around a castle and a church, and who served the King and the Bishop. The other word, "Heathen," had meant one who lived outside the town, on the heath;

but now it meant one who clung to the old beliefs that the towns were banishing.

The Heathen who thought he had married a Goddess walked home one evening in gloomy thought. Could it be that the death of Freya and all the company of Gods, foretold in the old poems, was at hand?

> Then burns the world, and all the Aesir bright
> Descend with it to everlasting night.

But there was to have been a great recompense—a last titanic battle, in which Thor and the mightiest of serpents slay each other, while Vithar steps between the open jaws of the wolf Giant, tears the monster apart and rips from his belly the flaming sun he has swallowed. There was not to have been such a quiet, unresisting, sick ending to all that grandeur. No, this was surely not the great Doom.

He walked home by a roundabout way, to be no longer alone, past a temple where they were sacrificing a bull to Niord because a ship had got in safely. He found himself looking strangely at the building, with an unaccustomed emotion which he suddenly realized was prophecy. The temple would soon not be there to be looked at: he could see it in flames. Angrily he shook this impossibility out of his head.

It was a long time before he got home. He was surprised to see his wife come out to meet him, which once she had done as a pleasant habit. Now he feared that something was the matter, perhaps with their son, and he hastened toward her.

But it was news that brought her out. She was bubbling and eager with it and poured it over him like a cascade. So delighted was she and so little did she understand him, that she thought he would be as pleased and excited as herself.

"A Priest!"—the King of Norway's own Priest, she emphasized, with satisfaction—"has come to live with us—"

He was startled, shocked. And silent, remembering who he had once thought she was.

"—he is not like what they say of Christians—A huge, handsome man with fierce proud eyes—Like an eagle!—He carries a sword—Oh, you will like him—"

16

Never, never! A sorcerer, an enemy, beneath his roof!

"—and by the King's wish, he makes our home his own. Think, think, what an honor! From here he says he will spread the Word—you know, the Word. In the beginning, he says, there was the Word—And God—*his* God spoke—and now everyone—everyone in Norway—all the Earls, that is—The King asks us to set an example—the Priest has already been speaking to Eric—"

She noticed her husband's stern, angry face as he turned abruptly from her to go searching for their son. Her voice died down as she tried to call after him that the Priest's name was Theobrand—Oh, such a splendid man—

Little Eric was by the brook with Turker, sailing his boat, when his father found him, knelt beside him and suddenly, almost roughly, snatched him to his side. "There are things I must tell you. Now, before it is too late. You are to listen and remember. As I did. And my father. And his father. And as your children shall." He dismissed Turker, sharply, meaning to deal with him later for having let the Priest come near Eric. Then he turned to the difficult problem at hand.

Articles of faith. He must tell them to his son, well and quickly, this moment, before a poisoned mist was spread about his mind. Now. He began with the tale of the beginning of things and how the world was created by his Gods. (The Word? The Word? What did it mean, that in the beginning was the Word? It sounded like a sorcerer's incantation.) He told the story, as he had often heard it rhymed, and the substance of it was this:

At first there was only Fire and Ice. They dwelt apart, each in its own vast land. Between, there lay a measureless, awful Gap in which there was nothing at all, except that now and again sparks would fly across from Fire-Home and hiss against the Ice, beginning the great war that was to go on forever.

The only living thing was a mighty Cow that roamed the dead Ice-World, stubbornly clinging to life by licking the salty rime from the frozen surface. On the first of the first three days, her great tongue melted the ice away until an immense head was revealed; the second day she released the Giant's shoulders and on the third his body. He stood erect, this son of cold and death, rushed upon his enemy the Sun and ravished her.

From that union was born the race of Giants, who bring all that is ill and who, like the ice and snow from which they stem, take strange forms. But three other sons were born, too, more like their mother, three shining Gods, who looked once upon their father, hated him and killed him.

They threw his body into the Gap in which there had been nothing, and he filled it. From his carcass they made this world; the rivers are his blood, the sky his skull. They hurled his brain up into the air and it turned into clouds. Through his heart they planted a great ash tree, whose roots are in Hell and whose topmost branches—

He did not finish the story, for his wife had come from the house and snatched the boy toward her as though to protect him, a startling thing which she had never dared before. Beside her was the Priest, handsome and huge indeed and with hand on sword; then, remembering he was a man of God, he used words instead.

"There was no ash tree!" he cried angrily, "but an apple tree from which we were forbidden to eat, and for the sin of disobeying—"

Little Eric's world was rocking, to hear his father contradicted. The latter knew it and felt he must redeem himself. His hand started for his sword but he desisted when he saw his wife's face, more astonished than alarmed. He remembered that the Priest, whatever he might be, was yet his guest and therefore sacred.

Thor's breath began to blow and make ripples on the brook. It cooled his head. Then he noticed, with a returning feeling of sanity, that ash trees were proving him right by growing there, while the stony ground beneath them gave the lie to the story which the Priest was telling, of a garden where fruits grew in original abundance in soil that needed no plough.

18

V

"GUEST" is one of the very oldest of all old words. Even in the tenth century its original meaning had long been forgotten and replaced by one very different.

Julius Caesar, who to the Vikings was merely an ancient fable, conquered their remote ancestors as much by double-dealing as by the sword. The victories by double-dealing were the more arduous, because Caesar's artless foemen did not trust his ambassadors and usually killed them before they could get to the deadly business of negotiating. Caesar it was, therefore, who for expediency's sake established the universal law that an ambassador is sacred; this he did by such bloody thousand-fold reprisals that the barbarians remembered the principle long after they had bargained away their freedom. A thousand years after Caesar and his empire were dead, the custom had grown even stronger because it had become intertwined with superstition, to the extent that any visitor from a foreign land was a safe and privileged being, to be entertained so bounteously that he could carry no ill tale back home. This concept developed in turn, until ultimately a host would seek to overwhelm his guest with such fabulous generosity that he would despise the country he had come from.

It is related of Thorolf Skalligrimsson that when King Harold Fairhair visited him, the entertainment was so splendid that the King became jealous and turned red in the face. Harold arrived with three hundred retainers, but Thorolf greeted him with five hundred of his own; this, he said, was the better to do honor to his exalted guest. The King murmured a hope that so large a following as his would not overcrowd his host's dwelling, but Thorolf led them to an immense new hall which he had built especially for the purpose. There followed a feast of unheard-of munificence, with gifts of gold to all and a famous Skald who composed songs in the King's honor. Throughout the traditional three-day visit, Thorolf's monumental hospitality continued while his guest grew ever more morose. When the time for parting came, they went together to the beach. There, instead of the ship in which Harold had arrived, was a much more handsome one, carved in the form of a dragon, with gaily colored tents on its deck and fitted with every kind of comfort. This Thorolf presented as a parting gift. They say the King never forgave him.

The feast in honor of Olaf's Priest was somewhat nearer to what Caesar had in mind. Here was more than a guest to be overpowered with bounty: he was an envoy from a King who, everybody felt, had it in his mind to conquer them.

His resentful host was trapped by custom into a semblance of graciousness, but could not bring himself to make the actual preparations. To others it would be a feast, to him a celebration of his own shame, however compensated by momentary distinction. He could not forget how his wife had snatched their son from him with the Priest looking on; that seemed to be a little foretaste of the future. He therefore steered a course that avoided all his varied feelings, as skillfully as ever he had guided a ship around hidden rocks. This he did by making his wife attend to everything, telling her that after all the Priest was more her guest than his.

And so he was: the guest of one of her wayward thoughts, who strangely refused to leave, with his furious eyes, his black, graying hair, his handsome frame and the way he had outfaced her husband. She was delighted to take charge, having already spread the news of their visitor by hint, boast, offhand reference and innuendo, so that by the time she began sending out invitations, every peak and plain in Iceland was wondering why she had been so long about it. The response was prodigious. For a while they thought they might have to do as Thorolf Skalligrimsson had, and build a special hall to hold the diners.

While his wife busied herself with the arrangements, tyrannizing rapturously over the servants, the size and relentless actuality of the coming event evoked a different preoccupation in him. He knew that some sort of public attitude would be expected of him. Trying this one and that, he found them all unsatisfactory, and was still undecided when the night of the feast arrived and the first guest was entering his door. At once, the many tentative postures rushed back into his mind for final, inevitable choice. He chose to be himself, that is, a defender of the old and loved against the new and odious. He managed to fulfill this role without sacrificing that of host, by binding them together under a covering of stubborn grandeur. As he greeted each arrival, he was conscious that he himself was a tall man and, therefore, literally as it were, eminent, like a boulder on a crag, which might topple one way or another or not at all. Everyone for miles around knew by gossip what was going on in his household and there had been much speculation as to how he would carry it off. He was on trial. But his manner and his wife's arrangements were alike magnificent and both had to be admired. That at length happened, not gradually but abruptly; all the guests suddenly and simultaneously admitted it, by small, almost imperceptible nods of admiration. Then he knew he had achieved success, of precisely the shape and color he wanted. He began to enjoy himself.

It was a curious enjoyment, flavored with danger. Most particularly he relished what he thought was the open envy of Theobrand the Priest. Envy it was not, truly not; certainly Theobrand himself thought it was not, although his astonishment as he noticed the tapestries, the wood-carvings, the golden dishes and the slaves, made him seem to be wishing they were his, or at least his master's. But his real wish, deeply felt and painfully reached, was that he might somehow have all he saw, everywhere, always, for the glory of his God. Such a wish was a much graver threat to these Icelanders, more terrible in its relentlessness, though they did not know it, than any devotion to a King could have been. It was their certain doom, whose messenger was their guest. Their swords were futile against it. Their bravery was futile. A troop of giant centuries was coming,

21

to stamp on them until nothing of them would remain but this shadowy tale, which we have forgotten how to believe. However, they felt alarm enough as they saw the Priest's all-devouring look, since all had, sometime and somewhere, felt the kind of envy they thought he felt now. Without a word being said about it, they looked at one another and mistook his purpose, but they knew that they and their island were in common peril.

Then they looked toward their host. He had earned respect by his behavior; now they expected leadership of him. He, too, was an Iceland Bonder and must see the danger. They stretched their legs beneath the great laden tables, leaving him the field.

He appreciated the honored position of standard-bearer, thus silently offered, and swiftly planned his battle. Back to his master must King Olaf's Priest be sent, with the news that wondrous Iceland and its Bonders were beyond the taking. By hint and indirection only should that message be entrusted to their enemy-guest, amid amenities and song, with no man eating or drinking less than the utmost. A redoubtable, worthy task. So be it. He looked about, to make sure there was no stint of roast or beer. Then, as if unsheathing a sword, he extended his right arm grandly toward Bjorn the Skald, who sat opposite him, and continued the gesture to the seat at his own right where Theobrand was, as though to say: "Let us have a song, Bjorn, in honor of our chief guest!"

Bjorn, who had been awaiting just such a signal, at once set his harp against his knee and, looking directly across the hall at Theobrand, swept his hand over the strings with a flourish that was both greeting and challenge. He continued strumming for a moment and staring at Theobrand, considering him and planning what his opening verse should say. It is a much graver thing to sing a thought about a man than it is to say it, especially when many people are listening; then it becomes a ritual, with the singer himself a kind of Priest, and all the extra meanings of the words, dimmed through being often spoken, are suddenly revealed anew. No one will lightly offend a Skald, nor refuse him any gift, lest he make a mocking little poem that may stick in the ear and be sung around the land. Worse, he might not sing of one at all, and of what use are great forgotten deeds, that otherwise were history?

"Priest of the King!" sang Bjorn suddenly. That was a skill-ful way to begin, stating completely in the very first line what all thought about Theobrand, as well as what he very likely thought about himself. Other phrases followed which fitted him in the same manner, such as "Bringer of Words," and "Servant of a Slain God." Having at length named Theobrand in so many ways that any vanity he could have must be surfeited, Bjorn went on to sing of Iceland, with hints of how it felt about its visitor. He used the past tense, making it sound as if all he sang had long been part of recorded history, which no one would question. The song told how Theobrand had come, how Iceland's Bonders had gathered to greet him, and how they had reached a peaceable understanding of each other. The song ended thus, with a sort of short summary:

The home of Odin welcomed the Priest of a foreign faith.
Over the food we were friendly. No sword itched in the scab-
    bard.
Empty, the fields of battle; vainly waited the vultures.

He stopped singing suddenly, leaving all inferences unsaid and looking expectantly toward his host. The latter took a gold ring from his finger and tossed it to Bjorn, who caught it dexterously, appraising it pleasurably with one eye while he drank to the giver's health.

But more than a ring was expected by the assembly. The harp was passed from hand to hand, up to the High Seat, for the master of the house to add authority to what had just been sung.

He chose as his theme the tale of Those Who Dwelt Here Before, of his great-grandfather Ingolf who was the first settler, because he would not be ruled in Norway by King Harold Fair-hair, but chose to be a ruler himself in unknown Iceland, if only over his own slaves. He set sail with others whose minds were like his own and they named him Sea-King, the first here to be

23

so called. When their ships came in sight of this cape, Ingolf cast overboard a wooden image of Thor; where it floated ashore, they landed and called the place Thor's Haven. The hill that overlooks it he named Thor's Hill and forbade any man to kill within sight of it or to walk upon its slopes unwashed. At the foot of the hill, covered by a huge mound of Iceland's earth, is buried the ship that brought Ingolf; he himself sits on its deck, in full armor, reminding us of the course he set for us to steer. On the hill, a temple to Thor was built—

"—and in it we worship Thor still"—the singer's voice rose, exulting—"and always shall, and so shall our children, remembering he found the place for us to land and live, and protects it and us with his great Hammer, which cracks even the sky. A hammer makes the sword"—he drew his sword halfway from its sheath—"and the sword guards the Hammer!"—He thrust it significantly back.

There was silence again, this time of a dead kind. Nothing was left to say, unless one should say too much and offend their guest. They did not even eat or drink for a while, but sat looking at Olaf's Priest, marveling a little at how different a meaning he now had for them because two songs had been sung.

Theobrand was silent, too, though he was in a rage that few men could have controlled. He understood everything that had been said or meant: hints, insults, threats and all. He had long since vowed that nothing, nothing, should ever get in the way of the task he had set himself, neither his own feelings nor anyone's feelings nor any amount of pain or destruction to mind or body, of all the world if need be. He buried his rage in the two pits he had dug at the corners of his mouth, in which earlier rages lay buried. He himself it was who spoke first. "Song for song," he said. "Give me the harp."

It was handed to him. He struck its strings once or twice, very much as Bjorn had done, except that his mind was made up as to what he would sing.

"I will relate to you," he said, "some of the great deeds of Olaf Tryggvesson, King of Norway by the grace of God."

VI

THE Priest began his song immediately, as one whose well-known tale needs no thinking out. He was no poet and did not speak in verse, but his theme, which had been smoldering in him while the others held forth, burst into such a fire when he freed it that he declaimed rather than spoke, letting the sounds billow from his huge body, while ever and again he marked a surge in his feelings by plucking at the harp. He was so sure that everything he said was as right and just and beyond doubt as the open sea, and he said it all so loudly, that his listeners found it hard to keep from agreeing with him, though their own interest ran the other way. Even when he mocked their deepest belief, calling it the evil cant of Heathendom, they sat like a group bewitched, helpless before the triple charm of great faith, great sound and the great danger they wanted to learn about.

The way he chose to tell them of the King whose shadow was falling across their lives was as the life-story of a little boy who grew up fighting against many foes. It was their own kind of life, made of weapons, magic, frenzy, pillage and the letting of blood, wherefore they listened, with very personal understanding, as often for Olaf as against him.

"He was born in a swamp"—so Theobrand began the story—"whither his mother had fled, and none but the stars and God looked down on Tryggve's royal son.

"In grim silence Astrid suffered the birth-pains. She granted herself neither moan nor murmur, for Earl Haakon's men and hounds were hunting them. Haakon would remember that silence twenty-five years later, and copy it, when Olaf's men

25

ABIGAIL E. WEEKS MEMORIAL LIBRARY
UNION COLLEGE
BARBOURVILLE, KENTUCKY

and hounds hunted him, as he hid in the pit beneath the pigsty.

"Astrid taught her son that the sky rests on the shoulders of the four dwarfs, along with other Heathen blasphemy, for mother and son were unbaptized still, and had the boy died in the caves or forests where his childhood passed, he would never have known Heaven. She taught him also that he was the great-grandson of Harold Fairhair and the son of Tryggve, whom she called the Rightful King, having yet to learn that only God's Church can make a King rightful. She taught him the name of the man who had killed his father and the name of the man who told him to do it: Haakon, whom the Heathen still call Haakon the Good, but whom the good now call Haakon the Heathen. And she taught him vengeance (though it is the Lord's), and who the friends were, in hall or cottage, who might one day help him have it. 'This land is yours,' she said. 'Every stone and tree and house and farm and cow and man and shrub, all things that walk or fly or crawl, or swim beneath the water or breathe below the sky, all are yours, to help, to hinder, to nourish or to kill, according as the whim strikes you, because you are my son and because I married as I did.' All this she told him, and he believed it, believing also, alas, the impious reasons why she said it all was his.

"To that vain and ungodly teaching of hers can be traced, I think, a certain rude way that Olaf has—though he tries to conquer it now—of rushing to seize that which he wants. He shouts, 'It is mine and I will have it!' where another, who has learned the virtue of tact, will advance his claim more gently, as a river eats away its banks.

"For their sin of human pride they were punished. God sent pirates to that shore, who seized them and sold them as slaves in distant lands. Olaf never saw his mother again.

"But the things she had taught him were carved upon his soul. He remembered them when he was a slave in Esthonia, twelve years old. He remembered them when he poured his master's ale or fenced his master's field. And he remembered them one day in the marketplace, when he heard a man called by the name that was the name of his father's murderer. He has often said that what he did then, he did without thought or plan, because it seemed the thing to do, that must be done, by

26

himself, then and there, on the instant. He seized the man's own axe and with a strength beyond his years he split him from crown to chin, so that the man fell like a dead tree. There was a great outcry at this, that a slave had slain a Bonder, and the people were for hanging him at once. But he set his back against a wall, the bloody axe in his hands, and faced them with determination, insisting that he was a King and merited the High justice, not the Low. Many thought him drunk or demented, but others were struck by his bearing, feeling that no one would dare make such a claim unless there was a reason back of it. So he was taken for judgment before the King of Novgorod, named Valdemar. To everyone's surprise, King Valdemar did not ask why the boy had been brought before him, but scanned his features sharply, looking at him from this side and from that, saying nothing but seeming to make up his mind by Olaf's looks alone, which, as the onlookers began to see, resembled the King's own. At last King Valdemar spoke, and his words have been made into a song which everyone in Norway knows:

> " 'Your face and mine are one,
> And each is like the other,
> For you are Astrid's son
> And I am Astrid's brother.'

"From that time on, Olaf was under King Valdemar's protection and all men were forbidden to do him injury, under threat of heavy punishment.

"Olaf should have given thanks for that miracle, for miracle it was, sent to prove that only Heaven could help him. But he was so deeply sunk in arrogance, he thought it merely proved his kin were Kings everywhere, seated on thrones by their very nature, as a tree puts forth roots. King Valdemar encouraged this belief, sharing it with him and scheming how Olaf might capture his Kingdom of Norway. He had famous champions teach him the arts of war and the many exercises that make the body strong. Olaf had the tall, long-boned frame of his great-grandfather, Harold Fairhair, and he surpassed everyone in strength and the courage to use it. He had moreover a fearful determination to be first in everything, as if a demon possessed

27

him. He could throw two javelins at once, and make both hit the mark. He climbed up the side of the great mountain they call the Smalsarhorn, to rescue a friend who tried to reach the top but lost courage halfway. Olaf ran up to him like a goat, carried him to the summit with him, left his shield hanging there to prove he had done it, then carried his friend to the ground in safety. He could run along the oars of a ship that was being rowed through the water, without so much as getting his feet wet. He has never lost these arts. He is today the most redoubtable man in Norway.

"There was another kind of knowledge that Valdemar would let no one teach him but himself. This was a store of tricks and methods by which a King gets what he covets and keeps what he lays hands upon. The thing they both wanted was the dream of every Heathen ruler: to have his Kingdom endure through eternity, for himself and his heirs. It was a hopeless quest while they remained Heathen, for eternity is given only by God, to His own elect. Nonetheless, Olaf and his uncle persisted. They studied how Charlemagne, King of the Franks, restored and ruled the ancient Holy Empire of Rome, when once he had Rome's Church beside him to proclaim his right Divine; how the great Constantine had done so before him in Byzantium; and how Olaf's great-grandfather had failed, through not seeking that kind of help. They planned not to make that mistake.

"As soon as Olaf was old enough, Valdemar arranged that he marry the daughter of King Burislav of Wendland, so that he might have wealth and an ally. Some said the bride was beautiful and that Olaf loved her, but if he did it was with a demon love, for he spoke to her in a kind of strange, unholy poetry, likening her to Fricka and Freya and Ran, and other filthy idols you call Goddesses and sprinkle with bullock's blood. After they were married and his wife was with child, Burislav deemed that Olaf's Kingdom would be a lasting one, bequeathed to Burislav's own grandchild. So he gave him a fleet of ships manned with warriors, with which to go and take it. Many secret friends of Olaf's father, who had been awaiting such a chance, joined him. It seemed to them he now had strength enough to get what he sought.

28

"But then a second Divine judgment fell upon Olaf. His wife died in childbirth and her Heathen infant with her. Who shall say it would have happened so, had they been baptized Christians?—for why should devil's spawn be loosed upon this world, to inherit and rule it?

"That is how it was whispered about by certain Irish slaves, who secretly had clung to their Christian faith to sustain them in their wretchedness. What they were saying was reported to Olaf, but instead of having them slain or tortured, he began to think soberly and deeply about the blow that had been dealt him. He has told me since, he wondered why those he loved were snatched away, and if indeed such a question had any answer. Wondering thus, he sailed with his fleet of ships, though no longer with an heir nor a wife to bear him another, nor, therefore, his father-in-law any longer for an ally. Little indeed that a King needs he seemed to have, as he sailed toward the place where God had stationed me, His unknowing, unworthy instrument, to await Olaf's coming."

Now that Theobrand had brought the tale to where his own path crossed Olaf's he deliberately paused, apparently to drink his ale, but really to consider what progress he was making.

As he lifted the horn to his lips, his arm was the only thing in the room that moved. Every Bonder sat, watching him drink, waiting. He noticed that they breathed as one, in and out, in and out, all at the same time. It could be heard.

There was one person present who had been on Theobrand's side from the start, whose eyes could not have left him even if their owner had wished. His hostess Helga watched his slightest move and look, like one in the spell of a Troll. She moved her lips with his, shaping them to the words he said, taking quick sharp breaths when his voice or face shifted from one emotion to another. The meaning of what he said went by her unperceived, but she drank the sound in. What she saw was neither Priest nor Ambassador, but only this huge, handsome man who could keep his temper and lose it at the same time and whose thoughts, even when he spoke them most softly, had so much frenzy in them.

And there were the Thralls. He had seen them watching him as they passed about, serving meat and drink, then listening furtively in the shadow beyond the doorway. There was a gleam in their faces, though they tried to dissemble it, a vague hope that somehow their life was going to be lightened, through the power of this new God before whom all were equals. Turker came toward him to refill the ale-horn as he set it down. When he was close by, Turker crossed himself, in such a way that only Theobrand could see it. "The slaves and a woman are Christians in their hearts," the Priest told himself. "Olaf will win a victory here." With strengthened faith, he resumed his tale.

"I dwelt in a cave, in the furthest of the Scilly Islands, where I mortified my flesh and lived upon scraps of food brought to me by pious fisherfolk whom I had baptized. Perhaps their piety was not of the best; they may have looked on me as one more idol whom they might as well placate, of which they had many. Whatever their reasons were, they held me in a kind of awe and often asked me to pray for the safe return of their boats. More than once those prayers were answered. Then I began to have influence. Not only my prayers were sought, but also my advice.

"There was a Christian Bishop in those islands, named Sigurd, a saintly man who had been to Rome, where he was highly thought of and entrusted with great and noble work. I had been a servant in his house, working as a groom in the stable. He it was who taught me what Latin and other knowledge I have, and looked with favor on my wish to live a simple and holy life. He took a certain pleasure in helping me find a cave to live in and often came to visit me there. After a time, during which he made sure that my zeal never abated, he gave my preaching Heaven's sanction by ordaining me a Priest. Then my cave became a little church, while an ampler one was built by my pious fishermen, stone by stone, for the glory of God.

"He it was, too, who gave me the name I bear. It had been Thangbrand, a Heathen name belonging to my grandfather. Bishop Sigurd christened me Theobrand, which in the sacred language of Scripture signifies Brand of God. He prayed that I might always burn with a sacred flame. Once or twice I felt

30

that he found me somehow amusing, but this suspicion was placed in my mind by Satan, and I crushed it.

"Very early one morning, before the sun was out of the ocean, he honored my humble cave-church with an unexpected visit. By the tight look of his brow and lips and the hasty way he had donned his robe, I saw that a very great matter had brought him.

" 'Prepare now, Brand of God!' he said. 'You have a mission to perform, far beyond the reach of most men. If you fulfill it well and truly, you will save more souls

> than a path has stones
> or a fish has bones.

Tryggve's son has landed here with a fleet of ships. His men want food and water and other lusts of the flesh, but Olaf is sad and thoughtful, a lonely man who only wants advice. He has heard of you.' With that, the Bishop gave me such a look that I felt as if the great Hand that shaped the world were laid upon my shoulder.

" 'Let me be given more than human strength!' I cried, 'so I may save his soul! It were better that one lost sheep—'

" 'A sheep,' the Bishop interrupted me, 'that will lead countless others into the fold! Let us see how you may be given that more-than-human strength you crave.'

"He remained there with me for hours, instructing me in my task, though it kept him from his meditations, so great was his zeal for one man's salvation. I was amazed at the endless pains he took and the vast store of knowledge he drew upon and freely gave. He told me how Olaf envied and admired the two great Kings, Constantine and Charlemagne. He told me the kind of man Olaf was, what things he loved or hated or sought or avoided or said or knew or even dreamed, all of which had been gathered from so many different places and put together so carefully and skillfully that I knew Olaf before ever I saw him. Lastly, he made me truly see how vast was the good I might achieve, which I had scarcely glimpsed, though my vanity had been telling me I saw it wholly. He said there should be a thousand church steeples pointing the way to Heaven, above scores of the devout, kneeling as they received the Word. This, I might bring about: I, who had been content to sit in my cave and meditate about the next world, never thinking to help mend this one. Such a chance has been given to few men since Adam wasted his. When my Bishop had raised me to this degree of understanding, we knelt together and prayed for me to have that strength, far beyond my own, which I needed so desperately. At once it crept into my limbs and tingled in my blood. When Bishop Sigurd left me, I felt an exaltation, a clarity, a purpose, which nothing shall ever diminish.

"When Olaf entered my cave, as the Bishop had prophesied he would, his appearance impressed me, even though I had been so well prepared for it. He is immensely tall, strong and handsome, and must indeed resemble his great-grandfather, who is said to have looked like that. I understood, as my Bishop had told me I would, why many ignorant people were ready to believe that Olaf was one of their own Gods, come to rule them on earth.

"How great is the power of prayer, how boundless! The thoughts I had hoped to implant in his mind were already there. He was thinking about the Christian life, although— since he was a Heathen—he thought about it for wrong reasons. But there it was nonetheless, like the thoughts of my half-believing fishermen, ready to grow into a great verdant tree of faith. I cannot truly say I baptized Olaf; it was rather as if he baptized himself.

"He began speaking at once, as if grudging the loss of an instant. 'You are Theobrand, the Christian Troll, are you not?' he asked. 'I am Theobrand, the Christian *Priest*,' I answered somewhat angrily, not liking the common jibe that the two are in some way the same. 'Troll or Priest,' he said impatiently, 'you are a Christian, and Christianity is what I want to know about.'

" 'It is the light that shines upon the world—' I began, but he stopped me, with that inelegant directness of which I complain. 'Save that kind of breath,' he said, 'to cool your food and warm your flock. There are certain things I want, and if this Church of yours can get them for me—' Then it was I who stopped him, thinking to humble him toward what he spoke of so bloodlessly. 'That Church,' I said, 'can do many things, and all of them by faith.' He turned to go, scornfully, as if from a quest which he had feared from the start would be fruitless, so I quickly added, 'And it knows many things. It knows what you want and who you are, Olaf Tryggvesson.' He turned, instantly and eagerly, like one who hears a longed-for signal, and cried, 'So you have been waiting for me, as I thought! Then let us have no delay and no pretense. Cast your line, Priest of Fishermen. Your fish is willing to be caught, if you throw me the bait I like.'

"His manner made me writhe inwardly. He treated me so like a huckster that I almost felt like one. There are so many ways of saying things that he might have chosen another. But I remembered my duty, held my temper in, and let him speak on.

"He told me he had heard many things concerning me and had formed his own notion besides. I cannot say he was wrong, except that his devils made him think I had devils' reasons for all I might say or do. He agreed with everything I urged upon him, but he agreed like a Heathen agreeing with another Heathen. When I offered him forgiveness for his sins, he assented indifferently, saying he would as lief not have his deeds held against him. When I threatened him with Hell-fire, he admitted it was great pain to be burnt, which he would like to avoid if he could. And when I promised him the peace that passeth understanding, he cried out in a very agony of longing that he wanted that above all, but could never have it while his other wants were unfulfilled. 'I must have my Kingdom!' he cried. 'Everything else eludes me like a wraith in a snow-storm, but my Kingdom at least I shall have!—and keep it too—if you will help me!' With that he stepped close to me and gripped my arms with such fury that I thought he had become berserk and I must fight for my life. 'You have your Church's ear!' he said fiercely. 'Tell them to help me! I will pray your prayers, and ring your bells, and stuff more souls down your throat than you can swallow. Earls, Bonders, Thanes, Thralls, myself, and the very cattle, if you like. Not one shall refuse, if I set my hand to it. But there must be this for that, with both sides gaining by it, or no bargain ever yet was kept.'

"My anger rose again, at the base word, but he rushed on, prodded by whatever was inside him, so that I had no time to shape the smallest sound. 'I know how Constantine was helped, and Charlemagne, too, and what they gave in payment. We can trade in the same coin and make it work as well, with no need for either of us to speak from the side of the mouth. Give me a Divine Right to be Norway's King, and I will give you a Royal Right to be Norway's Church! There, clear is clear, and plain is plain, and the answer can be Yes or No.'

"I saw it was a greater task than I had thought to make our minds see the same thing in the same manner. I began to wonder whether it might not be well to agree outwardly to what he asked, seemingly on his own blasphemous terms, while secretly having faith that he would one day do things for the right reasons. He suddenly made up my mind for me. He seized my wrist, dipped my hand into the holy basin and shook drops of water onto his own head, like the wind shaking a wet oak leaf. 'Say your spells!' he shouted. I said the sacred words that exorcise evil spirits and make a man a Christian. When it was done, he gave a grunt of satisfaction. 'There is your first soul,' he said. 'Come with me now and you shall have a thousand more.'

"I hesitated to follow him. Stepping outside my safe cave would mean being hurled into a life of perilous action. It was easy enough to speak learnedly, even ardently, of great, dead Kings, but actually to help Olaf take their path was another matter. They knew the traps that beset a conqueror's feet. Perhaps I should study further, before taking action.

"Olaf guessed my doubts and laughed at me, more heartily than I thought such an unfrolicsome man could laugh. 'Oh you of little faith!' he mocked. 'Are you afraid to see things come to life that you have helped beget?' He shamed me with the challenge and I followed him, humbled at his showing me my duty.

"I had been wrong in doubting. The strange thing about a Heavenly plan, which surprises and rewards the faithful, is how simple it is in the carrying out. Of course, it was a miracle, but oh! the rapture of taking part in a miracle! In fairness, though, it should be said that the quick way it was all accom-

34

plished was largely owing to that same vulgar directness of Olaf's that so made my skin creep.

"He waited not an instant to make good his pious boast about the thousand souls. As I followed him down the hill toward where his host was encamped, we saw a man walking alone, who showed by the way he came forward to greet Olaf, that he knew him. 'Here is our first convert,' said Olaf. 'His name is Bolli; he is a great Bonder with a hundred Thanes and Thralls. Let us save his soul!' With that he seized Bolli by the throat and forced him to his knees. Bolli would have had no chance against him, even were he not surprised, and Olaf held him thus with one hand, while with the other he drew his sword. "Choose now, Bolli!' he said. 'Shall I make you Earl of all Norwegian land within ten miles of Nidaros?—or shall I thrust this sword down your gullet and spear out the salmon you ate last night?' 'The Earldom, of course,' replied Bolli, watching the sword point; 'but surely there is some favor I must do, in return for so great a gift.'

" 'Nothing big enough to boggle at,' said Olaf. 'Merely that you became a Christian and acknowledge me as your Divinely appointed King, along with my heirs, forever.'

"Bolli gulped, and I thought he meant to fight. He rolled his eyes upward toward the sky, seeming to weigh the reward that might be his, both hereafter and here. 'Agreed,' he said, and I baptized him. Bolli swore fealty to Olaf. This he did in the names of both his old Gods and his New and gave his word besides, which I knew he would never break, because he was a Bonder. He rose to his feet and drew a breath down into his very toes, as if he had not expected to taste air again. 'Is it not a great comfort to have eternal life?' asked Olaf. 'Any kind will do,' answered Bolli, feeling his windpipe where Olaf had squeezed it, 'but I would feel more comfort still, when I return home, if a few others shared this eternity with me.' 'That is easily managed,' said Olaf; 'where is Hoskuld?' 'Sleeping,' said Bolli. The two of them took sword in hand and sought out Hoskuld, who was quickly baptized and made to swear fealty to Olaf. Three brothers named Floki, Dag and Gunnlaug were the next to whom we brought the Word. They drew their swords

35

and for a moment it seemed that they might stand Olaf off long enough to alarm the camp, for it was three against three. But I got behind one of them, seized him and turned the tide of battle, so that they were soon disarmed, whereupon they accepted baptism, and Olaf as their King. After that we decided to be more patient and convert them one at a time. In that way our numbers grew steadily larger, with Heathen Bonders being transformed into Christian Earls. When at last very few were left (and very few Earldoms left for them), that few accepted the Faith as a group. Then all had been saved, up to the number of thirty.

"But Bolli's faith was too new to him to be the prop it should. 'There are still our thousand men,' he said. 'They cannot all be Earls, nor can the thirty of us master them by force!' Glancing toward me, he added, '—although our strength now be doubled.'

"Olaf was quick with his reply. 'There are both slaves and free among them,' he said, 'and I know that most of the slaves are already secret Christians, dreaming of an eternity in which they are to be our equals. They will be on our side, against any who choose to remain Heathen.' Some grumbled at this, doubting the wisdom of letting a slave think, even once, that he might raise his hand against any of his masters, be they Heathen or not. But we were risking so much by then that this extra risk was taken. The thousand were summoned to a Thing, to be held the next morning, and bidden to bring their wooden image of Thor with them onto the plain.

"Rumors of what was afoot spread through the camp during the night, and Thor's worshipers placed food before him to make him strong for the next day's conflict. When morning came and he was wheeled to the Thing, we saw that they had smeared him all over with fat, so that his gold and silver ornaments shone brightly. They made a great show of bowing to him, very low.

"Olaf came to the point at once, which proved to be the right way to go about it, though no one else would have thought of doing it like that. He told them Thor was a false idol and they must bow only to God. He said nothing more, just that much, and said it with the air of one who has just passed a law.

But one among them, Dala-Gudbrand by name, whom they seemed to have made their spokesman, opposed Olaf with equal readiness. 'Where is this God of yours?' he asked, in a voice of scorn. 'It seems to me he is hiding because he is afraid Thor will see him. Let him show himself, if he dare, as Thor does. Let the two Gods face each other.' Many said that would be a fair test, and there was much laughing when a moment passed and Thor was still the only God they saw. This was a blow to us, for we had counted on everything except to be laughed at. But Olaf pointed suddenly at the sky, where the sun was coming out from behind a cloud, and cried out, 'There comes our God now, looking at us with one of his great eyes! Is there one of you who can meet his gaze?' 'Thor can meet it!' replied Dala-Gudbrand stubbornly, and truly Thor's wooden face was staring back at the sun without flinching, and seeming to gleam fiercely.

"In point of years I was but newly a Christian, and a chill of old Heathen fear crept back into my heart as the God I had once worshiped glared at the One for whom I had forsaken him. Demons tempted me, chanting in my brain that I had chosen wrongly. Nor was I alone in my agony of spirit. All about me, my recent converts sweated and doubted.

"Olaf restored our belief. He seized an axe and, pausing no longer than when he had split his father's slayer, he split Thor. The two halves crashed to the ground with a hollow booming sound that frightened away the Trolls who were beguiling us. 'Thor looks upon our God no more!' cried Olaf, and spat upon the fallen demon. 'Can any of you make our God as sightless as Thor is now?' None of the Heathen moved, all being shamed, but there came a sound from within Thor's burst body, as if he were dying. Olaf turned one of the halves over with his axe, and rats ran out, as big as small dogs. 'There is where the meat has gone which you laid before him,' said Olaf with his loud laugh, in which we all began to join, glad of a chance to set our feelings loose.

"With the laugh thus turned the other way, the matter was decided. We stripped the gold and silver from Thor and made a fire with what was left of him, around which we had a great feast to celebrate a thousand new baptisms. I gave thanks for the good food and ale and preached a sermon to my huge new flock, in which I showed them how right it is to have a God who rules forever in Heaven, and His appointed King, who rules forever here. When I finished, they cried 'Amen,' and a Skald made a song in which he asked God always to save the King. Olaf gave him a piece of gold because the song pleased him, and handed me a smaller piece of gold to give him also, to show that I, too, was pleased and that my approval as well as his must always be sought. Then everyone sang the song together.

"I felt very humble. I saw that an ageless, mighty plan was being followed, against which nothing can stand. It was clear that my small part of it was to join my lot to Olaf's, at whatever hardship to myself. So when he set sail for Norway, I sailed with him, my Bishop's blessing on my head, the Book in my hand, and a sword at my side.

"Now that a thousand and thirty of us had the same zeal, our task grew easier and its fulfillment quicker. At each place where we beached our ships, the same thing happened in the same manner, except that it took less and less time as word about us spread. First we would convert the Bonder or the Hirsir, and after him his men. From the top downward it was always done: from God, through the King, through the Earls, to the people, a mighty pyramid reaching from earth to Heaven, forever kept from crumbling by the servants of the Church.

"Conversion became easier still when Olaf let it be known that he would not harry or pillage any who took the true Faith. Another cause was the fearful lesson he taught to the few who resisted. There was, for example, a Viking named Raud, famed for his strength and stubbornness, who swore he would never take Olaf's God for his, nor Olaf for a King. Raud was said to be a wizard, and many thought he had spells to make Olaf helpless. But one night, after Raud had been drinking heavily, we stole upon him while he slept, bound him to a beam and asked him whether he would be baptized. He refused, with hideous blasphemies. Then Olaf put a piece of wood between his jaws, to hold his mouth open, and tried to make a poisonous adder crawl inside. Raud blew so strongly with his breath that the adder turned back. But Olaf was not to be turned from his purpose as the snake had been. He placed the small end of his hunting horn between Raud's teeth and put the adder in the horn; then he burned the adder's tail with a heated iron, and it crawled down Raud's throat and ate its way out through his stomach. Raud screamed blasphemies until he died, but when the story got out, there were only a few who would copy his stubbornness.

"One such was Eylan Kalda, who boasted that his mother had been a Troll. Many people believed it and went to him to have wounds cured or storms quieted or when some man wanted a woman to love him. Now they went to him to cause Olaf's death. He and his followers encircled Olaf's dwelling and called on all the Trolls and Weir-things to cast their dooms and diseases upon him. But Olaf caught them at their devil's work. He had them bound to a rocky skerry that juts up out of the water at low tide. He himself stood on the beach, within their view. 'My God against yours!' he called to them. 'Put all your spells upon me. If I fall dead, I hereby order that you are to be set free.' He waited, while the tide rose, ever higher, about them. They shrieked their curses at him. Then they shrieked to him to spare them. By the time the water reached their faces, they were merely shrieking, with no real words at all. Those who live near there have named the rocks The Shrieking Skerry. They say they still hear the sounds, at high tide. God will not let them forget.

"The final proof to the Gods of Valhalla that their day was done was the end of Earl Haakon, their champion. He sat smug and smiling when he heard Olaf had landed in Norway, saying to those about him, 'We are threatened by a baby born in a swamp who worships a baby born in a manger!' There was much laughter at this; it was called Haakon's Joke and retold from end to end of Norway. The laughter grew less as Olaf and the fame of his deeds came nearer, but Haakon made no move to defend himself, being unable to believe, after thirty years of ruling, that it could ever be otherwise. It was only when his closest friends were hastening to join Olaf, and the flames of Thor's temples lit the skies, that, too late, Haakon sent out the war-arrow. None answered. His halls were empty, save for a slave named Kark, who sat in chains, waiting to be hanged for killing a freeman. Haakon promised him his pardon and his freedom if he would help him save his life, though if his need had not been so pressing it is doubtful that he would have taken a slave's word. Kark led him to a pit beneath a pigsty, where he kept things he had stolen, by which he had hoped some day to buy his freedom. They jumped down into it, closing the opening above their heads with branches. There they waited, in darkness, silence and filth, until they heard Olaf's men and horses tramping overhead. Olaf knew that Haakon must be hiding somewhere near by, since no one for miles about had seen him leave, so there Olaf camped and waited, meaning to sit endlessly, until hunger and thirst should drag Haakon out from wherever he was. I saw the look of unforgiving remembrance on Olaf's face, and dared to say to him that a Christian turns the other cheek to the foe who strikes him. He bared his teeth like a wolf, and said, 'I must have this particular vengeance. Perhaps it will cleanse my soul.' Then he let it be known that he would give a helmet full of gold to the man who brought him Earl Haakon's head. The two men in the pit heard it proclaimed. After that the Earl and the slave watched each other for three days and nights. Neither of them dared to sleep, Haakon fearing that Kark would kill him, and Kark fearing to be killed because of Haakon's fear. On the fourth day Kark feigned sleep, to see what Haakon would do. Haakon crept toward him, either to see whether he was really asleep, or to be sure he slept forever. Whichever it was, as Haakon bent over him, Kark stabbed him in the heart, and Haakon's death-scream was heard above by Olaf's men. They hauled Kark out by his hair, and Olaf made his word good by giving him a helmet filled with gold. Then he had him hanged for his old crime of having killed a freeman, because Olaf did not want it thought that his was to be a lawless reign, with slaves daring to be more than God had meant they should.

"Now at last he had Norway, all of it, from top to bottom and side to side. No one dared resist him any longer, except a few wretches who fled to sea or to the icy wastes of Finland, whence they screamed vain prayers against Olaf to the unhearing air. Norway was his, wholly and undoubtedly, as his mother had hoped it would be, held more tightly by him than even she had dreamed, because he had an ally beyond her imagining.

"He had said he wanted only his Kingdom, to have peace in his soul. Why then is he still unsatisfied?

"Olaf has thought much about that, and about other things, so much that men say he is becoming a great sage as well as a great warrior, and are repeating his words, as the ancients repeated the words of Aristotle. God has so contrived our growth —says Olaf—that we are never the same when we finish a task as when we begin it. Olaf has a soul now, which he had not when he and his mother made their wish, and that soul will not let him rest while Norway is the only Christian land. Obscene idols are yet worshiped in Sweden, Finland, Denmark and islands beyond the mist. God made them all—says Olaf—and back to God they must all be brought. To the devout, good works have no end. It has been revealed to Olaf that his Kingdom must grow into a Holy Empire, united like those of Constantine and Charlemagne under the one great Sign. Heaven has decreed it so, and Heaven's warrior Olaf will carry out the decree.

"Icelanders! King Olaf sends this word to you, through me. He has looked upon the great task which is his to do. He sees where next he must plant the sacred seed: here in this land where, beyond all others, the soil of the spirit is like Norway's own. And it will be done in peace, as the Prince of Peace, whom Olaf serves, would wish. For Olaf cannot believe that the grandchildren of his own countrymen will, through stubborn pride, bring fire and death into their lovely island, so clearly ordained to be an outpost and sentinel of the Christian Faith. He does not question your bravery, but neither does he question your good sense. You would find the odds too great, a thousand to your one, of men as brave as you. He has the mightiest fleet of ships the world ever saw, to carry his thousands of men where he will. One of his ships is called The Crane. It is twice as long as any ship ever built before it. Another is called The Serpent. It is twice as long as The Crane. Still another is called The Long Serpent. It is half again as long as both the others. These three ships alone could carry more men than there are in Iceland, without his hundred others, all fully manned, all ready to sail, all awaiting his word. But Olaf has learned patience; he enjoined me not to hurry you. A hasty answer—Olaf says—has speed but not weight, which is bad in either ships or promises. He wants the mind, the heart and the spirit to deliberate together, so that when they have agreed, they will answer as one. He wants you to think carefully, deeply, completely, to consider the full meanings of Yes and No, with the blessings or ills that go with the one or the other. Then, when at last you see his great fleet of warships, with Olaf himself on the deck of The Long Serpent, he feels that your minds will have found truth and your souls peace, and you will welcome him joyously, prepared to join him in bringing light to other lands.

"That is all. I give you my thanks for the noble feast you have spread in my honor and for the fine songs that have been sung for me. In return, I have tried to help enliven this night by telling the tale, and bringing the message, of Olaf, King of Norway by the grace of God."

VII

THE feast ended abruptly, no one having much appetite left nor anything to add to what had been said or sung. All knew that a summons to a general Thing would have to be sent through the four Quarters of Iceland. But a good fortnight would pass before it could meet, and it was humanly impossible not to discuss the matter at once. So when the guests took their leave, while expressing their thanks for the food and entertainment, they whispered from one to the other that a small house-Thing would be held next day at the home of Bjorn the Skald.

Theobrand expected something of the sort, but he pretended not to notice the whispering, being glad they would soon start threshing the question out and reasoning their way toward where he felt they must go. With pointed tact, he retired for the night. As he made his way toward the room where he slept, someone scurried up behind him and plucked his sleeve. He turned and recognized Turker, who had crossed himself when he passed near him earlier.

"What is it, my son?" he asked him.

"I am a Christian," said Turker. "Look." He made sure no one was within sight or hearing, then put his hand inside his bosom and drew out a silver crucifix.

Theobrand approved with a smile, then remembered that silver is a thing of value. "Where did you get this?" he asked.

"It was a ring on the finger of Thor, who stands in the temple on the hill. I took it, and beat it into shape. Will you say a spell over it for me?"

"I will say a blessing," replied Theobrand, with a little frown, and did so.

Blessing or spell, Turker was pleased. He kissed it and replaced it in his blouse. "Now you will believe what I will tell you," he said.

"What is that, my son?"

"That I will do anything to help Olaf," said Turker. "Anything." Then, with a wide sweep of his arm that meant the other Thralls, "We all will."

Theobrand smiled benignly. "You would help Olaf spread the Faith?"

"The Faith!" exclaimed Turker, with impatience that gave way to fury. "I want these Icelanders to be slaves!—to Olaf or anyone else!" With that he was gone, leaving Theobrand with one more of the means that the end would justify.

Faith, old and new, was discussed all through that night between Bonders and their wives. In some cases there was bitterness over one another's easy surrender or unreasoning obstinacy; others were pleasantly surprised to find agreement where they had expected opposition, whether in upholding the old beliefs or in hoping for an Earldom.

Eric's father spoke to Eric's mother about what they should do. He found it very difficult, because he had for a long time avoided taking up with her any subject that was serious. She

43

turned her face toward him as he started speaking, without hearing what he said. Her ears were full of Theobrand's voice and the way it rose and fell.

"Eric—" her husband began, with an effort, then stopped. How could he explain to her how all this concerned Eric? How could he say, to that dull, fatuous face, that stranger's face, that Eric was what they must talk about—that Eric was his hope, the great recompense that had replaced *her*, his chance to live again, in old familiar ways that must not be changed? Since he could not, he left Eric out of it and spoke only of himself and her. He tried to make her see the threat that hung over his world, and why he loved that world, even the part of it which she had once been. He tried hard, so very hard, with unaccustomed patience, to make her know at last what he was really like, so that she might stand by his side, without love if need be but with understanding, in a great fight against any odds whatever.

She was not listening. She was dreaming of that other man who had spoken to all of them, earlier in the evening. When it was at length borne in upon her that someone was actually speaking to her there and then, and that it was her husband, all she could think to say was that the feast had ended very suddenly, that it must have been because the guests were displeased about something, that the servants were too slow, or too fast, that the meat was too cold or too hot or too this or too that, that the wrong songs had been sung, that her husband had offended Theobrand in some way, that, oh, that whatever it was, the evening was a failure and it would be said up and down the island that she was a bad hostess. When she reached that point, or rather just before she reached it, she broke into a fit of weeping, so that the last words could not be made out. Her husband saw the meaning coming and did not wait for it, but went out for a walk and to commune with his old friend, the night air.

It was fairly dark outside, with very little moonlight, but he could have followed the familiar footpath with no light at all. By the side, he saw some white shapes and recognized them as the muslin slave-clothes of a group of Thralls. They were talking earnestly together, and though he could not make out

44

the words, their voices had an excitement and exhilaration that was unusual for them. They stopped speaking when they heard his footsteps, and as he passed by they made a great show of bowing and wishing that good Lok should be with him, but he knew what they must have been saying and hoping. If slaves can lift their heads—! Again he had the sickening feeling that the bottom was dropping out of the ground.

By sheer walking, he made himself a little tired. Toward morning he went back home and slept uneasily, waking several times in the belief that it was time to go to Bjorn's house.

Only a dozen or so came to the house-Thing the next day. According to law they did not have to come at all, because there had not been five days' notice. Those who did attend were disheartened by those who did not, feeling they must have already made up their minds what they would do. Each man present had by now the clear intention of saying either Yes or No to Olaf, and they were sure that those who were absent had been thinking in the same manner and very likely reaching opposite conclusions. Resentment which had been felt against Olaf turned against the absentees, and suspicion against the few who straggled in late. The afternoon was nearly over when they decided it was useless to wait longer, for they could see there would be far from a full attendance. By that time there was a wide and angry split in the making between those who were there and those who were not, another between those there with differing opinions. When Bjorn, as host, declared the house-Thing opened, every man mistrusted every other, whether there or not.

When Eric's father arrived, he was peculiarly alert, as one often is after too little sleep, before exhaustion comes. He saw that there were too many ways in which these men differed from one another for them to stand together on what they had in common.

Here were those who would be Earls in Iceland and their sons after them; they were moving about grandly as if they already had the title. They had agreed on it with their wives. All that remained was to mouth a plausible reason and keep a good face before their friends, though they would forgo that if they had to.

Here were those, like himself, ready to fight. They, too, had talked it over with their wives and now acted either through zeal or fury, according to whether or not they had found agreement.

He saw Bjorn's Irish slaves, doubtless as Christian as slaves anywhere, laughing furtively with their eyes at the sight of their masters at odds. He remembered those he had seen in the darkness by the side of the road. Hope was spreading among them, had grown immeasurably in one night.

And between top and bottom were the Freemen, helpless as their fellows in Norway. All were readier to fight each other than Olaf.

He heard loud talk and calm talk, true and lying talk, talk of fighting gloriously or accepting fate. He had never felt before, at any Thing he attended, that the talk was so useless, so plainly aimed at nothing but to give a semblance of argument, with no one really hoping to convince anyone else. He, too, had his turn, and he talked of sending out the war-arrow, while the others listened with their ears but not with their eyes. At last they reached what sounded like a decision, though it made everything meaningless that had been said: they would wait a fortnight until the general Thing would meet, and be bound by what happened there. This brought a great sense of relief, as if it disposed of their difficulties. There would be a great gathering, many wise men would speak and someone would think of the right thing for them all to do. Meanwhile, no one would actually have to do anything, which was why the house-Thing had been such a comfort.

It seemed so to all but their host of the night before. He had led the attack against Olaf, and now felt they were deserting him. As the little meeting disintegrated, he murmured, "But time is short. We must do something now." He repeated the word "now," to make them see it was the point, but they smiled at his impatience, thinking it grew out of his having the Priest for a house-guest. A few of them, who had noticed how Helga had looked at the Priest, thought she was the reason.

He did not return home, as the others did. He needed sleep, but he had passed the point where he could have slept. He resented this terrible wakefulness, which was depriving him of the chance to have dreams. In a dream he had often found the answer to a difficult problem.

So he went to a place where he could sometimes have dreams with his eyes open: to the side of the Ocean. There he sat for a long time, on a piece of wreckage, looking at the water, listening to it, hoping it would send him the kind of strong, helpful thought he needed.

The Ocean is too big. It cannot really be any man's friend, or sympathize or help him get his thoughts in order, no matter how long he may sit at its side, peering into its huge, furrowed face. The Ocean has its own vast problems, which keep it troubled and seething and which it feels it has to solve.

Even the man who once thought he had married a Goddess got no help from this greatest of Giants. It was dusk when he called upon it by name—Aegir, Aegir, Aegir. But Aegir would not be diverted and merely sent his nine daughters scudding to the shore, one by one, to find out what the little man wanted. They are so light-minded and wanton that by the time they got to where he sat they forgot their errand, and told him only that their father's hall is built of emeralds and that if a man were to follow them to where it is strange and wonderful and deep, he would find nothing to disturb his dreams. Then each of them in turn got out of her sister's way and waited for another chance to seduce him. They kept up their steady whispering until little by little he began to listen to them, one after another, and to heed. "Down there, down there," he heard them say, "you can end your doubts, and never know what happens on the shore." He felt his kinship with the land fading, his thoughts mingling with the water's thoughts and a yearning to yield to the persistent invitation. But twilight suddenly made way for night, at which the Ocean felt no need for further disguise and became its dark, horrible, immense self, so that he saw it for the dread Giant it really is and no longer dared think its thoughts. He hastily stepped back, just as one of Aegir's daughters, bolder and more abandoned than her sisters, threw herself on the ground where he had been sitting.

He shuddered at the doom which had so nearly beguiled him.

He belonged to the land, and the land to him. Why should he take himself out of the way? Why not do something against his foes? Something mighty. Something berserk. Something with a sword. A sword, a sword, and something to split with it! Why had the Ocean not said that? Was there something that a sword could not subdue? Was the night hurrying in, so as to hide it from him? Again he scanned the blackening waters for an omen. The foam and shadows only told him what he was deeply telling himself. They said, "You know, you know." He turned and walked away, rapidly, trying as much not to hear as to hear, but he stopped, as the Ocean suddenly called after him, the name—Olaf!

Beyond any doubt the name had been said, clearly, and clearly heard. It may even be that he and the Ocean said it together, since they thought of it together. That was why the Ocean had not called for swords. It was Olaf against whom swords were helpless.

But only Fate was stronger than a sword. Then was Fate on Olaf's side? Yes. Of course. Long before he listened to the Priest's tale, he had been hearing from the crews of many ships, how Olaf did this or Olaf decreed that or Olaf the King commanded thus and such; until now, skimming the cream off his memories as they rushed past him, the names shone forth together. Olaf and Fate. Fate and Olaf. Not only Olaf. Not only Olaf's new God. Fate was upon them. That had been his dim foreboding since the first ships arrived with the news. What else could make Sea-Kings look like that, and put surrender in their faces? They were so quiet, so passive about the coming change. They sent out no war-call, as against any other invader. It is only Fate that thus numbs the sword-arm and lulls the will. He himself! How readily he accepted the King's Priest as a guest! King? Olaf was not his King, whatever he was in Norway, yet he was naming him so. "*The* King." And he had let the Priest talk him down, before his wife, before his son, as if the curse of helplessness lay on his own tongue. Olaf. The waves went on shouting to him and to each other, Olaf, Olaf, Olaf, Olaf, until he, who had just been so nearly one with them that he had learned a little of their language, began to understand why they were so certain, so insistent, why they kept repeating

48

that the world could not prevent what Olaf meant to do. Olaf the All-Powerful. Olaf the Spear-Breaker. Olaf the Doom.

He thanked Aegir, threw him a golden ring for his treasure-chest, inhaled deeply of his salty breath, and walked on, considering his new-found fact and the way it changed everything. If the battle was already decided, deep in the brain of Time, it was best to know it. Fate takes many forms and has a monstrous pleasure in seizing you unaware. A man is just the least bit better off who can recognize it when it comes. Then he has a better chance of doing whatever can still be done, of saving what can still be saved.

He needed a plan, one that was not already written down to be thwarted. He must consult with friends beyond suspicion, who had no hope of gain or fear of loss, who loved him and would advise him what he should do, what he must do, what he could do if they told him, without pausing or thinking. He had two such friends, and they were both dead: his great-grandfather Ingolf who was the first to settle here and his father Eric who had told him of it.

From the dead he would get the advice he needed. It was the end of their world, too, that was threatened. They would find that far more awesome than their own life's end had been, and no amount of glory with Odin in Valhall could pay for it. It is to earth that the dead cling most tightly, and they want the earth likewise to cling to them. The true solace of dying is to know that familiar things will remain, that familiar people will remember and perhaps make a song about the things you and they believed in common; a ghost, hearing such a song, may return and feel at home. That cannot be if there is nothing familiar to return to, if memory no longer cares about such as you or your Gods.

He walked toward the buried ship that was Ingolf's tomb. Not directly to the tomb. First to the temple of Thor on the hill which overlooked it. They say a dead man sometimes changes from what he was in life. A visit to the God would be a safeguard.

The wooden image of Thor, which many years ago had floated to the spot where he wanted Ingolf to land, still stood in the temple on the hill. The remains of an altar fire glowed before him through the night, making his greased face gleam out of the darkness at Ingolf's descendant, who came in to tell Thor what was afoot and ask whether he might borrow some light from the altar. It is very dark in a tomb, he explained to Thor, even an ancestor's tomb, and no ghost likes to be awakened. Light and the God's approval would lend him courage. He touched a pine torch to the embers and was gratified when Thor allowed the flame to catch. Holding the burning branch above his head, he promised Thor an ox and went on his way down the hill toward the buried ship.

The torch made a wide, bright circle, around whose rim danced shadows which really might not have been shadows at all, but something else waiting to close in if the light should happen to go out. The nearer he came to the ship-tomb, the greater grew his fears and the greater the courage with which he conquered them. It is hard to understand such courage and such fear. He was braving things he believed in. Have you ever heard the story of Hervod? Well, he had.

When the great earthen mound that covered the ship and its master loomed against the stars, he stopped suddenly where he was, despite courage, torch and Thor. On its top he saw, not the unexpected, but ever so much more terrible, something he had told himself he would have to see. What is sudden fright, compared to a nightmare come true? Pale, bluish ghost-lights flickered on the mound, waiting. For him. Expecting him, watching him. He had summoned them and they were there, to take part in the tomb-Thing. All of them, and himself.

Cowardly thoughts rushed into his mind and seized him from within. Go back! Be with living men! Say "Yes" to Olaf and his Priest! So many were going to! Were they right? At least they were safe. They did not have to face—*this*. What was shame? Be safe, be safe! Fling your torch at the ghosts, scream and run!

But from out of the deepest, oldest part of his memory arose the echo of a story. He had heard it as a very little boy, along with stories of the four dwarfs who hold up the sky, the deeds of the hero Hjalmar and all the other lore around which his little bones and flesh had wrapped themselves. This was the story about Odin, about how the father of the Gods obtained

50

wisdom, and the price he paid for it. His father had told it to him. It seemed to him now, as always, that his father and Odin looked alike.

"Wisdom lay at the bottom of a well. 'What price will you pay for it?' asked Mimir, the well-keeper. 'Any and all,' said Odin. 'Then any and all it shall be,' Mimir answered him. He plucked out one of Odin's eyes, stabbed him with a spear and hanged him to a tree. Nine days and nights the God hung there, suffering as none have suffered since, to learn how to rule us here on earth, and hereafter in Valhall.

> Nine days and nights hung Odin there,
>   Upon the dreadful tree
> To learn the Runes of earth and air
>   And sky and flame and sea.
> A spear within his heart was thrust,
>   And half his sight he gave,
> To learn how men, when turned to dust,
>   May live beyond the grave.

Say a prayer to Odin on the battlefield! Drink a toast to Odin at the feast! Never desert him!"

"No, never!" he cried, and the ghosts could hear him if they would. "Odin against Christ! Let my son be proud of me!" He ran, but toward the mound, not from it.

The stone entrance had long since fallen in, but thieves had made another through the earthen side and shored it up with wood. Through this he made his way, clutching his pine torch and having to crouch somewhat because the opening was low.

He straightened up when he reached the inner chamber and for a moment believed he was still outside, because he was conscious of stars above his head. Then he saw that they were not spread over the whole sky, but only here and there, and he knew that small animals had dug holes from above, both through the great shed that was built above the ship and the thick layer of earth and stones that was laid upon it.

This bit of reasoning led to more, leaving no room in his head for his fears, which raged in the air around him, looking for somewhere to roost. He looked about carefully and thoroughly, as he always did when he found himself in any sort of unexpected place. Also by habit, he took stock of himself, making sure that his sword was not jammed in its sheath, nor his belt unbuckled. His teeth were chattering. Not from fear; he knew what it was from. It was the cold, the piercing, gnawing cold, which had not been tempered by the sun in a hundred years. There is nothing so cold as a grave.

His torch-light showed him that he was standing outside the hull of the ship. Whoever had made the opening in the side of the mound had broken through this as well. He walked to the inside of the vessel and found that there, too, he was standing on ground. The keel had rotted away in the hundred years it had lain against the earth, and only the sides were standing. The only other wood that remained in place was the great shed above. Its beams were unusually thick, and must have been overlaid with stones before the dirt was thrown on, or they would surely have rotted as the keel had.

The ship was not an overly long one: a Karfi, with seats for twenty rowers. It was pointed toward the sea, which could be heard roaring, even here. He walked toward the prow, and there his feet trod on some moldering wooden planks that could not be part of the sides, because they lay below where the forecastle must have stood. He stopped, wondering why these planks alone could have lain on the open earth so long and not have decayed utterly. No one could have brought them there for any purpose whatever; they must have been part of the ship. After a little thought, he reasoned it out. Here, near the prow, the forecastle had stood; the deck, above which it rose, collapsed first and lay between earth and forecastle. This was an exciting thought, for if it were so, then Ingolf's dust must lie precisely here; those who were buried with their ships were always placed in the forecastle, seated, and in their full armor. He searched about in the rubble for that armor, holding his torch this way and that, so the glint of metal would show.

Any fear was now as far from his mind as if he had never known it. Only one passion at a time can possess a man, and his was the zeal of the quest. He was the reasoner, the searcher, the Viking who explored.

A small plank broke in two as he stepped on it. The ends fell inward and struck something which rang metallically. He kicked the plank away. Was it armor? It did not shine. Why, no, how could it? It was covered with rust. What was it? A shield? A helmet? He picked it up and held the flame near it. It was a helmet, made of bronze. The workmanship was very rich; despite the corrosion, he could make out handsome silver chasing. He looked away from it to the place where it had been lying. Had there been a skull under it? Ingolf's? He bent down to look closely.

And then something rushed at him from a shadow and put out the torch.

Now this is a strange thing. He had come here for the most important deed of his life, his greatest act, his greatest decision, his greatest heroism. He knew how much depended on it, and had all his faculties alert. He saw, heard, observed, more keenly than ever in his life. Then for just a moment a shock upset the balance, and the importance, which had urged him to be aware, became his enemy and overwhelmed his eyes and ears, so that afterward he was never sure what he had seen or heard, or how or when, or whether it was real.

Here is what Ingolf's great-grandson believed had happened, when he told it later:

He screamed when the torch went out, the deep chest-scream of a man dreaming hideously. He did not know what had brushed the torch from his hand, whether animal, demon or ghost, and did not dare to try to find out. He shrank to the ground and huddled there, covering his face with his arm so as not to see. It was dark, so he could not have seen anyway, but he dreaded that he somehow might. His teeth still chattered, and now not only from the cold. He wished they would stop. He has said that it was not he that was afraid. It was his teeth. They seemed so frightened that fear had come leaping back into him, through them.

Though his arm and the blackness kept him from seeing, he began to hear. There was a sound as of something moving about. At first he thought it was made by whatever had struck out the torch. Then it seemed rather to be made by many things. Then by many men. And the sound they made as they moved was familiar. It was the awkward, shuffling tread of men who are carrying heavy loads—*aboard a ship*. Then he heard two men together, carrying something unusually heavy and panting from the effort; after that there was no longer any mistaking the sound. A man shouted orders, the same that every ship's captain gives when leaving port. He remembered hearing those orders given by his father, the first time they sailed together, and by many captains since. And then, out of all the sounds that he was hearing or remembering, one voice arose, singing, a song that sailors have when the Ocean has called them and they cast off. It mingled with the splashing of waves and oars creaking against their locks. He knew the song, knew its every rise and fall. Everyone who sailed the North Sea knew it.

> I know an old man,
>   He has nine daughters,
> A wife named Ran,
>   And he rules the waters.
> I hear him call, and I cannot stay.
> Away!
>
> Far back on the land,
>   Where trees are shady,
> While hand in hand
>   With you, my lady,
> I thought of the wind and the flying spray.
> Away!
>
> Your hair was gold,
>   Your eyes were starry,
> The wind is cold,
>   And now I'm sorry.
> I'm going to live on the land some day.
> Away! Awa-a-a-ay!

He was never able to recall why and when he uncovered his eyes. All he could swear to was that presently they were open, seeing what was taking place about him, and it was the very same that he had been imagining when he had only the sounds to go by. There was no change which could make him notice

54

that his eyes were open, or to remind him that they had not been.

For one thing, he was not surprised to find he was no longer in the grave at night, but on the open sea in brilliant daylight. He had known that from the first, as he had known that the ship had become as strong and seaworthy as when it was put into the ground. The mast was raised, the sail bellied against the bright sky, the men bent strongly to their oars, and they were swiftly drawing away from land which he knew was Norway. Two other ships followed, raising their masts into place as this one had done and taking the course it set. And above, at the window of the forecastle was Ingolf, his graying hair falling below his bronze helmet, whose silver chasing gleamed in the sunlight.

The ghost of the first settler did not look down at the deck, even when his great-grandson found his voice and dared to call him by name, but stared out to sea with an obstinate fixity that nothing could shake. The crew, too, possessed by the same grim singleness of thought as their commander, were intent upon their oars and where they were heading, giving no sign that a visitant from another day was aboard, though he walked the length of the ship and back, telling them who he was and that he had come for their guidance and help, against their great, common doom. They gave him no answer. There was none they could give, nor could they see or hear him, for he was as unalive to them as they to him. These men were Those Who Dwelt Here Before, a hundred years before. The song came back to him, with which he had taunted Theobrand:

> Ingolf,
> Who was the first settler,
> Because he would not be ruled in Norway
> By King Harold Fairhair—

Here it was, that famous, stubborn journey to Iceland, for him to see, and concealed in it somehow, the answer to his question, how he and his son should meet Fate.

The sun went down behind the horizon as he looked at it, then magically up again on the other side; three times thus and the journey was done, and there lay the shore of Iceland, less

55

than a mile off their bow, with its distant mountains rising to offer an austere welcome.

They brought Thor up on deck, to behold his new home. He stared at it steadily, looking the same in every way as when he lent the fire in the temple. They lowered him over the side, dropped him into the waves and crowded to the rail, to see which landing-place he would choose. Because of his great weight he went almost full length under water, then bobbed back up into the air, fell on his back with a splash, floated for a moment while he made up his mind, and at last found a current to take him where he wanted to go.

Ingolf spoke to his crew. "Thor is finding what we seek," he said. "A new place for our old ways." The men yelled for joy and shouted insults back across the Ocean toward Harold Fairhair in Norway. Ingolf let them vent their feelings for a moment, then gave a sharp order. Instantly the men went back to their oars and rowed after Thor, toward land.

The journey would soon be done. The man who was aboard with them, whom they could not see, knew he must get an answer to his query, now, before they landed, or the chance would be gone. He must make them hear him. Calling upon all his strength, he shouted, loudly enough, as the saying goes, to wake the dead. "What shall we do?" he screamed. "My son and I—what shall we do?"

Ingolf, who was going back into the forecastle, turned and looked at the place where his great-grandson stood, although he did not see him and was looking through him into the distance. "Let those who come later," he said solemnly, "repay this debt to Thor." When he had said that, all the crew rested on their oars and looked in the direction he was looking, through the man who had come with them on the trip, to the horizon, behind which the future hides. They were giving him his answer, all the answer he would get. Its meaning was deep and hidden, and he would have to think it out, like the riddles that Odin was fond of asking and answering.

Then, very swiftly, the light began to fade, as when the sun sinks behind a hill. He tried, with all the power of his will, to go on seeing Ingolf and his crew, but suddenly everything was dark and the ship was back in its grave under the mound, rotting away as it had for a hundred years.

The darkness was no longer as black as when his torch went out. Overhead, through the little holes the animals had made, and at the side through the thieves' tunnel, bits of early morning light began to seep in. Ingolf's great-grandson groped about on the ground for the rusted helmet. As his eyes grew used to the graying light, he found it. He took it with him, out through the tunnel. He meant to wear it, on a certain sea-voyage he had decided to make. He knew how the debt to Thor could be repaid.

VIII

IT is very difficult to keep a big secret in a little place, and Iceland was little. The first thing that got into the air was that there was a secret. The second thing was that a certain small group of men, not more than half a dozen, and all of them close friends of Eric's father, were the ones who shared it. The third thing was that others near to them, who customarily learned a secret by simply waiting for it to be told them, were not learning this one.

All that was certain was this: the seven men had met in the woods near Thor's temple. A woman who was gathering berries saw them, but they saw her, too, and stopped talking until she was out of earshot, although she dawdled as much as she could. The next day one of them bought a ship from a trader, and they let it be known that in three days they would sail.

That was far from enough to satisfy curiosity, but there was no coping with the resistance of those who held the secret. When anyone questioned them, they said they were going raiding in the Orkneys. Nobody believed that, because one of the seven, when asked suddenly where they were going, had absent-mindedly started to say something else, then quickly corrected himself to say it was the Orkneys. He was seen to make the sign of Thor's Hammer as he walked away, as though to guard against another such near-slip. Evidently an oath had been sworn.

Theobrand the Priest was least ready of all to believe this story of a raiding-trip to the Orkneys. He felt that it might be—and suspicion changed "might be" to "doubtless was"—a trick to upset his plans, such as he himself would attempt were he in the place of these Icelanders.

He knew two ways to learn a secret: to think it out and to spy it out. He sent for Turker.

"Do you still wish to help Olaf spread the Faith?" he asked, choosing to forget the precise words the Thrall had said.

Turker did not correct him. He simply said, "Yes."

"Then here is what you are to do. First, you must go along on that ship. Can you find a way to do that?"

"Yes."

"At each port you touch, you are to send me an account of all that has happened. I will give you money, to pay messengers. Can you do that, too?"

"Yes."

Theobrand indicated that he had nothing further to say, but Turker did not leave. "Is there something you don't understand?" the Priest asked.

"Yes," said Turker. "Why am I to do this?"

"For the greatest of all rewards."

"In this world or the next?"

"In both. You shall be free here and happy hereafter."

"Then I will do it," said Turker, and left.

Having arranged for the secret to be spied out, the Priest turned to his second method: thinking it out. His mind did not function like the mind of Eric's father. He hated the cursed practice of meandering through old slow beliefs, of communing with Nature and idols in order to bring one's own thoughts laboriously to the surface—hated it the more because it had once been his own way. Chase away the Trolls who make the shadows! Let God's sunlight in! "Here are certain facts," thought Theobrand, "to be examined with the eyes and ears that Heaven gave me, and the nose, too, to track down the Heathen stench that seems to be in them. What are these facts? I will tell them off with my beads, calmly, knowing that the truth will prevail. So: One, for the Father; Two, for the Son; Three, for the Paraclete; Four, for the Gospels. Now there will be virtue in my reasoning."

But virtue or not, and truth or not, he counted his beads in vain, sifting fact by fact, over and over, so many times that they ceased to have any meaning whatever. The day before the ship was to sail, he still had only the suspicion he started with.

There had been time and ease enough for him to think it through. The traditional three-day visit was well over, but his hostess had pressed him to stay, with something more in her face than kindness to a guest. The remembrance of the look she had bestowed on him suddenly sent another idea racing through his blood: how desirable she was and his long continence. He dismissed this hurriedly, perceiving once again how Satan ever lurked in unexpected corners, and returned to his problem. Most suspect was the extreme hospitality of Helga's husband, who had lately been adding his persuasion to hers, begging him to stay and make the house his own, even after the ship would sail. "He hates me," thought the Priest, who knew other men's hatred as one knows an old friend turned enemy. "This is not hospitality, but disdain. He feeds me while he laughs at me in his heart. Something makes him confident." There was the first fact, to mark yet once again with the first blessed bead. Now to the next, trying to see it afresh, as if he never had before.

The Icelanders would sail in the morning. No waiting for the Thing, at which their Thor must fight for his life. They had so much to say, those singers about Ingolf and the idol that led him ashore, yet they could leave without saying it to all Iceland, at a moment when their Gods needed so badly to be sung about. That, too, was marked again, by the second bead, but it only made the same sound as always when it clicked against the first. No matter. Have faith. Light will come. To the next point.

They were not going to the Orkneys. Theobrand had seen the ship loading up with water and food. They had enough salted meat, herring and dried fruit to eat their way to the Orkneys and back six times. Didn't they mean to live off the land they sacked? What kind of woman's raiding was this? And they had driven live cattle aboard, and piled in fodder for them. "Why?" he had asked one of the men, and received the obvious, idiot's answer: "For milk." Did they expect to be becalmed in the middle of the Ocean, and have to live a year there, waiting for a breeze? There were seats for twenty rowers. Row, you fools! He almost shouted at their bland, annoying faces, though he was alone in the house and they were all at the harbor. Ah well, that was the third bead. Click.

And four. Four, the preposterous, mad item. The cargo! What was a cargo doing on a raiding trip? Perhaps they were really only going to trade with the Orkney Islanders, not harry them, and were ashamed to show they had so little courage. Even so, why such a cargo as this? Ploughs, chairs, beds: things to put in houses and keep farms growing. The Orkneys had no need of these; they made them as well as Icelanders did. He was losing his temper and was about to fling his beads on the floor, when a fifth fact ran into the room in the person of little Eric and shouted jubilantly, "I am going with my father on the raiding trip tomorrow!"

Well, it was possible, Theobrand reasoned, when he had digested the new surprise. A boy is taken on his first sea-journey some time or other. But not yet. Not quite so young as this. He sat Eric on his knee, trying to seem jovial, but frightening him with his ferreting look. He had to let him play with the rosary and break the string before his young confidence was restored. Then Theobrand, kneeling to gather the beads from the floor and with his avid face thus averted, asked in a casual tone, "Where is the ship going?"

"To the Orkneys," answered Eric, both meaning it and liking the sound.

"But aren't you afraid to go raiding?" asked Theobrand, and somehow remembered a verse that was sung to him in his own childhood, in a woman's voice.

Some day your sword will win renown—
Not yet.
Some day another sword will strike it down—
Not yet.
Some day you will be borne to Odin's hall,
But oh, not yet!—you are so very small.

Oh no, Eric wasn't afraid. "Stand there, against the wall!"
he commanded. "Now, look!" He made the Priest pretend to be
an Orkney Islander and ran him through with a fancied sword.
Then, satisfied that his victim was impaled, he ran out of the
house, shouting to any and all that he was going raiding with
his father.

Eric's mother came into the room. She was the sixth fact
connected with the secret that was trying to be kept, though
no one knew it, except perhaps Odin and Thor and Frey and
Freya and the other Divinities of Valhall, who had once let
her pretend to be one of them. Had she made the most of that
chance years ago, Theobrand would not now be here, in their
house, seeking an augury in his beads.

She came in diffidently, asked whether he was comfortable
and hoped that her little boy had not disturbed his meditations.
She seemed wholly taken up with household affairs, of which
her guest's tranquility was part, and of which her husband's
departure on the morrow only made her more conscious. This
was indicated at once, not only from the quick, practiced look
she cast about the room, but from her housewifely attire, with
its apron and the big bunch of keys dangling from her hip. The
only detail that belied this impression was the way she wore her
hair: it hung down over her back and shoulders and the ends
were tucked into her belt in the fashion of unmarried girls.
That suggested that she was younger than one would suppose,
but was bravely performing mature duties thrust upon her by
life.

She blew a speck of dust from the lectern that held Theobrand's book, and gave him a little unobtrusive smile which told
him to go on with whatever he was doing. She was tiptoeing
out when it occurred to him that God might have sent her, to
help him learn the truth about the raiding-trip to the Orkneys.

He remembered her rapt look when he was speaking at the feast.

"Don't go," he said.

"I don't want to interrupt—" she began.

"A welcome interruption," he assured her, and removed a roll of parchment from a chair, to make a place for her. After a moment's fluttering doubt that such an honor could really be hers, she sat timidly on the edge of the chair, as if poised for quick departure when the time should come for him to return to his great thoughts and herself to her little tasks. She waited in modest silence, to let him choose the subject of discourse.

"What did you think," he asked her at length, "of what was said at the feast the other evening?"

"I do not remember what the others said," she replied. "Your words have driven theirs away."

"They were not my words," he gently reproved her. "God placed them in my mouth."

"I see that, now that you have pointed it out to me," she said, and contritely echoed him: "God placed the words in your mouth."

"You speak of God. Have you lost faith then, in your own Gods?"

"My life is very unhappy." Her eyes abruptly filled with tears. "It is the old Gods who have made it so." She had an impulse to tell him of her sorrows and disappointments, but remembered he was a stranger. He eased the way for her to do it. "If it will make you feel at peace to unburden your soul," he said, "no one but God and I will be listening, and it will never be retold."

She was encouraged by his manner and the Cross he drew in the air. "Seven years," she said, then stopped, as if it were a complete explanation.

"Have you been unhappy all that time?"

"I have been lonely. And at my father's house before that. No one ever seemed to—to—"

"To love you?"

"—to want to speak to me. Only to each other. When I would ask something, they were annoyed, having to answer me."

62

"But your husband?—and your son?"

"My husband least of all. At the start—oh, yes! oh, yes!—but it passed, so quickly! And he never let me be with my son, not really. He took him away for whole days. They would come back, laughing together and talking together at the table, just as my father and brothers had done. Never to me. No one ever—until now—until you—" Her feelings suddenly got the better of her. She reached across to him, seized one of his hands and kissed it.

"You need be alone no longer, my daughter," he said. "You may speak with God, whenever you wish, and He will answer you."

"Yes!" she exclaimed, with a force and fire he did not know she had. "I want to follow your God! Tell me how I can serve him!"

As if a new and arresting thought had suddenly forced itself upon him, Theobrand stepped back and studied her intently, remaining thus a long time, until she grew uneasy and asked what made him stare at her.

"Your face."

"Oh," she said bitterly, "my face is not what it was. Neglect and scorn have changed me. You will think me vain, but I once was praised for my beauty. I was called by the names of a Goddess!" she added proudly.

"A Goddess!" cried Theobrand indignantly. "Your face is the face of a Saint!" He pressed on, with so much earnestness that he began to mean it a little. "I never until now saw a Saint's face," he said, with a trace of sadness because of the long deprivation, "but I have long known what it would be like. My Bishop told me of such a face. He saw it in the wall of a church in Byzantium. It was made of a thousand little squares of marble, variously colored, but the glory of the Heavenly face held it all together as one. People stood before it throughout the day, bound by its divine spell, and no one who saw it could ever forget its double promise: of love for those who need love"—Helga's heart glowed with kinship for the distant, beautiful mosaic—"or help," he added, "for those who are sunk in evil. A Saint fulfills both these holy duties," he explained, softening his voice to ease her double, saintly burden.

"Both are ways to serve God, and the opportunities are ever present. There is one now, near by, who has an evil secret in his heart, placed there by Satan, who hopes thus to thwart the God you and I serve. It has been granted you to learn this secret, my daughter, so that his soul may be saved and our God not thwarted."

"I will do whatever you wish," said Helga.

Deeming it safe by now, he told her he meant her husband. Placing his hand gently upon her head, as if to steady her for her task, he suggested to her how the secret might be learned on this her husband's last night at home. It was another of the means justified by the great good end, that otherwise were dubious.

Later, when he was alone, he wondered whether she really could regain her husband's trust, after relinquishing it for seven years. He felt just the least bit sorry for her, in case she should fail and be humiliated. Instantly he banished such compassion, lest it give birth to fleshly appetite, and resisted the impulse to call her back. To purge himself of any possible impurity, he prayed in this fashion:

"Oh, Lord, You know all things. You see into my heart and search the darkest corners. Even if I wished to deceive You, I could not. You know I do not desire this woman or want anything soever from her for myself. You know that all I do, Lord, is for You. To serve You I will endure any trial, suffer any shame. Therefore, forgive me, Lord, for the deception I have practiced upon her, nor let it count against me on the last great day. Amen." He rose from his knees, refreshed, cleansed and secure.

Helga had no such recourse as his, not having yet learned the tranquilizing power of prayer. Her only religious acts had been sacrificing before idols, which among Icelanders usually led to deeds, often of a violent kind. Now she was between two faiths, had neither and felt spiritually aimless. She seized the one thing she could be sure of and clung to it. Out of all the complicated things Theobrand had said to her, she gleaned there was a particular task he wanted done. She would try to do it, to please him.

IX

IT was Theobrand's own fault that he could not reason out the carefully kept secret. He had six facts to work with, but there was a seventh which would have made all the others clear, and he was refusing to admit that it existed. That seventh fact was Thor. Were it not for the Priest's stubborn blindness to the Heathen God, he would have seen that once these men sailed from Iceland, they were never coming back. Here is what had happened in the woods near Thor's temple:

The little group of Bonders whom Eric's father had summoned there were those out of all he knew who could be relied upon with absolute certainty. He wanted no would-be Earls trying to prevent his sailing in the hope that Olaf would hear of it and be pleased. At the general Thing, votes would certainly be taken and laws passed, all on Olaf's behalf, so they must sail before it took place. There was no chance that he was guessing wrong about how it would go, for he had had a little taste of it at the house-Thing. As the saying went, he did not need to eat the whole egg to know it was addled.

He spent an entire precious night considering those he knew who, for whatever reason, would be willing to leave Iceland at once and forever and keep the news to themselves. In the six he chose, he made no mistake. The number could have been greater, but less sure. All of them believed in the old Gods and the old habits and privileges they symbolized. In addition, one had debts which he did not want to spend the rest of his life paying, one wanted to avoid trial at the Thing for murder and one was a Norwegian who fled from Olaf to Iceland and had no wish to be pointed out to him by Theobrand. All had the necessary quality of desperation.

Feeling, however, that their personal reasons, though ever so urgent, were not sufficient guarantee of secrecy, he first made them go with him into the temple, where he sacrificed the ox which he had promised Thor. Then they dipped the altar-ring in the animal's blood, swore secrecy and begged the God that if ever they broke their oath, they should be changed into women. But even an oath enforced by a God was not enough. A man may break an oath and brave the consequences. Eric's father wanted an assurance that could not be broken, no matter what a man might be willing to do. That assurance was given, by all seven of them. They gave each other their word.

Had the townspeople known that, they would have realized it was impossible to learn the secret, and stopped trying. To give a word was an awesome, literal action, full of magic, because a word and the thing it stood for were one and the same. To say a man's name, for example, was to affect his flesh, and therefore, not to be said lightly. You had a certain number of words, which were your power over the things you named; if you *gave* a word, the thing it stood for went with it, and if you broke the word—which of course you wouldn't dare do—you broke the thing, too. Thus, if I said to you: "I give you my word that I will not speak of this," and then I did speak of it after all, the broken word would break my power to speak, and I could never speak again. Several things happened to a word when it was thus used as a hostage: first it was given; then someone else took it; then the one who had taken it said he "had" the first man's word; and when at last the first man made the word good, it was his again, so that he was able to say he kept it after all. Therefore, the giving of words was a most solemn deed, fatal to the giver if not redeemed. Except by monsters, a word was never broken until Christianity came and changed "keeping your word" to "telling the truth," which was an entirely different thing and almost impossible to do; nobody could be sure of telling the truth even if he wanted to, and no threat of Hell-fire could compel it. The old way was more practical.

When the seven Bonders had thus made completely sure of

one another, they went into the woods, for even in the temple someone might be listening. Some of them expected a proposal that they go to Norway and try to kill Olaf, and asked if that were it. The answer was "No"; he had thought of it, but it would be a hopeless attempt, with so few against all Norway; they would be throwing their lives away with nothing gained. They agreed that this was so.

Then he told them what he did have in mind. When they heard it, they knew he had been right to insist on so many safeguards.

He related what he had seen and heard in Ingolf's tomb, the advice Ingolf had given, and how by heeding it and repaying the old debt, they could save all they most highly prized. Just as Thor had found a new home for their ancestors in the old days, they must now find a new home for Thor.

He knew of a place where such a home could be, but no one besides themselves must know, lest Olaf send a fleet and bring them back. Before telling them where it was, he warned them that they would have to build it up from the very ground, losing everything in Iceland that they had worked for, fought for or inherited. They would have to people it, too, so let them bring their children. Let them bring their wives, too, if their wives wanted to come and could be trusted; if not, leave them for Olaf and Christ, and new women would be captured in raids, to breed new families. The crew would have to be chosen carefully, being told they were going to the Orkneys, but they would be such men as would most likely stay with them when they heard the truth, which would be when they were well off shore. Dissenters would then be fed to the fishes. After that, they would bring the image of Thor up from the hold and tell him and the others where they were really heading. They were not going to the Orkneys, of course.

The site of their new home had not been revealed to him by his great-grandfather Ingolf, in a dream or elsewhere, but by his father Eric, or what was the same thing to him, by a vivid memory of his father Eric, with his flaming red beard looking like the sunset. They were going to Greenland.

There, amid rocks and snow would rise new altars. They would have to fight ice and bitter wind and hard, stubborn

67

ground, but that was easier, in this dark moment of their world's life, than fighting Olaf. The Aesir-creed would live. And if things changed as none could now foresee, their sons might bring it back to Iceland at the point of their swords. Small streams become big rivers. This world itself contained nothing at all at first, before Odin and his brothers molded it for our delight.

> Odin and Villi and Vay,
> They say,
> Found nothing but darkness and snow,
> And so
> They filled it with beauty, and then,
> My men,
> Created a female and male.
> Wassail!

A great cheer went up as he finished, heartier and louder than their small numbers seemed able to give forth. Even the woman who had been unable to overhear what they were saying, heard the cheer when she was a long distance away. It meant that they were with him completely. It meant that they agreed as we only agree with one who says what we would like to have said ourselves. It meant that they were now seven, instead of only one. And they rewarded him with the prize he valued most: they acclaimed him their Sea-King.

Sea-King! When they called him that, the two ends of his life came together and rhymed. Memories by the dozen mingled with the present reality, so that he could not tell which was which. A rush of all the thoughts he had ever had about anything were in his old nickname, which was now his real name, and between the two lay all the things that had happened to him, of which he now was made. He could not think of anything, because he was thinking of too much. Sea-King! The sound of it was all he could take in.

X

HELGA was, by habit, unfitted for conniving. Her scheme for how she would draw the secret out of her husband was simple and transparent, built around the fact that he was to sail next morning and this would be their last night together.

What she meant to do, with no previous practice in such difficult magic, was to bring back their past, and that without ever having understood what it was. She still had the dress she had been wearing when he first saw her. While she was putting it on, before dinner, she imagined what would happen—or, rather, what she would like to have happen, being unused to distinguishing the two. As she saw it, the conversation would not move gradually from step to step, as usually happens. In her thoughts it galloped and leaped, from peak to peak.

"Do I remind you of someone?" she was going to ask.

"Yes," he was going to reply, as memories crept back upon him. "Freya!"

"And you believe in me still?"

"Always! You are the Most Gently Born of the Gods, Wearer of the Flaming Necklace, Bringer of Love, Weeper of Gold!"

"How will you prove this to me?"

"By giving you all that I most dearly prize: my love, my wealth—my *secret!*"

After that, there would be an embrace—At that point, she stopped thinking about it, because her desire was now for Theobrand. She would manage that detail in the easy, effective way known as "somehow." The great thing was that the prize would be hers, to bring back to Theobrand in triumph.

But good Lok was not with her, because she had renounced him, and so did not suffer anything to turn out as she had planned. She waited vainly, all through dinner, for her husband to say something about the dress. He showed no sign of recognizing it, or even of noticing it. The fact is, he had decided to confide in her. He was silent and waiting, because Theobrand was at the table with them.

Like his wife, he, too, had imagined how he would begin, but he meant to stick to truth and fact. "As a matter of justice to Eric," he was going to say, "I think his mother should be given the choice of coming with us." This would lead to all the rest, as it had led him to his decision to tell her.

He knew that trusting to her silence would be a risk. As ship's master, he alone did not have the privilege of making a mistake, but after weighing his duty to his ship against his duty to his son, he felt it was a risk that had to be taken. Reasonable safety could be had through an oath from her, threats from himself, and waiting until the night before they sailed, and he would have no regrets for want of one last effort to make her understand.

> Rather wish you had not tried
> Than wish you had.

When they went to their bedroom, he undressed at once, wanting rest for the next day's trying tasks. Helga opened one of the light-holes in the wall and let the moon shine on her face. Just as he was about to begin speaking, she asked him whether she didn't remind him of someone. That distracted him and he had to reassemble his thoughts. He did not answer, because he had not been paying attention to her, but only to what he meant to say to her. She repeated the question, and pouted.

"What did you say?" he asked, becoming conscious that she was speaking to him. He was annoyed by the interruption and became mindful that she still had time to spread the news, through folly or malice.

70

She asked the question for the third time, now fairly shouting it. "I asked whether I don't *remind* you of someone!"

To that he could not resist answering yes, she reminded him of her father, whom she was growing to look more like every day (and whom he disliked, probably for being her father). He made up his mind to wait with telling her until morning, the very last instant before they sailed. He was in bed by now. He turned over onto his side with his back toward her and shut his eyes.

Things were turning out in grotesque opposition to the way Helga had daydreamed them. She became impatient, then irritable, then lost what self-possession she had and made the mistake of improvising. In a petulant tone, she accused him of never confiding in her any more. He and his friends knew where that ship was really bound: why didn't he tell her? Half asleep, he grunted: "The Orkneys." That brought a flood of tears and mild hysterics, through which she denounced him as a Heathen, told him he was helping Satan, thwarting God and other bits of Christian sermonizing whose source was unmistakable. That brought him sitting up, wide awake and appreciating his narrow escape. She was encouraged by his attention, thinking it meant she was making headway at last, and went on exhorting. He began to be mirthful over her ill-fitting role of zealot, and when she told him earnestly that it was one of her holy duties to save his soul, he saw the whole thing very close to the way it had happened. At that he let out such a roar of laughter, and kept it up so long, that she knew he was beyond her reach. With her looked-for triumph thus snatched from her, and any hope of praise or reward with it, she ran from the room holding her breath and gave full vent to hysterics outside. When she returned, somewhat later, tearful but no longer convulsed, he was asleep. She miserably followed him into bed and cried softly until she, too, fell asleep. When she awoke in the morning, he was gone. She learned from the servants that he was at the harbor, with their son.

Recollection of her failure made her weep again, and she went to Theobrand for sympathy. She told him what had happened, looking very appealing with her tear-stained, immature face. He realized that all she had accomplished was to make the holders of the secret more tight-lipped than ever; they would sail today with it still held from him. But he was not angry. His only feeling toward her was the sympathy she had come for. She had suffered the humiliation he had feared. The misgivings about her which had flitted through his mind the day before returned upon him in a great wave, filling him with reproach toward himself and tenderness toward her. He took her hands in his and called her his sister.

Until now neither of them had spoken of whether she should be baptized. Now, with neither of them yet speaking of it, because there was no need between two whose thoughts were so in accord, he dipped his fingers in Holy Water and spoke the Latin words that brought her into his faith. After it was done, they knelt together and prayed. He spoke the prayer and she said it after him, repeating not only his words, but his intonation, too, as if she were his voice's own reassuring echo. When they came to the end, he added a little silent prayer for himself, which differed from his prayer of the day before in the more insistent way it forswore any desire for her. Besides guarding his soul, he wanted to assure himself, as a man, that he had not been so warped by his years as a hermit that he could be falling in love with an old woman of twenty-six.

Helga presently withdrew her hand from his and left him, because she had to go to the harbor and say good-bye to her husband. But in a few moments she was back, burning with a strange bit of news she had just gathered from the servants. It had been discovered that the image of Thor was not in the temple. Word of this had spread everywhere, causing many to believe that Thor had fled, unable to face the banishment that would be voted him at the Thing. In a way, that belief was correct, and she had no sooner babbled it excitedly to Theobrand than the servant who had told it to her came in with proof. Thor had been carried aboard the ship in the early hours of the morning and was now in the hold waiting for the tide, along with the ploughs, tableware, bed-clothes and the rest of the strange cargo. There was no doubt of it: two men had seen it being done. Everyone was saying now that Thor had given up the fight and Olaf had already won. Helga praised the man for bringing the news, then sent him back to his labors so that she might receive from Theobrand the kiss of victory and exultation which she saw waiting on his lips.

To Theobrand alone, of all who were not going on the ship, the embarkation of Thor revealed the truth about the expedition. He had studied the ways of idols in studying the people who worship them. He knew that a man expects his God to guard his home when he is away, and that when both of them go, leaving neither to guard, it is because they have a new home in mind. So went the Israelites toward Canaan, forty years homeless, but carrying their Ark all the while. So fled the survivors of Troy, escaping through the broken walls with their Lares and Penates, with which they founded Rome. So came Ingolf to this very harbor with this selfsame idol, with which his great-grandson now—

At last the final bead of the rosary was in place and Theobrand had his final fact, giving meaning to all the others. He knew the reasons for the secrecy, the lying, the cargo, the haste and the careless kindness to himself. But he knew it only at the last scanty instant, an hour before the tide would come to snatch the ship away. They had tricked him after all, keeping back the tell-tale action till the end.

He and Helga exchanged the kiss in which they rejoiced together over Thor's surrender, so warmly that no amount of praying would ever explain it away; but even while his arms were around her, his two-fold mind was wondering whether there was not some way, some inspired, Heaven-shown way, by which he could keep that defiant handful of Heathen fish in Olaf's net and make God's victory complete.

XI

AS Eric and his father walked along the path that led from their farm to the harbor, they looked at the same things, each in his own way. The man was observing them for the last time, the boy for the first. They both enjoyed the same rare vividness.

Remember this tree, my son. Do you see how its root grows out above the ground? It looks like a knee, as if the tree is going to lift its leg out of the earth and climb out after it. When I was your age, I used to challenge it to race me to the water. Pat it, so, with the palm of your hand, to remember how the bark feels.

Do you see that heap of rocks? I put them there, I, with my own hands. I cleared them out of the way of this path. It had to wind around them before that. It still must go around those bushes and that boulder. I meant to clear them away, too. Remember this path, its every twist and turn. Close your eyes for a moment and go on walking. You see, we do know it, very well indeed.

And that mound that covers our fathers, that we sit on when we free a Thrall. That makes them understand that they get their freedom from all the Bonders who ever lived here. And the level place where duels are fought. If you step back off the cowhide, remember it will count against you, but if you step outside the square you are disgraced. And this rise in the ground where we are now: remember how much of Iceland we can see from here. All the way to the cottage where Grypti lives. He is descended from the Vanir and can make broken

74

bones mend; this right arm that I carry whole from Iceland would be shorter but for him.

Now look back, before we go down the other side of the hill. A long, long look, so it will bite its way deep into the mind. There is our farm, with its houses and cattle and the fence around it for which I let you split some rails. In silence now, steadily. So. Yes, we will remember that.

And look there, quickly! Those two birds flying over it toward the woods! For all we know, they may be Odin's ravens, Hugin and Munin, flying to perch on his shoulders and tell him they saw us leaving Iceland.

And always remember this moment, as we turn our backs and go upon our way. Of such a memory songs are made.

Now on we go, with never a regret, to meet the tide. There is the harbor below us and our ship waiting and a crowd to see us sail and wish that good Lok will be with us.

There are two birds that whisper in Odin's ear:
    "Caw! Caw!"
They tell him all the things we are doing here,
    "Caw! Caw!"
The things distinct and things that do not appear.
    "Caw! Caw!" they say,
    "Caw! Caw!
    We saw!"

They stopped singing, well before they got to where the ship and the crowd awaited them, and walked instead with the dignity befitting a Sea-King and his son.

Their companions of the coming journey were already there, hoping that nothing would delay their Sea-King or their sailing. They were worried, and not only about whether they might miss the tide. It was because the departure of Thor was now considered a surrender, and nothing less, by faithful and renegades alike. Both groups were becoming hostile and were almost ready to combine and hold them for Olaf. They must put to sea as fast as possible.

They could not, even had they wished, have changed their minds and remained. Each of them had done something or

75

other to lock that door, past any hope of reopening it. Some had sold their farms, never thinking what they would do with the money, save for a hazy notion that some day they might return. Two of them had confided in their wives, found them in agreement and brought them along, which prompted the onlookers to tell each other that the ship's commander had lost his mind from walking too much in the moonlight. One Bonder who had confided in his wife had done so mistakenly; she was rabidly on the other side and threatened to get help and stop him. He had to bind and gag her and lock her in the house, and now was on edge to be off before she could get loose and spread an alarm. There were a number of sons along, too, some as young as Eric and some old enough to be in the crew. There were a few old parents who would be in the way, and a few daughters whom they must watch in the midst of so many men. The presence of all these kinfolk aroused suspicion: the trip was beginning to look like the flight without a return, which it was. The story of a raiding-trip to the Orkneys had so far served its purpose, by bringing them this far without being interfered with, but any attempt to continue the deception would be useless. Speed was the necessity now. They fretted and wished they could start, meanwhile taking refuge in a sulky refusal to answer any more questions, especially the question about where they were really going. Their surliness aggravated the growing resentment against them.

The crew was on hand, with the exception, which was always expected, of the few who had changed their minds. Of those who had put in an appearance, several had been made dubious about the journey by their fellow-townsmen and were beginning to drift away. Their number was soon reduced by about a third, leaving just enough to man the ship if the grown sons were used as a reserve.

At this well-chosen moment Turker approached one of the Bonders and asked to be taken along as an oarsman. He offered as a special reason his attachment to little Eric and knowledge of caring for children. They might have refused his request on the ground that a slave cannot be trusted, but they were becoming dangerously short-handed. His eagerness offset their hesitancy. They accepted him, subject to the Sea-King's approval. Then they were glad they had, for his example stemmed the stream of desertions, for a while at least.

The ship had been drawn up on the beach, where it waited, supported by props, ready to be pushed to the water on its wooden rollers. It was not a war-ship, such as Vikings customarily used in raiding, but a Knorr, larger and slower than a fighting vessel, though that alone would not have caused suspicion, for merchant-ships could be used in battle and occasionally were.

Apart from the doubts it evoked, could anyone there have observed it in a detached way, it was a handsome vessel, worthy of admiration. It had been beautifully and strikingly decorated, to do honor to its divine passenger. The sides were striped, red and white, the sail was red and blue, while a huge gilt dragon's head and tail reared themselves from prow and stern. On the deck brilliantly colored tents had been pitched, and some of the families were already in them. Along the outer edge of the rail, reaching from the bow to the first oar-lock, the shields were hung; it was their customary place, where they were at hand yet out of the way, but they seemed to be an additional bright ornament, overlapping one another, rim to boss, and all of them gleaming in the sun.

"That is our ship!" said the Sea-King as they reached the harbor. What a satisfactory thing that was for a man to tell his son about his ship, when he was so proud of both of them! His spirit glowed. He was a Sea-King, in command for the first time. He walked with a buoyant step, conscious that the crowd was making way for him and that his son was beside him, participating in his dignity. One of the Bonders pushed his way toward him through the crowd, told him of the growing danger and that they had best cast off quickly. He took the warning lightly, with no intention of hastening through his enjoyment. When the Bonder asked him whether he approved of Turker's joining the crew, he felt so well disposed toward all the world that he said "Of course!" with immense geniality.

A hand was laid upon his arm and he turned, to see his wife. "I came to wish you a good journey," she said. This surprised him, for though farewells were being said all around him he had not thought of this one. She offered her face for a kiss and he kissed her. There was no feeling in it for him, unless a memory of a memory is a feeling. All it did was impress upon him the actuality of departure. Over her shoulder he saw his horses and wagon standing where she had tethered them. Ground-Spurner and Wind-Borne. Good horses. He might have taken them with him. It would be too difficult now. Oh, well.

He looked about for something else that he was leaving, Theobrand—and saw him, close by. The Priest came forward and held out his hand. The Sea-King took it in his own. Why not?

"I wish you a pleasant journey," said Theobrand.

"Thank you."

"And I have prayed that you will soon come back to us."

"Thank you." He turned from them and gave the order to put to sea.

The women who were going along, but were not yet aboard, climbed up, stepping from the men's clasped hands to their shoulders and thence to the deck. The children were handed up to them.

The ship's props were knocked away and the crew began pushing it toward the water, over the wooden rollers. Some of them pushed with poles which they pressed against the rail, holding them like spears as if they were goading the vessel along. Others put their shoulders to the hull, all of them taking great care to keep it upright, for the sake of those on deck. The ship moved at a constant rate of speed, so that as each roller was left behind, the men were able to bring it around to the front without pause. This took careful watching, and Eric's father felt proud to have his son observe his skill, as he selected the precise moment to order each roller laid in place. The crew had done it often before and very likely needed no such orders, but the pleasure of conspicuously giving them was a privilege of his rank. Eric followed, absorbed in the process, holding his mother's hand.

Then, while all were intent on the launching, Theobrand whispered to Turker. Now that he had deduced what they were planning, he had to change his instructions. He managed it quickly, unobserved. "Listen closely. I must be quick. Your task is different from what it was. You are to see that they come back. Don't argue. Don't ask questions. Do as I say. *Bring them back.* Do you understand?"

"Yes." Turker said it without turning his head or letting go of the pole he was pressing against the hull. No one would have thought the two men were speaking to each other.

"All of them. Olaf must have them all. If you do this, I will see that you are freed and sent back to your own country. You want that, don't you?"

"Yes." Just the one word. He did not, could not say how much he wanted it.

Theobrand persisted. He wanted to be sure. "You know you can accept my promise—the word of a man of God!"

Turker turned deep-set eyes upon him. "I must accept it," he said. "It is all I have."

The slope toward the water suddenly increased, and so did the speed of the ship. The Sea-King ran rapidly from stern to stem, to see the final rollers accurately placed, so that when the ship reached the water, a final shove would send her in far and deep enough to float. His excitement was as high as anyone's but he could not, as they could, stand by to enjoy it. He could not even turn around to see whether his son was admiring him.

The ship hit the water and got the great final shove that all were waiting to see. The crew waded in along, waist-deep, to give her an extra ell or two. She floated, and a great shout went up from everybody. Animosities were forgotten in the pleasure of seeing a ship floated. The crew climbed aboard, water streaming from their clothing. The Bonders followed. The Sea-King had to be the last aboard. He stood by the water's edge, watching his ship. She looked even handsomer with the water setting off her colors than when she was propped up on shore. When he saw that all were on deck, he turned back to get his son, meaning to carry him aboard in triumph on his shoulder.

And then he noticed that Eric was not there. Neither was Helga. He called him by name, he called both of them by name, but there was no answer. He took a sharp, convulsive breath, but then realized what must have happened. Eric had of course been carried aboard by Turker. He waded quickly into the water and had to swim a little, because the ship was floating comfortably now and had begun to drift. He was hauled up onto the deck, dripping and triumphant. He and one of his friends clapped each other jovially on the back and they had a great, satisfying laugh together. Then he turned to look for Eric.

The boy was not on the ship. A quick search proved it. "Did one of you bring my son aboard?" he asked the men nearest him. They said they had not. He shouted the same question up and down the ship, getting the same answer. A vague apprehension filled him. He turned about, to find Turker waiting to speak to him.

"I saw him," said Turker.

"Ah! Where is he, then?"

"With his mother."

"But she—? Where is she?"

"Why, I don't know. I think she went home. I saw her— and the Priest—and Eric between them—they were driving the wagon back—"

"What! And you let them?"

"I? Stop his mother? I saw you speaking with her. I thought—"

The Sea-King waited to hear no more. "Take command until I come back," he said to the Bonder nearest him, and started to climb over the rail.

"Where are you going?" asked the Bonder, and caught hold of one of his arms.

"Home!" snapped the Sea-King, trying to shake himself loose. "I'm going home, to get my son."

"No!" cried the Bonder, clinging to him. "You can't leave! We're ready to sail!" He called to another of the Bonders to help him. Between them, they hauled the Sea-King back to the deck, where he suddenly went into a blind fury and began roaring like a bull and fighting so desperately that it took all six of his friends to hold him. Throughout this, they urged him in an undertone not to behave so before the crew, but he could not hear them because he himself was shouting that no one was going to steal his son. At last they forced him into the forecastle and shut the door behind them, though there was scarcely room for the seven of them. There at last, by one of them clapping a hand over his mouth while another spoke to him and the others held him, they made him listen to reason.

The council they held was very brief. It had to be, because of the bad effect they were having on the crew. The Sea-King's six companions were agreed on one thing: he could on no account leave the ship. They had staked everything on the journey and would let nothing imperil it. If the prime mover of the expedition, the man who had thought of it, were to leave it now and perhaps not come back—No, they could not risk it. The whole thing would fall apart. They would accept neither his oath nor promise that he would return. He might not be able to. He might be waylaid. Some land-Troll might be trying to keep them from leaving; it was beginning to feel that way. No.

At last they reached an agreement, and it was the most they would concede to him. Three of the Bonders were chosen to return to his farm and bring Eric back with them to the ship, by force if they had to. They would take all the time they could, merely making sure to return before the tide receded. With this he had to be content. And for it he had to swear by Thor, and give his word besides, that when they returned to the ship, with or without Eric, he would take command, make for the open sea and go ahead with the plans they had made in the woods near Thor's temple.

He watched from the forecastle window while the three clambered over the side and swam and waded ashore. He saw them talking to people in the crowd, which was still on the beach wondering why the ship did not get under way. He saw them pay out money, mount horses which they were evidently hiring and ride off swiftly along the road that led to his farm.

There followed an endless, tortured wait, which he spent alternately reproaching himself for not foreseeing his wife's treachery and assuring himself that she had not really taken Eric away, even if Turker did think he had seen her do it. What did a slave know? Eric had just wandered somewhere. He would turn up at any moment. He was only a boy after all, and the like. Since the Sea-King was not a Christian, he did not have the consolations of prayer and faith; he was a Heathen and could only look anxiously toward shore and hope that Fate had not chosen this moment to wreck him and all his careful plans.

A little before the tide was due to recede, two of the emissaries were seen returning, with the horse of the third, and without Eric. They gave the animals back to their owners, and were ferried to the ship in a rowboat, because by now the water was high and strong. They came aboard silently, paid their ferrymen and went directly to the forecastle, pretending not to hear the crew's questions. When they got inside they told their news. It was simple and bad.

They had ridden directly to the house. Helga was not there, but the Priest was. He knew at once why they had come and answered their question before they asked it. Eric's mother, he said, had decided the boy was too young to go on a raiding-trip, so she had taken him to her father and brothers. The three Bonders did not believe him. Mindful of their promise, they drew their swords, meaning to force their way into the house and search it. But Theobrand evidently expected something of the kind, for he drew his own sword and gave a loud shout, whereat a dozen Thralls came running to his side, armed with spears and axes. A furious fight took place, in which the third Bonder was killed and the other two overpowered by numbers and disarmed. They thought they would be killed, too, but Theobrand would not let the Thralls harm them, saying he wanted a message carried back to Eric's father by someone he would believe. "Tell him," the Priest had said, "that Eric's grandfather and uncles will see that he is safe, *until his father returns,*" and the Bonders emphasized the words, just as the Priest had done. "Tell him also," he said, "that there is no need to worry about the boy's welfare. They have decided that they and Eric shall all become Christians and be under God's protection."

Eric's father tried hard to keep from going berserk again. He wanted to shout that he would kill Theobrand, that he would cut a blood-eagle in his back. He realized, however, that everyone on deck was listening, as he could tell from the silence there. So he managed to speak lower. He said, what he had known was true from the start, that they were holding Eric as a hostage. "Until his father returns." What else could it mean? Very well, why not let him go back and exchange himself for his son? Let Olaf take what vengeance he liked on him, while the rest went on to their new home, with Eric.

They would not hear of it, nor that they all go back and try to rescue Eric together, nor any other new scheme, sane or wild. They would follow only one plan: that he keep the word he had given, now made doubly binding by the death of one of their number.

By this time several small boats were putting off from shore, filled with persons who could no longer restrain their curiosity, as well as by those who sensed that there was disorder aboard and hoped to turn it somehow to their own advantage. When the Sea-King saw that, he knew he could waste no more time. He kept his word, as there had never been any doubt that he would. He left the forecastle, went to his place at the tiller and gave the order: "Out oars!" In a moment they were moving out to sea. The occupants of the small boats, seeing this, stopped rowing and contented themselves with shouting derision after them.

He paid no attention to them, though he was conscious of being insulted. He kept grimly to his task of steering, taking a perverse satisfaction in getting further and further from shore. The sight of the land receding, the impression that the ship was leaping ahead as the oars bit the water, the realization that their fateful journey was beginning at last, all had their effect upon him, but a very different effect from that which he had promised himself. Now there was only vengeance in his mind, a determination to come back, sometime, somehow, and snatch his son from them. Never mind how; he would find a way. He had no plan, only fury because he had no plan, and a wild vision of fighting his way back from Greenland, alone, in a small boat, in this boat, in any boat, by night, in winter when they would not expect him, when they would think no one would brave the sea. Ah, but a Sea-King would! They forgot they were dealing with a Sea-King! There would be a silent, unseen landing, a stealthy approach, a sudden attack, then back to the boat with his son in his arms, who would say in his ear: "I knew you would come for me!" Of course Eric knew he would, and would go on knowing it. They could never change him now, after all he had taught him. He was like his father, not his mother. "He shall not take this new canting Faith, wherein the mouth says one thing and the hand does another! Odin, Odin, I pledge him to you, with a battle-cry on his lips and a sword to follow it! Straight ahead and know where we are going, as the axe cleaves the foeman!"

Straight ahead it was, steering the way he was thinking, until they were well out of the harbor and the open sea stood ready to receive them. Then one of the Bonders walked the length of the ship and reminded him that it was time to rid themselves of any Olaf-men who might be aboard. At once he gave the order: "Up oars!" And the men stopped rowing, wondering what new quirk their commander had.

He spoke to them directly, saying exactly what he was thinking. "They have stolen my son," he said, "but they shall not bring me back, not until I have brought all of us to our new home, where we shall pay a certain old debt to Thor. If any of you, however, wants to serve Christ—Well, they say he walked upon the waters, so his servants can surely swim through them." He waited for a response, with an insane, traitorous hope that the crew might rebel and force them back to Iceland. But not one spoke up. It was clear that the nature of the journey was understood before they left, and all the Olaf-men had stayed ashore. "Well, then," he said, looking aimlessly across the water, "out oars—for Greenland!" There was a little stir as the men realized their precise destination at last. Then off they went, all of them now with a single plan, all, that is, except their Sea-King, who had made the plan for them but who now had none for himself. He did what had been agreed upon: steering southeast as if indeed for the Orkneys, for the sake of any who were watching from the shore. When once out of sight of land, they would change to their true course.

Someone started to sing:

> I know an old man
> Who has nine daughters—

and then he felt that he had done all this before, which he had, in Ingolf's tomb. He found it difficult to know whether he had dreamed it and was now doing it, or was dreaming what once he had done. He could not bring himself to decide. He had been through so much in this last little while, had been forced to reason his way painfully through such difficult problems, that he did not feel equal to facing this extra small one. He just steered, whether in a dream or a reality, across the roof of Aegir's great green hall, toward whatever dream might be next.

XII

WHEN Odin's ravens Hugin and Munin perched on his shoulders and told him the ship had left, the All-Father was seen to give one of his rare smiles. This was the first favorable news he had heard since it became known that the death of all the Gods was near. The sorrow that filled him came not from the approaching doom, but from the approaching ingratitude. This green and growing world, which they had so painfully made out of the body of an Ice-Giant, would go on without them into other times, unremembering and uncaring.

The Gods would have known they were soon to die, even if it had not been foretold, by the great number of people who were willing to stop believing in them. The blood in a God's veins was nothing but the faith that was placed in them by people; if the faith died, so did the Gods. But they never let the people know their power, pretending to them that it was the faith which kept the worshipers alive. The result, however, could not be changed: no faith, no Gods. So out of pure self-preservation, they encouraged those who did believe in them, performing miracles in their behalf, or at least natural prodigies that could be mistaken for miracles, such as rainfall after there has been a drought, or a breeze after a ship has been becalmed.

In the present case, Odin was particularly anxious to help his servant, the Sea-King. So he granted his deepest wish: he conferred on his son Eric a strange kind of memory, by which he would never forget anything his father had taught him. In addition, he made the wind so favorable and the sky so clear that the ship found its way easily into the current that flows forever westward.

The travelers were especially glad, when they were out of sight of land, to find that Aegir had decided to be friendly. They could never be sure about him. Standing on the shore and feeling safe while he cajoled them was not the same as being in his arms and at the mercy of his whims, though both were ways of finding out what he was like. There was a third way, too: to be washed overboard when he was in one of his stormy moods; then the seafarer found that he had fallen in Aegir's mouth and was being swallowed. The few who were hauled back out of those dreadful jaws were terribly shaken by the experience and full of fear afterward. But when Aegir smiled, as he was smiling (at Odin's behest) on this Greenland-bound ship, none could be a more delightful companion. He made these voyagers feel they were his guests, under his protection, and filled them with such zest they were eager to pay him more such visits. He even used one of his greatest spells: he made the land they had left seem further away than it was, thus loosening the hold of the troubles that concerned them there, even if they were the very troubles that had made them set sail. The brightness of where they were was greater than the sadness of what they were leaving; furthermore, the brightness remained for them to look at, while the sadness moved further and further back. Turker helped Aegir cheer them, by singing a little song of his native land; it was a way they had there of saying: "Out of sight, out of mind," and went something like this:

> Here and There are brothers.
> Here is my friend.
> There is not.
> For Here stays near me,
> But There stays far away.

They began to like Turker more than they had, after that, and were readier to accept him as one of themselves, despite his being a Thrall. They asked him for more songs of his country and he sang them one about the famous King Atyl, after whom his own little boy was named. They had all heard of Atyl, under their Norse name for him, Atli. They had heard, too, that there was a Christian prayer against him in Rome, where he was known as Attila, which said: "From fire, pestilence and the Hun, good Lord deliver us!" Turker's song added a personal note to their ideas about Atyl, and about Turker, too, for the fire with which he sang it showed that he considered his legendary hero an example to himself.

> Atyl the Great was a dwarf,
> Less than four feet tall,
> Yet he built a pyramid a thousand feet high
> With the skulls of his enemies.

> Atyl the Great was a dwarf,
> His head below other Kings' belts,
> Yet he made them bow so low before him,
> That their heads were under his feet.

> Atyl the Great was a dwarf,
> His bed was four feet long,
> Yet his enemies are sleeping forever,
> And their bed is all of Europe.

> Atyl the Great was a dwarf,
> Half the size of a man,
> Yet the fear he brought into the world
> Lives longer than time itself.

There had been a little doubt about Turker's usefulness before that, because of his own short stature, but this helped banish it, along with the hearty way he did his part at the oars. The Sea-King became well disposed toward him, too, as toward a friend with the same grief as his own, who yet was helping make the trip easier.

Thanks to Aegir's friendliness, and thanks a good deal to

Turker, the first day passed bravely, even buoyantly, that otherwise might have been given over to tears, or what was worse, to manly suppression of tears.

The second day Aegir's favor continued. But since he was a Giant as well as a God, there was a speck of hidden malice in his gifts. In this case he was raising their spirits so high that they would become overly confident, readier to fall into traps that were always being planned in his crazy, green mind.

It is about two hundred and fifty miles to Greenland. Three days will take a ship there, if only it has a reasonable wind, a sail, oars, a skillful helmsman and a foolish desire to get there. One day was gone. There seemed no possible reason to have doubts, or take precautions, or feel any way except the way the ocean felt. It said: "I am big. I am strong. I do as I please. Nothing can stop me." They had breathed so much of his breath that they felt that way about themselves. The men shook their fists in the direction of Norway, and defied Olaf, in a strange, haunting redoing of what had happened in Ingolf's tomb. It disturbed the Sea-King, who alone had no reason for wholeheartedness. "The living are haunting the dead!" he muttered. "Are we only ghosts?" He looked at the sun for an answer, and Ingolf's helmet, which he wore newly burnished, flashed so vividly that it can be seen today, by us, to whom he is a ghost indeed.

The defying of Olaf developed into a sort of boasting-contest, in which the men vied with each other in saying what they would do to him, were he there, face to face with them, man to man. "It would be my sword against his," said the first, "and for a while I would let him think he was winning, but then I would use a certain trick which I learned from a Troll, and overboard Olaf would go, down, down, through the water, to be eaten by the fishes, who would cry out: 'Give us no more Kings to eat who rule by Divine Right! We don't like the way they taste!'" There was great laughter at this, and the boaster rowed with renewed energy, pleased with his success.

Another spoke up, and everyone thought he outdid the first, not for how he said he would kill Olaf, but for what he would do with him afterward. He would cut his head off and bury him sitting on his own face. Then he would be ashamed to return as a ghost, because he would know how he looked to the rest of the world.

The third and best boaster was Turker. He said he would insult Olaf if he got the chance. Now an insult was a much worse injury to a man than killing him, and there were especially severe laws, telling how much of a fine you had to pay a man for each particular way you might insult him. The way Turker said he would insult Olaf must have been the most dreadful that existed, for its meaning is buried in such deep silence that there is no hope of rediscovering it. He said, that if he ever saw Olaf, he would stick his tongue out at him. After that, there was no use in trying to make greater boasts. The game was over and had been won. In fact, it was felt that Turker had gone too far in saying such a thing with children aboard, and the men hid their embarrassment by a sudden, conscientious application to the oars.

A small, awkward qualm like that could not bother them for long, while wind and current were with them, great distance being covered with little effort, and sky and water so beautiful. "How," they perversely began asking themselves, "can we make this delicious day pass more swiftly?" There was a well-known way of accomplishing that, and both children and grown-ups liked nothing better. They all thought of it together, during a silent moment, and looked toward their Sea-King to grant what all were wishing. He did, because it was one of his duties. He announced that he would tell a story.

Having made the offer, he began to miss his son, who had been his best listener, and Turker gave a little sorrowful look, to show he missed him, too. But the Sea-King had little time in which to think of his loss. He had to consider, very carefully, which tale should be told and how to go about it. Story-telling was a very difficult art. Old, familiar stories were wanted, not new ones, so the teller did not have novelty to help him hold the interest. Listeners got their pleasure from making sure that everything was told correctly, and stood ready to protest the change of a single, traditional word. What they did was memorize together, memory being their only library.

The story he told was a favorite. It was about a Giant, named Jokul—who was named after the mountain-range, or it after him, one of the two. Jokul wanted some of the famous mead that the Gods drank. So he climbed the mountain up to Asgard, where the Gods live, but where Thor had sternly ordered all Giants not to go. Jokul filled his pail from the magic udders of the she-goat that supplied the mead and was about to drink, when Thor saw him and gave him a stupendous kick that sent him whizzing back to the bottom of the mountain. Jokul broke his head as he landed, and when his sister Jill tried what he had tried, she was sent tumbling down after him. They still do it, every night and day, for Jokul is the moon and Jill is the sun, and Thor is forever kicking them back into the Ocean, with the spilled mead all around them. Jokul really does break his crown, and on successive nights it can be seen that his head always has a different shape.

When the story was ended, they all sang, with great enthusiasm:

> Jokul and Jill
> Went up the hill—

and then called loudly for another. So he told them the story of Hamlet.

The Hamlet he described was not a Prince. He did come from Denmark, however, where he was the son of a free farmer, but he had no liking for wealth or possessions of any kind, which made him as popular with slaves as with Bonders. He wanted only to live from day to day and induce others to do likewise. More grasping men could not endure his homely wisdom, because it made them seem mean and base, so they consoled themselves by saying he was mad. He was content to let them say so, for it was always clear who was really mad. There was, for example, the incident of the Runes. All the high and mighty ones were forever carving Runes, which told who their ancestors were. One day, when they saw Hamlet carving some meaningless scratches on a stone slab, they asked him, with mock seriousness: "What do you carve?" He replied: "Runes! Runes!" and this time they could not say he was mad, because it would have made them seem mad, too. He was a greater Hero than the conventional Heroes with whom he matched wits and everyone loved him because of his sly way of hinting that there might be something better than the accepted best.

There were cries of "One more! One more!" which no story-teller was ever allowed to resist, no matter what personal woes were on his mind, so the men rested on their oars and let Greenland wait while they heard a tale which had been told of many Kings and Earls, and lately was being told of Olaf.

"Last Yule-Tide, which Olaf and his followers were mis-using to celebrate Christmas, and making the sign of the Cross instead of the sign of the Hammer, an old man entered the hall and seated himself on the bench that was kept for unexpected guests. He wore a broad-brimmed hat which he kept pulled down over his face, but his white beard bespoke years and wisdom. After he had eaten, Olaf asked him what he could tell them that would add to their store of knowledge. The warriors, expecting sport, leaned forward to hear his answer.

" 'I can tell you three things,' said the old man. 'The first is, why wolves have not come into this hall and eaten you. The second is, why serpents have not crawled into this hall and stung you. The third is, why death has not burst into this hall and seized you.'

" 'I can answer that myself!' cried Olaf. 'God and my sword hold all three at a distance.'

"The old stranger smiled indulgently. 'You walked twenty-nine years upon this earth,' he said, 'not always with a sword, and with other Gods. Who protected you then?' Olaf was abashed by this, and silent, and the white-beard went on. 'There was a time, before the first sword was made, when wolves ruled Norway and feasted upon men as they willed. Their King, who ruled over them as you rule over Norway's men, was named Fenris. He was a Giant wolf with a Giant's strength and jaws big enough to swallow all the men on earth. The Gods planned to prevent that. So they taunted Fenris, saying he was not strong enough to break a chain. He accepted the wager and burst the chain with which they bound him. Chain after chain he burst in this manner, until they had made him vain. Then they had a magic chain made by the Dwarfs. It was made out of six things: a woman's beard, the noise of a cat's footsteps, a mountain's anchor, the shadow of the sun, a fish's breath and

91

a bird's spittle. This time Fenris suspected a trap and would not be bound with the chain until the God Tyr put his right hand in the wolf's mouth as a pledge to release him. Fenris could not break the chain and the Gods would not release him. In a rage, he bit off Tyr's right hand. But Fenris will never break that chain until the day of the last great battle, and his followers were all banished to the forests. Tyr's sword, which he could never wield again, was given to a man to protect himself, and all other swords were copied from it.

> " 'The wolf no longer dares appear.
> All honor to the great God Tyr!'

"At mention of a God he had deserted, Olaf tried to leap to his feet and slay the stranger, but he was in a spell and could not move, nor could his warriors. The white-beard went on:

" 'Before Fenris was born, the world was ruled by serpents, who bit and poisoned men as they wished. Their King was a Giant snake named Ormungunder and he was Fenris' older brother. His jaws were so huge that he could swallow all men, living, dead and yet unborn, and the Gods planned how to prevent it. Now Ormungunder could not be slain, because he lay around the whole world, holding it together with his tail in his mouth, and if he ever let go, it would all fly apart. So the strongest God, Thor, held the world together by wrapping one of his arms around it, while with his other hand he tore Ormungunder loose and flung him into the deepest part of the Ocean. He lies there now, with his tail in his mouth, holding the world together, through fear of Thor. He will stay there until he comes forth for the last great battle, and his followers were all banished to pits and caves.

> " 'The snakes shall rule you nevermore.
> All honor to the great god Thor!'

"Again Olaf tried to rise and draw his sword, but the old man's first word froze him where he was.

" 'Death,' he said, 'ruled the world before the wolf or snake, and was their elder sister. She had no followers, because where she walked, no one could live. Nothing bloomed, nothing bore, nothing breathed. Ice and darkness covered the earth, and the

Gods feared that life would never begin. Only Odin could deal with her. He made a bargain with her, by which she agreed to make her home in a dark place under the earth, and which she named Hel. She reigns there over the dead who do not go to Valhall, but they come to her only after they have had a share of life on earth. There she will remain, until the last great battle. Odin's part of the bargain, by which he made her agree to this, was that he gave her his only son.

" 'By living men this earth is trod.
All honor to the One-Eyed God!'

"Thereupon the stranger arose and they saw that he had only one eye. They knew then that this was Odin. 'The Gods of Asgard,' he said sternly, 'made it possible for you to enjoy this beautiful world. Now the day of the last great battle is at hand, when Wolf, Snake, Death and all their hosts come forth, seeking to destroy the Gods for what they did for you. It is not fitting, nor manly, that you should desert them now.' With that, he strode from the hall in silent dignity. When they came to their senses and could move again, he was gone, although the gates were still locked from within and the watch-dogs had not barked."

That was the end of the last story. For a while no one spoke, thinking about how much depended on them. They vowed silently not to fail in their duty. They would keep the Gods alive, in one small corner of the world at least.

If their silent resolve was heard in Valhall, it must have been a comfort amid great gloom, for on the next day the General Thing was to meet in Iceland, which Fate had decided would renounce the Gods. Odin sent out Hugin and Munin, the one to watch the Thing that would break his heart, the other to watch the ship that carried the last of his life-blood.

From his mountain peak, the All-Father looked down into Hel with his single eye, and saw Death preparing to come forth with her two monstrous brothers and all their followers, seeking revenge for their long banishment. Tomorrow it was coming, at last and for certain, the Great Battle, Ragnarok. All that the Gods could do was to set an example in bravery to a world that no longer believed in them. So Odin summoned

Heimdal, who could see the stars by day and hear the grass grow, and told him to blow his horn at the least alarm. Next he ordered the Gods and the dead Heroes to be ready with their weapons and wield them with the knowledge that it was the last time.

Throughout the night Odin sat in his great chair. In his hand was one last hornful of the magic mead, and on the table before him was the severed head of the wisest of all dwarfs. He and it spoke together till morning about the world as they had known it.

XIII

WHEN the first daylight came, Munin, who had been flying all night, saw the ship far below him and realized at once that everything was not as it should be. Aegir had taken advantage of Odin's many troubles, and being unwatched had set a trap, far ahead, at Greenland itself. Part of the trap was a storm and part of it was worse, and the people on the ship had no way of knowing about it or guarding against it. For Greenland's storms are sudden and freezing, unlike those of Iceland whose name it should have had; and Greenland's people, especially if you do not know they exist, can strike as suddenly and savagely as their storms.

These Greenlanders had, it is true, been spoken of by Thorgest Drangar's kinfolk, but in so slighting a way and with so few words, that they received less notice than Greenland's weather or currents and were dismissed completely from the hearers' memory. Those who told the story were ashamed of what had happened, and so passed over that part of it briefly and with evident contempt, pausing only long enough to give the Greenlanders one of the three names they went by. They called them Skraelings which, in the Norse tongue, signified dwarfish men. It was not a true description—though the concept of shortness has clung to them—but came from their flat, furry bonnets and their wide, fur clothing, which gave them a squat look. The second of the names by which they were known was given them by a tribe of their enemies whom they had driven from Greenland: by them they were called Eskimos, which meant "eaters of raw flesh," and may have been a figure of speech suggesting their fierceness when aroused. Their third name—by which they preferred to be called—was Innuits; this was a word in their own language, which simply meant "people." If they had been thought of as that, instead of as Skraelings or not at all, the seafarers would have avoided a great misfortune.

The Skraelings differed from the Icelanders and from everyone else, in that they had no past and no songs. They might have had songs if they had had a past to sing about, but the nature of their land prevented their remembering their past, which was very much like not having one. Their world was made entirely and solely of snow and rocks. If they built a house of snow, it would some day melt; if they built it of rocks, it would some day be hidden under snow. So nothing that they built could ever remind one generation that another had lived before it. The rocks were dead, unyielding and black; the snow was still, unending and white. There was no color beyond that, anywhere or ever, but the Skraelings did not hunger for color because they had never known it. They did not even know such words as "never" or "ever," because those imply that there have been many moments and will be many more, some of them different from the present. To the Skraelings all moments were so exactly alike that they all seemed to be the same, and it was called "Now." Their single problem was how to live through it.

With no past, there was no original Creation to wonder about, and therefore no Gods to have done the creating. But they did try to account for why the world was so difficult and dreadful, so they had a Devil. His name was Tarnasook and the tribe paid him to be allowed to live. The way he exacted his bribe was to crack the ice suddenly under someone's feet, drag him down and, of course, eat him. When that happened, no attempt must be made to save the victim; instead, everyone said in unison: "Tarnasook is taking his pay." The dead man was neither mourned nor remembered. Since there was no past, he simply never had been.

Of course, no story of theirs could begin with "Once upon a time." It had to be about the deadly present and teach some trick for keeping alive. Stories were a necessity and were told anywhere at any time, as, for example, while sitting in an igloo, fishing through a hole in the ice. The story-teller would suddenly, with neither warning nor skillful introduction, grasp his listener by the arm, and holding his attention thus, say with great intensity: "You are in a canoe. It overturns. Your spear floats out of reach. A hungry bear is sitting on an ice-floe. He sees that you are helpless. He swims toward you." Then there comes a pause, followed by the point of the story: *"What will you do?"* The listener finishes the story by answering with a quick improvisation, thus sharpening his wits against real accidents and real bears. Or the story might be this: "You are following a wounded caribou. You have no other food. You must capture him or starve. But it is snowing heavily. Every mark is being covered. If you do not start for home, you will not find your way back, and you will freeze to death." Then the pause, and the point: *"What will you do?"*

In various parts of the world, four separate accounts had been given of trips to Greenland. The people on the ship were in great peril, through knowing only three. First, there was the one told by Ulf the Crow, who said he saw the place as he scudded past it in a storm, and that was true. Then there was the Sea-King's father, Red Eric, who told how desolate it was and how he had tricked his enemies into going there, and that was true, too. And then there was the tale told by those enemies, Thorgest Drangar's kinfolk, who said it was an icy Hel where no man could live, but that was only partly true. By their own account, Skraelings lived there, despite the pretense that Skraelings were not really men and could well be forgotten. But for anyone to be safe who was going to Greenland, it was necessary to know the story that was told by the Skraelings themselves.

It was the only story they had which was concerned with the past, although, to be sure, they told it with their strange, present-tense vividness and always thought they were inventing it. It had happened thirty-two years before, but was so full of shock and horror to them that it could never be forgotten and was forever being retold. It was their version of how Thorgest's kinfolk had visited Greenland.

"You are standing on the shore!" they would begin abruptly, as usual. "The whole tribe is there. You are all looking at a strange kind of canoe which is coming toward land. It is very large and has many oars, and a square skin tied to a pole, and on its front end is the head of a huge animal. It rides onto the beach. Tall men with yellow hair jump out and pull the canoe safely from the waves. We do not know who they are, but they are on our shore and they are our guests. We help them pull the canoe up the beach. We lead the men to our huts. We warm them. We feed them. We lend them our wives. In the morning they all stand together, away from us, talking by themselves. They divide into two groups. One takes all the women and drives them toward the big canoe. The others attack us with big knives. They kill several of us. The rest of us run. The women get away and run with us. We run where we know the ice is thin. The yellow-haired men are bigger and heavier than we are. The ice breaks. Tarnasook takes three of them. The others stop running after us. They try to pull the three away from Tarnasook. We get our spears. We will not let Tarnasook be cheated. We fight. Tarnasook makes us strong and brave. The strangers run back to their big canoe. We let them go. They sail around the point of land. They try to live in another place. We hunt them. We kill many. Very few are left. They are sick and gloomy. They get into the big canoe, and go back, into the sea." Then the pause in the story, and the point: "Again you are standing on the shore. You see a big canoe coming out of the sea. It has a square skin tied to a pole, and many oars, and an animal's head on the front. Think now, and answer quickly. *What will you do?*"

And while the answer was being thought out, another square-sailed ship with a dragon-head prow, the one that was trying to save Thor from Olaf, came nearer to Greenland. To those on board, unaware of anything but fair weather, this was the third day of a perfect three-day journey. Nightfall—or morning at latest—would see them safely ashore, dividing the land that was to be their new farms. There had been some question in the Bonders' minds, whether the crew should have as much land as themselves, but since the crew heavily outnumbered them it seemed wiser to be fair, so they announced that the distribution would be the same for all. This news was received with enthusiasm. It was said on all sides that this was the right way to begin building their new world, but a few of the Bonders muttered that they were showing disrespect for the old ways they had set out to preserve. Turker was a source of embarrassment, being the only Thrall aboard. They could not really treat him like themselves unless they were prepared to abandon much of their thinking and all of their social structure; on the other hand he had performed his tasks as well as any: launching, rowing and being cheerful. For a moment the daring thought crossed a few minds that perhaps there should be no slaves in their new home, but the other changes which that suggested—such as, who would do the hardest, basest work?—were so drastic that they dismissed the idea, shocked, and were readier to hold to the old and tried. They consoled Turker (and themselves) by telling him they would bear his case in mind and find a way of dealing with it justly, some other time.

The nearer they drew to Greenland, the more they felt the need of preparing for practical difficulties. Among these was one that was so pressing that they called a Thing on deck, to discuss it. This was, how they could increase the supply of women. There were only five aboard, except for a couple of grandmothers who, when looked at practically, did not really count as women. Of the five, two were wives. The other three were daughters, two of whom were fifteen years old and therefore marriageable, while the third was twelve and developing rapidly, or as these free farmers expressed it, she would soon be ripe. Clearly, five were far from enough, for there were thirty-seven men aboard. A raid for women would be necessary very soon. But where, when and how? They had best make an immediate decision because it might alter their course. The men tried to discuss it objectively and frankly, as if no women were present, while the women tried to keep out of the argument and for a while succeeded.

The men began by calling it a problem in navigation. The trouble was, there is no land of any kind between Iceland and Greenland. So they must either turn back and raid the Orkneys after all—or perhaps the Shetlands or Faroes—or else they must go on to Greenland, leave the women and children there with a few men to guard them and then sail back a much greater distance to do their raiding.

The second plan was adopted because one of the wives could not be silent any longer and gave a practical reason which was decisive. She said that the women would need time ashore to set up housekeeping. The other women said this was true. They had another reason which they did not give and perhaps were not aware of: it was pleasant to be the only women on the expedition and they wanted that to last as long as possible. They did not dare oppose the raid altogether; the men would not have tolerated that and would have given a lofty reason of their own: the duty of peopling the new homeland.

Having decided when they would raid, the question remained, where? The first suggestion was a bold one. This was, that they raid Norway. They could make a sudden attack, which would succeed because no one could possibly expect it, and carry off the wives and daughters of those very Bonders who had become Christian Earls. What a gesture of defiance to Olaf that would be! They shouted to one another their various guesses as to how many ships he would send after them, and still not find them. A hundred! No, two hundred! No, all he had! And he'd build more! Olaf's probable fury was delightful. But they had to decide against that plan. They did not say the odds against them were too great and their destruction too certain. They would never entertain such a cowardly reason, especially with women present. They said Norway was too far away.

The second of the two wives then offered a suggestion that

was dear to her own heart. Her idea was that they raid Ireland. She herself was Irish and had been captured in a raid when she was fourteen. She was extremely beautiful at that time, which was the reason for her being taken, as well as why she was able to raise herself from the position of concubine to that of wife. Now she had a longing to see some of her relatives and former friends and thought this was a good way to do it. She offered to guide the men through the bog that led to her native village and show them where to hide until nightfall. She described, with pathetic eagerness, the excellent qualities of the Irish girls, dwelling on their beauty, habitual virginity, and fidelity when once they were mastered. She only failed to gain her end because other places were nearer and because her husband thought it might be a scheme to drown them all in a bog.

They came back at last to their first scheme: to raid the Orkneys. That would be as satisfying a defiance of Olaf as raiding Norway, because they had told all Iceland of their intention. He would never believe they would keep their word. Keeping one's word meant nothing to Olaf, now that he had forsaken Odin. Oh, his amazement, when the news reached him!

> But by the time he follows us there,
> We'll be away and he won't know where.

Then hurray! hurray! for now they had a plan!

> To Greenland first and the Orkneys next,
> And Christian Olaf will be perplexed.

There was not a dissenting voice, except that the Sea-King said he meant to live without women from then on, but he would help the other men to get some for themselves. The two wives and three daughters thought privately that this mood would pass and presently they would see what they could do about it. But one or two of the men said he should not be allowed to make an exception of himself. If he alone were wifeless and one day began to feel a love-lust, as they were sure he would, he might hunger for someone else's wife and there would be trouble. They were about to vote that he must get a woman for himself whether he wanted one or not, when land was sighted in the distance and everything else was forgotten.

It was immeasurably far off, scarcely distinguishable from the rest of the horizon-line, visible only to eyes sharpened, like theirs, by peering across great distances. Even if the wind held up, they would be most of the day reaching it. But it was Greenland, beyond any doubt. They knew the stars and they knew the course taken on the three earlier voyages. They knew everything that was known about it at the time, except the storm which Aegir was brewing there. Only the Skraelings knew about that, because they and their kayaks were trying to be safe from it there, in a haven where the ship with the square sail and the dragon-head prow would also seek shelter. The Icelanders might perhaps have been prepared for Aegir's treachery, but never for a fight with Skraelings. How could a people, who had no past, be imagined by people who had little else?

XIV

NIGHT was approaching when the ship reached the projecting cape which is the foot of Greenland. Wind and waves had been rising for some time. The storm was obviously on the very verge of breaking, so they headed into an inlet that looked like a safe place in which to wait for morning. The seafarers felt that good Lok was with them in showing them this haven while there was still light enough to see by, for they would not have dared to come near an unknown rocky coast in the dark, and would be forced to ride out the storm off shore all through the night. The inlet, which continued to be deep and navigable as they moved along it, cut directly into the land. Here and there ice appeared, floating on the surface, but not enough of it to be dangerous. It all looked very much like the fjords which they knew so well, except that the cliffs which formed its walls were somber and forbidding, being made of a solid mass of some kind of stone that was black as iron, with patches of snow that made it seem blacker still. These cliffs were very tall, too, so that the sky seemed far away and as if seen through a slit, across which the storm-clouds rushed. All on board felt subdued and found themselves unaccountably lowering their voices. There was none of the excitement and jubilation over coming into port, to which they had looked forward. They began to wonder whether all Greenland were as awesome and chilling as this part of it, then, remembering Red Eric's account, they feared the rest might be worse.

The inlet grew narrower and curved considerably as they rowed inland, until the boiling Ocean was cut off from view behind them by those black cliffs. Up ahead, the sheets of ice on the surface grew more dense. It would probably be best to ride at anchor until the storm ended, and then to sail further around the coast in search of land that was greener, or at least less black and white. They would go around the shoulder of just one more of the great cliffs, to see what lay beyond. As they did, it happened.

There was a sudden sound of screaming and yelping, as of a pack of wolves, and the Skraelings were upon them. They came from everywhere at once, out of crevices and from behind boulders, in their little skin boats, of which their furry hats and jackets made them seem a part. They paddled furiously toward the ship, covering distance with a speed that seemed incredible, and all the while keeping up their appalling screaming and yelping. A whole tribe was there, so many men and boats that they could not be counted. Indeed, no one thought to count, because of the surprise and the noise. No one thought of anything at all for a moment, and that moment was all the Skraelings needed, for it brought them close enough to the ship to throw their spears. Short weapons like javelins they were, with broad heads and handles of bone, and they threw them so straight and hard that there were dead men among the Icelanders before they knew an attack was being made.

There was no time to reach for shields or spears, or to string bows. Luckily, sword and dagger always hung at a man's belt, or there would have been no weapons at all. But even with these, it was not possible to strike a clean blow at the Skraelings, for they darted by too swiftly in their little witch-boats, and dodged and wheeled about in them as a man does on his own feet. Time had to be lost, too, in herding the women and children to the center of the ship, not only to be out of danger, but because a woman sometimes thinks she is protecting a man by flinging her arms about him, when what he wants is freedom to swing a sword. But the worst disadvantage of the Icelanders was that they had never known this kind of warfare, whereas the Skraelings seemed to know very well how Vikings fought, and were prepared for it. A number of them suddenly rowed to the very side of the ship, as if they were going to try climbing aboard. But this was a ruse, as was seen too late, for when one of the men leaned over the side to strike at them with a sword, the Skraeling at whom the blow was aimed turned suddenly upside down, boat and all, so that he was under the water and his boat above it. The Icelander's sword cut through air instead of a neck, and he lost his balance; thereupon other Skraelings darted forward in their boats, seized him and hauled him overboard, helped by their capsized companion, who righted himself as expertly as he had turned over. They seized two of the crew in this way and dragged them through the water toward shore, two Skraelings in boats holding a man between them while each rowed with his free hand. When they got their captives to the side of the fjord, they shoved them under the ice which floated there, and that was the last that was seen of them.

This much of the fight had taken place with lightning speed, so to say that the Sea-King had regained his wits by now, does not mean he had been at all slow about it. It is hard to think at all in the midst of sudden death. Before it was too late he saw what he must do, and that is better than many would have done, especially as he weighed all the possibilities in that short time and chose correctly. He ruled out trying to fight these men, who would not come near enough for sword-play. Nor would it do any good to come ashore and try to settle matters there, for there was scarcely any level space to set foot, with the cliffs beginning immediately and rising straight up. Skraelings were perched up on the sides wherever they could find a ledge, waiting to throw down spears and rocks if anyone should try to land, or even if the ship came near enough. He saw now that they had a large number of dogs, too, almost the size of wolves and looking very much like them, which were doing part of the yelping and were eager to get into the fight. If the Icelanders tried to come ashore, most of them would be pounced on and drowned at the water's edge. But neither could they stay where they were, because night was coming very fast, and with darkness it was they who would be boarded. They must not continue further into the fjord, because it grew ever narrower as they advanced and with a surface more ice-covered; if they went on, they would be frozen into the fjord and speared from the cliffs. A single, desperate choice was theirs. They must go back into the open sea. A frightful storm was waiting for them there, and a glance upward at the strip of sky showed the blackening clouds, but on the Ocean there was a chance, however slight, to escape death. He gave the order to back out, for turning would bring them too near shore in that narrow place. Back they went, toward the sea, less seven of their number, while their victorious foes shouted mockery at them in a language they did not understand and had no heart to answer.

The crew and the Bonders put their whole strength and will into the oars, thinking and straining for only one thing: how to stay alive. But the master of the ship could not grant himself such single-minded luxury. A question had arisen in his mind for which he must find an answer and have it ready before the others got around to asking it.

Where were they to go? It could not be Greenland. Not any longer. Not any part of it. The Skraelings would harry them wherever they might land. They would be watching from every cliff. He could see, by the way they fought and the way they knew how Vikings fought, that something had happened in the past to cause their hate and frenzy. Thorgest Drangar's kinfolk had left some tale untold, hoping for one more shift in the vengeance game, and it had happened. The old debt to Thor could not be paid here.

104

Then where? Greenland and this ship were the only places in the world where they could be, and Olaf not find out. Then must they stay forever on the ship, making it their only home, raiding for what they needed when they needed it? Sooner or later they would all be killed, sooner or later the ship would rot, sooner or later they must put into port, to be seized and held for Olaf. Were they to fall into his hands then, at last? Was Iceland lost, for nothing? Their homes gone, for nothing? His son stolen, for nothing? Was there no escape from Olaf or his new God? Olaf the Pursuer. Olaf the Sure. Olaf the Doom.

The Ocean was waiting for them ravenously when they backed into it, and Aegir laughed in their faces when they recognized his perfidy at last. Now that they and the Gods who protected them were alike in deadly peril, he had chosen to be more a Giant than a God, and faced these die-hards who were on Odin's side, sending a raging army of billows against them. Darkness would be complete in a very little while; Aegir knew they must try to get clear of the land whilst they could see at all, or risk being wrecked on unknown rocks. As they veered around, so as to strike him with their dragon-headed prow, he did his best to capsize them, and nearly succeeded, because seven rowers were missing and others had been wounded. But he was dealing with great sailors, the greatest in the world, and turn about they did, despite him. Time after time he tried furiously to throw them back upon the land, where the ship would be destroyed by rocks and themselves by spears. But they fought him valiantly with their oars, and his brother the Wind with their sail, and steadily pulled away from the danger.

The night now became wholly black. They could see no stars by which to guide themselves, nor even the land itself to steer away from; it had ceased being a black bulk against an almost black sky and had become part of the total blackness that enclosed everything. All they could do was listen for the breakers and steer so that the sound would remain behind them and grow ever fainter. Thor tried to help them, but he could do very little, being busy preparing the defense of Asgard; still, he did manage to toss an occasional lightning-bolt at Aegir, which lighted up the patches of snow and showed where the cliffs were lurking.

Failing to tear their keel out on the rocks, Aegir tried to flood them. He threw great quantities of water into the ship, but the women and children seized bailing-scoops and threw it back in his face, so that the men did not have to let go of the oars. Throughout the night that double battle went on: to get far away from the black cliffs and to keep Aegir in his place. Everybody did all they could, without stint: rowing, bailing, or singing to encourage the others. The Sea-King sang, while he steered and agonized over the problem of where his unhappy ship would ever make harbor. The song had a good lilt and rhythm for rowing. You could scarcely call it a cheery song— what song could be, with that darkness about and that surge beneath?—and this was about a man's grave. But it cheered nonetheless, because it reminded them that there was land as well as water.

> I shall not die at sea;
> There is a house ashore, awaiting me.
>
> That house is very small,
> No broader than myself, from wall to wall,
>
> Not long, nor wide, nor high,
> But room enough wherein a man can lie,
>
> It has not any door,
> But once inside, I shall come out no more.
>
> I shall escape the deep;
> There is a house ashore, where I shall sleep.

This did their spirits so much good that he sang again, a somewhat lighter song. Again it could not be called truly frolic-some, but it instilled courage of a cynical kind, derived from a cynical opinion of women and whether their devotion could ever be counted upon.

> If I were drowned at sea,
> How many girls would mourn for me?

106

How many girls would weep and wail and pine?
Nine?

How many girls would grieve about my fate?
Eight?

How many girls would wish me back from Heaven?
Seven?

How many girls their bread with tears would mix?
Six?

How many girls would hope I was alive?
Five?

How many girls would sigh forevermore?
Four?

How many girls would cry "Oh miseree!"?
Three?

How many girls would still continue true?
Two?

How many girls would think their lives were done?
One?

No, my son,
Not one—
None.

Well then, since not one girl would mourn for me,
I'll not be drowned at sea.

Though this was a bit more light-minded than the first song,
it did not quite give them the animation they needed. So he
stopped trying to remember songs that were made to cheer,
and instead made up a song that might stir them in another
way. It was about fighting, and concerned their recent battle
with the Skraelings, but he sang of it in such a way as to make
it seem somehow like a victory.

They hid in their shadowy fjords,
The cowards.
They kept out of reach of our swords,

The cowards,
Let them but come where we can reach them!
Oh what a lesson we will teach them!
We will slay them,
We will flay them,
We will split them,
We will spit them,
Their hands we'll chop off,
Their ears we'll lop off,
Their arms we'll break off,
Their heads we'll take off,
And leave their skulls
To feed the gulls,
And leave their eyes
To feed the flies,
For their men we'll find graves,
Of their women make slaves,
Then their Chief we will seize,
Force him down on his knees,
And with daggers we'll hack
Eagle's wings on his back.

This song produced wild enthusiasm, particularly the way it ended. There was no more satisfactory way of killing a foe than by cutting the design of a flying eagle deep into his back. His screams indeed resembled an eagle's, while the way he writhed made the bloody wings look as if they were flapping. The notion of doing this to a Skraeling Chief roused them to the same elation they had felt when boasting what they would like to do to Olaf. Now they boasted again, each describing the part he had taken in the fight, albeit the least bit exaggerated. Even Turker had struck some brave blows, and when he said so no one denied it. They all began to feel proud of themselves and of each other.

Their high spirits infuriated Aegir, who had been hoping to break their will. He watched them malevolently, then, seizing a moment when they were most jubilant and least alert, he threw one of his most enormous waves over the rail, flooding so much of the ship that they almost foundered then and there.

That wave extinguished their glee as it would a fire. Panic seized them. With unanimity born of their sudden joint plight, all stopped whatever they were doing, even rowing, and bailed frantically, with scoops, helmets or hands. After a few perilous minutes they were safe again and panting as they resumed their regular tasks, but those few minutes had brought them so near death that they were sobered, and faced things as they were, not as they wished they were. They saw that they must wage a long desperate fight, as easy to lose as win. No more thinking about anything else.

They managed to get a short breathing space. They poured barrels of whale-oil on the water about them, and Aegir, sickened by having his children's blood thus poured into his face, was unable to attack them until it washed away.

The Sea-King followed a custom of all masters whose ships were threatened. He removed the golden spirals which he wore around his arm, broke off bits and gave them to all who had no gold. Now, if indeed they were to travel downward into Aegir's hall, it would be said there that people from Earth were rich and worthy of respect.

Then, with every precaution taken, everyone grimly at work, every sinew strained to the utmost, he went back to wondering what port awaited them, or if there was any port for them at all. In all that cold he sweated as he wondered. A King, whether he is a Sea-King or any other kind, must never be in doubt. Well, he had no doubt about this particular moment: they must go wherever that rocky coast was not. But afterward, when the storm ended, when they found themselves once more on the open sea, by daylight and still alive: what then? That was the moment for which the crew was striving, for which they were giving up their last crumb of strength. That was when they would fall exhausted on their benches and wait for him to say which of the four corners of the sky they should head for.

Aegir's daughters slapped him across the face with their wet hands, their Giant father spat at him, and his brother the Wind turned icy and froze the spittle on his cheeks. The Sea-King made no attempt to brush away these tokens of their scorn. He leaned his full weight to steer-board, so as to retain his mastery of the rudder, and turned his eyes in the darkness toward the part of the ship's hold where he knew the image of Thor was. He prayed silently to the God for whose sake he had embarked not to let him be that most piteous of all creatures: a ship's master who did not know what course to take. He prayed hopelessly, because it was certain to happen. His companions must find it out. He would have to say to them: "We are lost. We have no place to go. It is my fault." Then—Sea-King! Sea-King! They would take the name and the honor from him. He saw himself suddenly, as he was when he first called himself that, at the age of seven. That seven-year-old self of his looked as if he wanted to cry.

XV

HELGA'S father, old Jatmund Jatmundson, had been congratulating himself for seven years on having got a husband for his unexciting daughter. Therefore, when the Sea-King sailed without her, amid rumors that he was never coming back, Jatmund gloomily faced the prospect of having to do it all over again.

This time it would be a much harder task. Those same seven years had made her that much older and had given her a son to prove it. Jatmund was not rich, could endow her with little, and even desirable daughters were costly things to get rid of. The Sea-King had not haggled over her lack of a dowry, but he was an odd, moon-struck man. Where could they ever find such another?

When she arrived at her father's house with Eric, she got no welcome.

"If your husband wants you and your son," Jatmund shouted in her face, "why stop him?"

"He does not want me. He only wants Eric."

"Couldn't you make a bargain with him, to take both?"

Helga replied meekly that she was only following Theobrand's advice. Her father growled that Theobrand should stick to his beads. Her three brothers, who had their own futures to think about, echoed the growl. That made her fly to Theobrand's defense, with more spirit than they had ever known her to show about anything.

Theobrand, she said, was a man who knew more than other men.

Theobrand, she said, had the kind of knowledge that came from God, which no Heathen could understand.

Theobrand, she said—

At the third mention of Theobrand, Helga's father began to see a little hope. At the fourth, her brothers, who were not so quick-witted as their father, began to see it, too. At the fifth, father and brothers looked at one another to see whether they all had the same idea, and at the sixth, Jatmund began to ask her a number of questions. She answered some, indignantly refused to answer some, wept at some, and finally took the high religious stand that the whole thing was God's business alone.

When Jatmund had found out from her all that he needed to know, he said, "On second thought, this Priest of yours has given you good advice. Remain here. Your brothers and I are going to visit him." He told his sons to get the horses ready.

Helga immediately feared that they meant some harm to Theobrand and wanted to go with them to prevent it. Jatmund assured her that there was very little chance of anything violent happening. She did not believe him and was ready to fight. They had never seen her like this. Finally he spoke to her severely.

"You should be grateful that we are still willing to trouble ourselves about you. Throughout your whole life you have been a great trial, because you are a girl in the first place, and older than your three brothers in the second. The only thing you have in your favor is that you are lucky. While most girls find it none too easy to get a husband, it seems that you have a chance to have two. Now, if you interfere while we try to take advantage of this great luck of yours, I will give you such a beating that there will be no man at all who will find you pleasant to look at—not even this woman-starved monk out of a cave."

When Helga thus learned that her father was only looking out for her welfare, she agreed to do as he asked and offered to help in any way she could. Jatmund praised her then for being a dutiful daughter and gave her certain instructions, impressing upon her that she was to carry them out exactly as he said and on no account to use her own judgment. After that, she was to follow them to her own house. He kissed her, shook his head in a baffled sort of way, as if her shortcomings were her fault and not his, then he and his three sons mounted their horses and set out to visit Theobrand.

On the way there, her oldest brother, Gorm, asked, "Why is our sister so lucky?"

"Because she is a fool," Jatmund answered. "Fools have to be lucky, to live."

Her brother Rolf took a gloomy view. "She has had her luck. Why should it continue?"

Their father replied with an old proverb: "When Odin wants to, he takes his bow and arrows and shoots at a broom."

"Whatever she may be," said Brother Hlod, who was the practical one, "I am not sure this Theobrand is a fool."

"Neither is it sure," responded Jatmund, "that he is lucky."

For Theobrand to have been really lucky, he would have had to live a century or two later, when his Church adopted a policy of celibacy for its servants. But the Church was then only beginning to wonder whether a Priest could love God and women, too, and rather thought he could. A Priest might even marry, if he liked. It was at that moment in the history of theological theorizing that Theobrand saw Helga's father and three brothers riding toward him.

He had just ordered the Thralls to bury the Bonder they had killed in the attempted rescue of Eric—in an unmarked grave, since he was a Heathen. At first he thought the news of the fight had somehow reached Jatmund's farm and they were coming to help, but the leisurely, deliberate way they trotted

112

their horses showed that it was not so. They dismounted, gave him a curiously sober greeting and asked whether they might have a word with him.

He invited them into the house and had beer brought to them. Hlod raised his drinking-horn in Theobrand's direction.

"May you have a long life!" he said.

"Thank you," Theobrand replied dubiously. The toast was a friendly one as far as its words went, but its tone somehow suggested that there was the possibility of a short life, too.

"We have set our hearts," Jatmund began abruptly, "on being the first Iceland family to be baptized."

"My heart rejoices at your zeal."

"It is Helga who has made us see the light."

Instantly the father and three sons all began talking about Helga, very earnestly and very eagerly, hardly waiting for one another to finish. Helga had told them, they said, of the joy this Christianity would bring them. They valued her opinions. She had always been so clear-sighted. And so high-minded. And so unselfish. Thinking only of others' good.

"A Saint," said Gorm.

Theobrand was a bit startled by that. She might have told all that had passed between them, because she was such a— because she was so guileless.

On they went, praising Helga, as if they never meant to speak of anything else. She had a fine character. So unswerving. Loyal to those she loved. An excellent housekeeper. Modest. Quiet. And beautiful, too, when you stop and think of it—in a very unusual way.

"—but unfortunately lacking one thing," said her father. "A Christian husband."

After that, it was impossible for Theobrand any longer to avoid knowing what they meant, especially as they all stopped speaking at that point and waited for him to reply.

It was not entirely a surprise. He had, already, once or twice imagined himself her husband, through envy of the man who was. He merely had never thought it would come to that. Well, now it had. Helga's face suddenly got inside his head, and the rest of her joined it. His blood drained downward, carrying his mind with it. He opened his mouth to give the answer they

113

wanted, but it was his male sense of self-protection which spoke instead, as if it had been thinking independently of him.

"It is a great pity," he found himself saying, "that her husband is a Heathen. But he is her husband, and what is done, is done."

"I do not think he is coming back," said Jatmund.

"No?" asked the Priest, as if he thought otherwise.

"No. That is why she may as well divorce him. I have told her to get three witnesses and come here."

"Witnesses?" asked the Priest tremulously, feeling this somehow concerned him.

"You will want to know something of our laws," said Jatmund. "Allow me to explain this one. A wife divorces her husband by denouncing him three times, before at least three witnesses. The first time is in bed, the second on the threshold, and the third at the Thing. Since the Thing is only three days away, we are attending to the bed and threshold at once."

Then they sat back, as if the explanation had settled everything—which it had—and waited for Helga and her witnesses, meanwhile drinking beer and uttering the toast: "God save King Olaf!" Jatmund's three sons silently toasted their father for his skill and speed.

With each swallow, Theobrand drank in more of the idea that he was to be married soon, though he had not yet fully realized he was to be married at all. Those were two big facts to absorb so suddenly, and a great deal of the Sea-King's beer was needed to wash them down.

Helga and beer were a persuasive combination. The prospect began to seem agreeable, though unexpected. A certain dignity added itself to his desire. Before this, his imaginings had been lustful; now he saw himself walking through a town with Helga's hand upon his arm, her light step beside his strong, sedate one, respected, deferred to, a leader of the social order with his wife.

When Helga arrived with her witnesses, they went immediately about the business of the divorce. She linked her arm with Theobrand's, as if for courage and protection, and together they led the way from room to room, making it seem that Theobrand was in charge and it was all being done to benefit him. The

114

three witnesses beamed on the pair, with the peculiar, conspiratorial smile used toward those about to be married and for whom no escape is possible.

They went first to the bedroom. There Helga turned toward all of them and said, "My husband has treated me very cruelly. I say to you that I wish no longer to be his wife." Then she got into bed and pulled the cover up to her chin. "I ask you to witness," she said, "that my husband is not in bed with me." The others indicated that they observed this, then all went together to the front door. Helga stood exactly on the threshold, and said: "This is the house in which we have lived as man and wife. I ask you to witness that now I come and go alone." With that, she stepped outside and then back in, and again they all gestured that they observed what she spoke of.

"Now there remains only the consent of those at the Thing," said her father, almost jubilantly, and turned to the Priest. "There will be no question about their giving it, especially if *you* support her plea." Then everyone had a final hornful of beer, with a toast to the health of the three witnesses, after which Helga thanked them for their help and they left, promising to help her present her case at the Thing. Her three brothers also left, each of them pausing to shake hands with Theobrand, in the special, impressive way that hands are shaken to acknowledge a bargain, though in this case no bargain had been mentioned. Then Theobrand turned to her father, thinking and hoping that he would leave, too, for by this time he was tingling to be alone with Helga.

But Jatmund did not leave and it soon became clear he did not mean to. He said so. He was going to live here for the next three days and nights, he said, until after the Thing. He stated it with candor and even a kind of hearty cooperation, as something of which Theobrand would approve. "Helga's good name may get into people's mouths," he said, "so you and I must keep it tasting sweet." Theobrand had to agree with this fine sentiment, thereby setting his blood to boil for three days more, which was the guarantee the old man wanted that his daughter would be married, or as they used to say, married *off*.

Theobrand hoped Helga would elude her father during the night and come to him, but she didn't. Not that she didn't want to. But in those days (wrongly called The Dark Ages) a woman learned to be both warm and cold at the same time, in self-protection. He spent the night wanting her, and the next two nights as well. He could not sleep. He listened at his door, thinking that every sound was her footstep.

Life in his cave had been an almost exact reverse of this. Women often had come to him there for counsel, while Satan whispered temptations from the crevices in the rock. But Theobrand had no confidence in himself then and was always afraid of being rebuffed, so he made himself want Heaven instead and prayed that he would get it. Now there was no such need to transfer his desires. He still prayed, not to be delivered from temptation, but that he possess her soon, very soon, *now*. He was past the stage of recognizing that his long asceticism had lent her an unnatural allure. She had blue eyes, yellow hair and a submissive look. So had many other women, all over Northern Europe. The difference between her and them was that she was the one he was going to get.

He passed the three days more easily than the three nights. He spent the first two walking about the farm and its various buildings, imagining himself already the head of the household, planning how he would change this and that and scorning his predecessor who had failed to make such obvious improvements. His excitement took him about the grounds rapidly and he returned full of enthusiasm, thinking he had achieved a great deal when he had merely been walking very fast.

Eric was a flaw in his enjoyment. They had lied to him to get him away from the ship, telling him his father was not sailing to the Orkneys after all and was coming right back to the house. Now he asked questions about it, and the deception had to be continued and new lies invented as the hours passed. Theobrand did his best to make Eric like him, with the idea that it would please Helga, but it was a strain, because he could not make himself like Eric. Eric was the legal heir to the estate, divorce or not. And he looked like his father.

On the third day, Helga's brothers called for them and they all walked together to the Thing, which was held not far from where they lived. Eric was brought along to see the gaily colored booths and the interesting things that were for sale, though he was not expected to understand the issues that would be discussed. He was beginning to understand more than they suspected, but he had a child's reluctance to embarrass his elders by showing he saw through their deception. Once he asked his grandfather, with startling abruptness, whether his father was really coming back, and was told to be quiet and enjoy the sights. He did not ask the question again, of anyone.

Helga's father suggested to Theobrand that they let the others walk on ahead, so that they two could have a chance to go into certain matters. This was done, and as they continued on their way in two little groups, Theobrand watched Helga, and her father watched him watching her, and decided that this was the ideal moment to get an agreement about her dowry.

Helga's brothers, who knew what the maneuver was for, whispered to one another that their father would cook a fine dish over Theobrand's heat; and so he did, for though he had little to offer, he managed to make that little sound big. He had only two articles of value, outside of Helga herself, with which to pay Theobrand for taking her off his hands. These were a quarter of her father's farm—the other three quarters being kept for her brothers—and the guardianship of Eric, with which would go the management of Eric's estate.

"If he has brothers or sisters," commented the old bargainer, "he will of course want to share everything with them. And she will bear children. You may depend upon it. She is as fruitful as her mother, who had four, as you see. With a husband she really loves—" He broke off with a lewd wink, and at that moment Helga turned and looked back at Theobrand with her blue eyes.

There being no further need to stay divided, the two groups rejoined. Helga clung to Theobrand's arm, while her father and brothers seemed somehow to be keeping them surrounded, as if afraid Theobrand would escape in the crowd. Helga bought a belt for Theobrand and presented it to him shyly. He bought a pin for her hair, feeling both pleased with himself and foolish. He also bought a game of draughts for Eric; then Helga said, "This is your new father, Eric. You must love him." Theobrand twitched uncomfortably, but Eric gave no sign of being affected.

The Thing was held on a plain, large enough for the great throng that was expected. It was near the harbor, for the sake of those who came by ship. These preparations proved warranted, for the Thing was the largest ever held in Iceland. Men were there from every part, and many more women than usually attended. It was evident that the importance of the meeting was understood. All seemed to feel, perhaps because it was exactly the year 1000, that an era of history was ending precisely then, and another beginning.

Wooden statues of the old Gods were there, greased and gleaming for the occasion, but mostly for old times' sake. Their regime had really ended some time ago, when it was first suspected that their usefulness was gone. Only a formal vote was lacking to make them part of a fading past, remembered as empty images, without the spark that was once thought to be in them. Everyone felt a certain pleasure in going through the old motions and rituals, as in enjoying for the last time the company of departing friends.

Some were less sentimental about it. A Skald sang a vengeful little song in an undertone to a group of his friends, telling how Odin and his fellow-Gods were at that moment trembling in Valhall, hoping, as piteously as they had ever let men hope, that the unexpected would save them, and knowing all the time that nothing could. A few smiled cynically at this, but a few others shuddered, not having quite got over their old fears.

Presently the leading Bonders selected one of their number to be Chief of the Thing, and it was declared open. There was a question whether they should begin, as they always had, with a prayer to Odin for guidance. Many were in favor of omitting it, especially with Theobrand present. Legal hair-splitting was a popular pastime and here was a chance to indulge in it. It was maintained that since the Gods had not yet actually been deposed by vote, the laws which derived from them were still in force, and unless these were lived up to, nothing done here would be binding. So Odin and Thor and their kin were allowed to preside this one last time, in order to let themselves be slain.

So pray to Odin they did, with sidelong looks of apology to Theobrand and a shrug of the shoulders as though to say: "Once more won't matter." A turmoil was in the minds of these people who were thus praying while they changed faiths. Some prayed to a God in whom they no longer believed; some prayed for the last time to a God in whom they did believe; and some, only half sure, one way or the other, prayed so as to be safe. But, as Theobrand had often said, great is the power of prayer. For whatever mixed reasons they prayed, when it was done all were united in a vague, solemn feeling that they were all in this together now and had better get it settled.

Smaller matters were always disposed of at the beginning. The fate of the Gods waited until the Thing decided land-disputes and declared certain wrong-doers to be outlaws.

Late in the day came Helga's final appeal for divorce. She spoke up bravely before all these people, accusing her husband of cruelty, neglect and desertion. Theobrand watched Eric while his father was thus spoken of, but the boy gave no sign of understanding the matter under discussion, nor showed whether it disturbed him. But then Eric had seen Theobrand turn toward him and he may have been on his guard, so there was no way of making sure.

Helga brought forward her three witnesses, who told how she had complied with the first two steps of the suit, and urged that the Thing complete the action with its approval. There was a little adverse mumbling here and there, because some men felt that the Sea-King should be given more time. They did not know with absolute certainty, they said, that he was not coming back. Furthermore, it was bad to let wives think they could get free the instant their husbands sailed. Then Helga's father and brothers indicated to Theobrand that it was time for him to speak in her behalf, and they moved toward him a little, as if to press him in case he should refuse. He did not refuse; he spoke, eloquently. His words were all that were needed to make them decide as Helga wished, for the desire to do him a visible favor was so great that men were shouting approval before he finished speaking. Helga was so moved by the success of his oratory that she threw her arms about his neck and kissed him with everyone looking on. After that, the Thing moved on to its main subject, and then Odin's fate was settled as definitely as Theobrand's.

Two laws were quickly passed, both of them realistic and

to the point. The first law stated: "The Asa-Creed shall be un-lawful. If any man is found praying before idols, or asking help of Trolls, or eating horseflesh at Yule-tide, or wishing beside magic wells or beside magic stones or inside graves, he shall pay a fine of two ounces of gold."

The second law (which was proposed by Theobrand) said: "The worship of Christ shall be the only faith practiced in Iceland. Christian Priests shall have all the rights formerly held by the Godi or Hersir, and shall be allowed to charge the same fees as were formerly charged by them."

Both laws were passed without dissent and with scarcely any discussion. It took only a few minutes for the land to change its entire system of thought, or, rather, to record the fact that it had been changing for some time and now needed to be officially recognized. Those present were a little shocked to find how fast they had got rid of what they had so long believed.

The Thing broke up after that, and Theobrand received many congratulations, some of them on the victory of Christ and some on his own imminent marriage, so that the two were somehow identified. All the good wishes evoked a great elation in him, which stifled a weaker feeling that he was committing an act of folly.

It was night by now, and they went to Jatmund's house for the feast and the wedding. The ceremony was very simple, what you might call a civil marriage. First, Helga's father re-stated the terms of the dowry before witnesses, and Theobrand said, "I agree to the terms of this dowry." Then he placed a gold coin in Jatmund's hand and said, "For this money, paid into your hand, I buy this woman from you."

That was all. They were man and wife now.

The feast was a modest one, with only a few friends present. Neither did it last into the late hours of the night, for Jatmund did not have the heart to keep Theobrand lusting any longer. The pair was permitted to drive away to Helga's house, amid shouted wishes that they would have many children. Eric was among those who stood at the doorway to see them depart. He stayed at his grandfather's house for the night. He knew why. He was a little farm-boy and he knew all about mating.

When they reached their home, Theobrand and Helga embraced and kissed ardently at the threshold, then he carried her to their bedroom. When they got there, Helga found it a strange and exciting experience to see the man of God disrobe. He found it just as strange, though a trifle unnerving, to follow her into the Sea-King's bed.

XVI

THE storm at sea continued for three days after the Icelanders were driven from Greenland and Odin from Iceland. The escapes from death were so many and so close together that courage in meeting them became a habit. It was more surprise than relief when, on the morning of the fourth day, the storm suddenly stopped and went screaming away across the horizon. It left them alive and afloat, but in the Sea-King's opinion not much better for its absence, as it seemed a question to him whether it was worse to be wrecked or to drift aimlessly until they starved.

None but he knew they had no course and he kept it to himself, merely telling the others to rest on their oars for a spell and let the sail do the work, as there might be a great deal of rowing presently. When they asked him, as he knew they would, where they were heading, he answered, "Westward," with an air of weary patience which implied that he knew what he was doing. As they could tell this was true by the sun, which was climbing over the clouds, and as they were so tired they would have taken almost anything for an answer, they asked no further questions and fell asleep on their benches.

He took a common-sense view, wherewith he justified his

behavior. He had said his prayer to the Gods. If Odin and Thor had a course for him to set, let them say so. It was their current which was pulling the ship to the west. He knew—that is, it was generally thought—that if they went on sailing westward they would fall off the edge of the world, into— Into what? Straight into Hel, perhaps. No one knew. No one had ever before been called upon to sail toward nowhere and away from everywhere. Westward it had to be.

A great calm settled over the water, as overwhelming in its way as the storm had been. The wind stopped so completely that it seemed never to have blown. The sail sagged. There were no more great waves, just small soothing ones that rocked the ship like a cradle, as if the Gods were saying, "Sleep, sleep, it is in our hands now." The sun climbed, higher and warmer, drawing the dampness out of them.

Three days is a painfully long time to be without sleep. Ingolf's helmet felt very heavy. It made his head droop. He did not struggle to stay awake, but welcomed this drowsiness. In sleep we get messages from such as cannot approach us when awake. He needed advice, some kind, any kind. There was no reason to stay awake. He had lashed his right hand to the tiller. Any movement of wind or water would rouse him. All his habits would be on guard.

But his sleep was dreamless, except for his doubts and worries. The day was well advanced when he awoke, but even so he was the first to open his eyes. It was expected of him, and in his sleep he had been telling himself to wake up. Everyone else still slept, in strange contorted postures, sitting or lying, with their heads on one another's shoulders or laps or prone bodies. They were fairly dry by now, but stiff and wretched from their exertions and the uncomfortable way they were sleeping; every now and then one of them moaned and tried to shift the angle of his tormented neck. As if he had never stopped thinking of it, the Sea-King remembered what they would sooner or later ask him: where? where? where? They would be in no mood for half-answers.

It was a satisfaction at least that the storm was unlikely to return. It had poured the very last drop of its watery blood upon them and seemed anxious only to get back to its home and gain new life. He was glad of that: they could not have found the strength to fight it off again. But though Aegir and his brother had abandoned the struggle, the ice-Giants now joined it. A great fog (which is their breath) was floating toward the ship. There was an immense bank of it, drifting from the west, thick, perilous, looking like the white ghost of the black cliffs. Once it was about them, they would be able to see neither rocks nor any other enemy. The westward current held them, carrying them relentlessly into this blind, silent whiteness. The rowers were exhausted, beyond any possibility of struggling against it. The sail was limp and useless. In a few moments they would be in the midst of it, helpless, being carried ever nearer the edge of the world. When the fated time came for them to fall off, there would be no warning, no chance to see it coming and sing a death-song.

His companions began to wake as the chill of the fog touched them. They sat up, unrefreshed, staring vaguely at the misty shroud which was enclosing them, feeling not as if coming out of sleep into wakefulness, but as if moving out of one dream into another. They turned to their Sea-King, to set their wits to rights.

"Where are we?" someone asked him.

"West of Greenland," he answered.

They digested this for a moment, distastefully. Their bodies were stiff and their spirits rueful and the mention of Greenland brought back to mind their defeat by the Skraelings, now shorn of vainglory. They tried to look through the fog, but it was growing too thick. They might have been anywhere. They felt confused, and that irritated them.

"How far west of Greenland?" another asked him.

He replied, "One night's rowing and one day's drifting."

Was it coming now, the question for which he had been waiting? It was all about him, in the air, trying to be said. *Where are we going?* He almost said it himself, but resisted the impulse and instead gave the order: "Out oars!" The next moment they were rowing with the current, making great headway with little effort. Just as well, he thought, noting the speed. Whatever is to happen, let it be soon.

Bending their backs to the oars was painful at first but it

helped later, limbering their stiffened muscles and offsetting the chill. And it took their thoughts off the subject he dreaded.

Just as he felt safe, he heard someone ask it.

"Where are we going?"

But the question was not addressed to him. Turker had asked it, of the man who sat beside him and rowed with the same oar. His companion gave a little laugh, even as they rowed, and told him it was the business of the Sea-King. "Why don't you ask him?" he finished slyly, and waited, grinning, for Turker to get into trouble.

Turker seemed to fall into the trap, and dared to question the ship's master. The Sea-King had heard the whole thing and was ready for him. "We are going westward!" he said sharply. "Tend your oar and leave the course to me!" There was a laugh at Turker's expense as he learned his beginner's lesson. But the Sea-King was not pleased. The danger was past for the moment, but the question had been uttered and would be remembered and asked again, perhaps not by a Thrall.

The fog clung to them through the rest of the day and all the night. They rowed until morning, kept warm by the exertion. Now that the ship had steadied, the women managed to prepare some hot food. They could be seen in the glow cast by the fire of the ship's little oven which they laboriously tended; nothing else was visible in the darkness, and the illumined group of female faces became a point of fascination. The food was passed from hand to hand in the darkness. There were no tense feelings left.

The fog lifted in the morning when the sun came up. They saw that they were still in a broad expanse of open sea. The all-night rowing had tired them, and as before, the Sea-King let them do their sleeping through the day, while they drifted, west, west, west. He himself slept a little, but was alert nonetheless, once more being the first to wake. Again, as evening approached, a bank of fog marched toward them and surrounded them, waking the sleepers with its chill, and again he ordered them to the oars and a night of rowing.

The women had their duties arranged in a more orderly way by now, with the fire lit in the oven and supper prepared

124

before darkness overtook them. During this Turker spoke again to his companion at the oar. What he said seemed to be a continuation of the previous night's question, as if there had been no rebuff and no time between.

"—because," he said abruptly, "if we *don't* know where we are going—" He stopped, with a semblance of reluctance.

"Yes?" asked his neighbor, amused, and the rowers before and behind them listened as their bodies moved near with the motion of the oars.

"I was going to say," said Turker, "that if we *don't* know, there is always one thing we can do."

"And what is that?"

"We can go back to Iceland, and throw ourselves on Olaf's mercy."

The merriment ceased. No one thought this was funny. The man who rowed with Turker moved slightly away from him and muttered something about a Thrall being a Thrall. Turker heard it and admitted humbly that it must be true. He seemed to be embarrassed and took enormous pains to excuse himself. He had bad habits, he said, which he had picked up from other Thralls; he was not used to the company of Freemen; it had come into his head and he had said it because to a Thrall's mind it seemed a good idea; he would have to guard his tongue if he hoped to be worthy of his companions; his place was to listen and learn, not thrust himself forward; he hoped they would forgive him; whether they did or not, he would never forgive himself; yield to Olaf, indeed!—he would die first; and so on, at such great length that he kept the suggestion alive that much longer, by the device of continuing to cry it down. By the time he finished his show of contrition, they were sorry they had made him feel so badly. One of them even said that Turker mustn't be too ready to condemn his own suggestion. Good ideas often sounded shocking at first, like cold water that feels warm after you swim in it for a while. Soon Turker was the center of attention, standing higher than he had before, with everyone teaching him how to behave like a Freeman.

That led to one of the Bonders' approaching the Sea-King and hinting to him that he ought to set Turker free.

125

"It is uncomfortable," he said, "to have one man along as a Thrall, especially one whom everybody likes. When we start raiding, there will be slaves enough."

"I will think about it," said the Sea-King.

But he did not. What he thought about was that the notion of turning back had been suggested, had been said for the first time, in the way that the question about their course had been asked, and by the same mouth. He must watch Turker. A slave's feelings, far from his own country, where he had been free—slaves might have memories, the same as men. He buried the thought at the bottom of his mind, as he always did with what troubled him, and waited for the Gods to make it blossom.

Another night and day, and another, and another, all oddly the same: clear and pleasant after the sun rose, and then toward evening, the fog. They began expecting the fog, planning for it, working at the oars when it was upon them, sleeping in the sunlight when it was not. It was their main concern, around which all else moved. It ruled their lives. The Sea-King wondered about the regular way it met them. It came from the west, always from the west, where there were no ice-Giants. Nothing was there but the edge of the world. It was that, and what it was thought to be, which led them at last to the moment he was dreading.

Again it was Turker's fault. Evening was coming on—no one could say whether it was evening of the sixth or seventh or eighth or whatever day, because they had lost count—and they were still rowing with that eternal westward current. The fog that was rolling toward them this time was so dense that it seemed surely to portend something. Someone said, "Grey-Fellow is in time for dinner again." Turker had been circumspect since his advice about turning back, and no one, not even the Sea-King, had been paying special heed to him. Now he abruptly asked his neighbor another question, an apparently innocent one, asked with the reasonable air of one who merely seeks to increase his knowledge.

"If one were to go westward long enough," he asked, "what place would he reach?"

"Why, no place at all. He would fall off the edge of the earth." His neighbor stopped short, realizing what he had said.

126

Turker gasped, as if the reply surprised and shocked him. Others heard it, too, and remembered, startled, that they had heard it before. For a moment there was confusion, as some of the oars fouled each other. Several men stopped rowing and spoke together in excited whispers; then everyone stopped rowing, except Turker, who made a brave show of trying to handle his oar alone, without his partner; then he gave up the attempt, smiling apologetically at the Sea-King as though to say: "It's too heavy for one man." All the crew were speaking now, to each other, to the Bonders, to the women, about the forgotten legend. No one would row another stroke; a few even made an effort to back, but the current was too strong.

Then at last it came. One of the Bonders did it, with due regard for a Sea-King's position, but feeling it had to be done for the general good.

"Perhaps it would be best," he said, "if you would tell us what course you are taking."

Before the Sea-King answered, some had a horrid foreboding of what he was going to say and wished he wouldn't say it. But he did. Now that the moment was here, he was glad to have it over and done. He replied, very quietly and simply, "I don't know."

After that, nothing was said for a very long time. They were trying to understand all that his answer implied, each in his or her own way. The fog grew denser and chillier. They noticed it much more than they lately had, and huddled together here and there, seeming to form little groups, though really there were only two groups: the Sea-King and everyone else. These two had suddenly become no longer the same, and now were facing each other. At last a man said, "You *don't know?*"

"No," he replied, and uttered the phrase yet once more. Then he explained what he meant and why he meant it. He was brief, truthful and direct. They could no longer go to Greenland, because of the Skraelings. They could no longer go anywhere else, because of Olaf. They were in a trap, because of himself. That was all. No excuses. No arguments. No pleas. He waited for them to say something, if they wished.

The Bonder who had spoken to him before asked him, "Have you a plan?"

"No," he answered, "there is no plan to have."

"What steps have you taken, to save us?"

"I have done all that I know, and since there are many things I do not know, I have prayed."

"What are you going to do now?"

"Hope that good Lok is with us."

"And if he is not?"

The Sea-King was about to answer, "I don't know," but he didn't, because at that instant something very strange went through his mind and put a different answer into his mouth. He said, so sharply that he startled them and himself, too, "Good Lok *is* with us!" He did not know why he said it, nor why he was so sure. From hoping Lok was with them to knowing he was, was an enormous step. Nothing had happened except that the tiniest little breeze had blown for an instant, stirred the fog and stopped. Assuredly that brief flutter could not help them, for the sail again hung, as limp as ever. But he knew he had found what he was seeking: the way out of their difficulties. The Gods had given him his answer. It was at the back of all his other thoughts, trying to hide from him, not yet clear enough for him to see its face, but he would, he would. He had been trying to find it for days, and now his mind—his *other* mind—had hold of it. What was it? Oh, what was it?

"Why are you so sure Lok is with us?" the Bonder asked.

"Because tomorrow morning we will reach land."

Everyone strained forward. The Bonder was startled, for it had been said with an air of complete assurance. "In that case—" he began apologetically, almost ready to drop the subject. "I thought—the men seemed uneasy—"

"I understand."

"Would you be willing to tell us what land it is?"

"Gladly"—every breath was held—"if I knew."

"Oh." There was disappointment again. "Has anyone ever been there?"

"I don't know."

"Then you have heard about it?—from your father, perhaps?"

"No."

128

"From someone else?"

"No."

The disappointment grew into restlessness, almost into hostility. "Then why—are you so sure—we will reach it?"

"I don't know." The Sea-King closed his eyes and motioned the Bonder to silence. "Let me think it out," he said. Without letting go of the tiller, he put his free elbow on his knee and rested his face on his hand.

The Bonder shrugged his shoulders helplessly, turned from him and addressed the other men. "I think," he said, "we must hold a Thing, at once." He did not add, "without our Sea-King," but that was understood. He went to the far end of the ship and the men followed him. One or two of the women made a move to go along, but the men who saw it shook their heads and they desisted. Turker did not even try to join them and no one invited him. The Sea-King was left with the Thrall and the women. But he did not notice where anyone was. His mind was full of the Gods, wondering whether they were doing what he thought they were, from certain indications that were there for all to see, though only he had perceived them.

It was dark by the time the Thing ended and the men returned to the stern. One of them held a lighted torch, which cast a huge halo in the fog above their heads. The Sea-King's face was calmest of all as he waited for what they had to say to him.

Their spokesman was the Bonder who had convoked the Thing. "I will tell you what has been decided," he said. "We can do nothing until daylight. But when the fog lifts in the morning, if we sight land—as you seem so sure we will"—the Sea-King nodded affirmation—"why then, well and good. It will show that the Gods are with us and that you have been doing their will. But if, when the fog lifts, there is no land"— he hesitated, not liking to say it—"that will mean that the Gods are displeased with us and that you have misled us. If that is what happens, we have voted that you shall be sacrificed to Odin, so we may regain his favor. After that, we shall take the advice which Turker gave, the other day: we shall return to Iceland and throw ourselves on Olaf's mercy. We reached this decision after praying to Odin for guidance, and we trust

129

him to soften Olaf's heart. I tell you that, so that you may see we are only following the All-Father's counsel."

"I see several things," replied the Sea-King. "For one thing, I see you mean to tell Olaf I was to blame."

The Bonder was ashamed, but tried not to be. "The men feel that what has happened has been your fault."

"Let them remember that tomorrow, when the fog lifts."

"You still believe we shall see land?"

"I am sure of it. In the meantime, am I still Sea-King of this ship?"

"No one else would take command, at night and in fog. Do you want the men to start rowing?"

"Not tonight. I do not wish to run upon land in the dark."

That was the end of it, and it appeared to all that the Sea-King had shown to the best advantage. Some of them began to be sorry that they had rendered such a harsh verdict and almost wished they could unsay it, though none would be the first to admit having been wrong. They returned to their benches, or lay down to rest—though they were too wrought up to be easy—or talked among themselves in an undertone, as people talk when a man is dying and no one can help him. They eased their qualms by hoping that the Sea-King would be proven right, though they were sure he would not, and saved their faces by keeping far away from him. All but Turker. He approached him, urged partly by curiosity, partly to be ready to shift his plans if need be, and a little by a wish to gloat.

"Why do you believe in Lok?" he asked him.

"Because he has always stood by me. I think he will even give me back my son."

"But *now?*" Turker insisted. *"Now?* How can you think he is with you *now?"*

"Because there is land less than ten miles away."

"Have you found out what makes you so sure?"

"Yes."

His certainty was impressive. Turker was awed by it. He became less aggressive, more cajoling, as he asked, "Will you tell me?"

"Yes. There are three reasons why I know it. They have been in the darkness at the back of my mind, but the Gods have just unlocked it, for me to see. First, there is the current. A current does not run *into* land; it turns when it comes near land and runs beside it. The westward current which has pulled us for days has lately been turning a little to the south. Then there is the fog, which is the breath of ice-Giants. It has been getting thicker. We are coming nearer to the Giant whose breath it is. And third—third—" He smiled a little, a strangely tender little smile, the kind that goes with old, beloved memories. "Early this evening, a little breeze found its way through the fog. All of you were excited and frightened from thinking about the edge of the world, so none of you noticed what I did, about that little breeze. It brought me the faint, distant scent of a pine forest."

Turker, no longer perceived by him, crept back through the darkness toward his companions, wondering whether he should tell them what he had just heard. It would encourage them, revive their trust in their Sea-King, make them readier to go on, harder to pull back to Iceland. But they would hear it anyway, so he had better get the credit for having found it out. He must keep their esteem and await his chance. *Then* they would listen when he advised—Ah, his chance, his chance! When would it come? Patience, he told himself for the hundredth, the thousandth time. No trial is too great. To make himself endure yet once again, he thought of his own little boy, for whom he was doing this terrible, endless waiting.

"I must tell the others what I have learned," he admitted to himself, gloomily, "but oh, ghost of Atyl the Great, grant there will be no land when the fog lifts!"

Even had the crew not got into the habit of sleeping by day and rowing by night, there would have been no sleeping on this night. They were too excited, speculating over what the lifting of the fog would reveal. The Sea-King's confidence had produced so marked an effect that many were wishing they had a good excuse to say they had changed their minds. And when Turker repeated to them what he had just heard, they believed to a man that they would sight land in the morning. They even believed they had thought so all along and tried to out-shout each other in claiming to have been in the believing minority.

Their ready acceptance of the Sea-King's reasons was not

warranted. A westerly current may turn south for other causes than merely to run beside a body of land. A fog may rise from floating icebergs. As for the distant scent of a pine forest, there is a question how far that can be wafted, and besides he may have imagined it. The best that could be justly said was that he might be right and might be wrong. But they now agreed with him more unreasonably than they had recently condemned him, since it was pleasanter to feel safe than frightened. They transferred their animosity to the Bonder who had convoked the Thing, mumbling that he would be a more fitting sacrifice to Odin than the man they had voted should be. Soon they were saying they should take another vote and undo the first.

The Sea-King, however, overheard this and inveighed against it sternly.

"You have made a bargain with Odin," he reminded them, "and you must live up to it. Odin is not to be cheated. He will have his sacrifice if he wants it, no matter what you decide or how many votes you take. The only thing that is in your power to do is show good faith."

As some of them were still inclined to risk the anger of the Gods, he saw that it was his duty to convince them. So he told them the story of Vikar.

"He was a Host-King, was Vikar, who commanded many men, and had many victories and successful raids which brought him wealth and fame. He made a great show of saying that Odin helped him win, but in his heart he thought it was his own doing. He praised Odin only to make his men more ready to die in battle, since they would do more for the God than for the King.

"On one of his raids, he decided that they would draw lots to see who would be sacrificed to Odin, never thinking in his pride that it would fall to himself. But the All-Father arranged that it turned out thus, and when it did, all became silent, no one daring either to say that the King must die or that the God must be cheated. It was decided to meet again the following day, and think about it in the meanwhile.

"During the night Odin appeared to one of the men, whose name was Stark, and said to him, 'At your birth I was your foster-father and have watched over you ever since. Will you admit that you have been fortunate in everything you have undertaken?' Stark thought a moment and then agreed that he had never been poor, unloved or defeated. 'Very well, foster-son,' said Odin, 'then it is your turn to help me. You must get Vikar for me tomorrow.' And he explained to Stark how it was to be done.

"When the meeting was held the next day, Stark said to Vikar, 'The proper course for us to follow, King Vikar, in order that we may neither offend Odin nor lose you, is to go through all the motions of sacrificing you without really doing so.' 'That is excellent,' assented Vikar, 'but I do not see how it is to be done.' Stark thereupon showed him two articles which he carried in his hand: a small piece of string tied to a twig, and a reed. 'We will pretend,' he said, 'that the string tied to a twig is a gallows and the reed is a spear. I will put the string around your neck and touch you with the reed. Then Odin will be satisfied, for we shall have gone through the form of sacrifice to which he is accustomed.' Vikar looked at the small objects and thought they were so harmless that even Odin could not injure him with them, so he allowed Stark to put the string about his neck. Then Stark touched him with the reed and said, 'I give you to Odin.' At once, everyone saw that they had been the victims of an illusion, that the reed was really a spear which pierced Vikar's body and that the string and twig were really a gallows, for they saw Vikar hoisted up by them above the ground, where he died.

"The death of Vikar shows that we cannot escape the will of the Gods, for this world is otherwise than as they let us see it, full of traps of which we are not aware until we are caught in them."

The Sea-King's telling of this tale and his willingness to lose his life if Odin pleased to take it made the listeners admire his pure, simple faith and be surer than ever that he would be rewarded for it by finding land next day. Many who had not gone into a temple in years vowed that they would be more religious in the future and would sacrifice regularly to whichever of the Gods they had been neglecting. And as they felt this surge of increasing piety, the first light of morning shone through the fog.

XVII

UNLIKE the men on the ship, Odin did not think it undignified to consult women on matters of life and death. His handful of storm-tossed followers must be given a home, so the All-Father turned to where he would get the best advice.

He summoned the oldest and wisest of his wives. She was an ancient Goddess named Erda, or Eartha, or as she was affectionately called by people: Mother Earth. He had long since deserted her for younger mates, but she did not reproach him, merely waiting patiently to learn what he wanted, prepared as ever to forgive him and grant it. "Have you no place upon your vast bosom," he asked her, "where my children may rest their heads? If not in the known world, then let it be in the unknown world!"

There was indeed such a refuge, she told him. But just as there were things so small they could scarcely be seen, this was so huge it could scarcely be imagined. It was boundless, endless, a great double continent, half of all the world, three thousand miles across and stretching from above the Northern Lights to a great frozen sea South of the South. It was spacious enough, she said, to shelter every man in the world, and each could bring all his wives and all his concubines, and they in turn could bring their lovers if they had them and would find places to conceal them, and all of them together could bring all their children to start new lineages with, and even then there would be so much room left that the same thing could be done again by other men and women, from the Moon perhaps, or from wherever else people might be seeking shelter, and again, and yet again forever. All comforts were in it, Erda said, that make life pleasant or make people want to live. It held food of every kind, fertile ground to grow more, sweet water to sprinkle it with or to drink, salt water to sail to and from it, woods, climate to please every liking, whether sleepy or pleasant or bracing, hills, valleys, sun, rain, flowers, birds, fish, animals, changing seasons, coasts, harbors, gold, silver, iron, copper, everything hard and soft and in between, lakes, brooks, rivers, plains, peaks, grass, granite, vast distances, near-by nooks, skies that were blue by day and starry by night, beauty, health, happiness, strength and wonder, and all in such prodigious, fabulous, unheard-of, unbelievable, unreasoning abundance, that the human race could be rid of all its hardships there, once and for all time, with hardly the effort of setting its mind to it.

This was no undiscovered world, oddly enough, that Erda was describing to her husband. It had been discovered many times, though neglected and forgotten as many. It was known to the ancients as a Paradise that had somehow been lost, and Plato, Aristotle and Seneca mentioned it as "the wonderful country hidden in the Western Ocean." It bore many names which expressed the deathless longing with which it was remembered, some of which were from time to time wistfully bestowed on other places, and among these were Atlantis, Moo, The Fortunate Isles and The Lost Island of the Seven Cities. And there were men and women living there, many tribes of them, handsome, copper-colored people, with gaily feathered dress, language, religion, customs, traditions and pleasures, who had long since discovered the beauty and marvel of the place and made up tales about it, and who had their own wonderful names for it, according to the part in which they dwelt. It would be as wrong to call it undiscovered because no European had found it, as to call Europe undiscovered because none of the copper-colored men had been there.

As a matter of fact, there were legends that Europeans had been there, ever since stories of the Lost Continent first were told. There was an Irish monk named Brendan—renamed Saint Brendan for what he did—of the Christian Culdee sect, who is said to have miraculously crossed the Ocean in a coracle about the year 700, landed on those mighty shores, preached to the copper-colored people and lived to return and tell about it. And the Aztecs worshipped an idol with a fair complexion and a golden beard; it represented a divinity who long ago had come from across the sea, had ruled them for a time and then departed, promising to return. And there was a yellow man from Cathay, named Lo-Fen, who reached the western side in a funny little square ship, in the funny little year 400. And long before any of these, the copper-colored people themselves discovered the land, coming from no one knows where, but certainly from somewhere. Where did those of the North get their high cheekbones, that look so Chinese? Where did those of the South get their pyramids, that look so Egyptian? Where did that tribe in the Andes get their skin, that looks so white? Wherever they got these things, and wherever they came from on their voyages of discovery, there were other people living there when they landed who had discovered it earlier still, imaginative, *building* people, who made giant mounds in the exact shape of bears and snakes. Countless times it had been discovered, by different kinds of people from different kinds of places, in the names of their different Gods, and they had discovered different things about the land, different ways of enjoying it, or ignoring or forgetting it. It may be that some were only laughed at when they went back home and said they had found it, but at least they would have kept alive the legend of the Lost Continent, to inspire other adventurers yet unborn. Erda had never tired of telling the secret, to whatever ears would listen, hoping that the rest of the world would taste its delights, and now in the portentous year 1000 she was telling it again to Odin, so that it might be newly discovered by the Sea-King, Red Eric's son Leif.

Well, there it was when the fog had cleared away, and all his unsound reasons were correct. It lay to steer-board, about ten miles off, and they were drifting along parallel to it, not head on, all just as he had said. There were no forests visible at this distance, of pine or any other tree; nothing, as far as they could make out, but snow and glaciers, nor did the aspect change when they put in toward shore for a better look. But he had found land, with or without pine, and that excused any discrepancy. The crew were ready to deny that he had mentioned a pine forest, so completely were they on his side now; at most, they claimed that if he *had* said it, then they must have drifted past the forest in the night. It was impossible for him to be wrong now. They would have believed any statement of his, obeyed any order. Had he wished, he could have had the Bonder sacrificed to Odin. Had he wished, and had it been possible, he could even have had Odin sacrificed. He could have had anything he wanted.

His only wish, however, was to bring their tired bodies into port, and he did not know whether to land here or seek further. Neither he nor the crew liked the look of this particular spot, which was as glacier-covered as Greenland but lacked even Greenland's black granite. They longed for just a patch of green to indicate that something might grow, and were prepared for any amount of back-breaking tillage. They were seamen, these Vikings, because they had to be, but in their hearts they were sailing farmers, looking for farm land.

The choice was not theirs. It was Thor's. His image was released from the cords which secured it and carried to the prow, to look at the land and decide for them as it had for Ingolf. It was soon made clear that Thor did not care to land there any more than the Icelanders did, for when they dropped him overboard he made no move to drift ashore, but remained floating close beside the ship. That was all the hint they needed. They hauled him aboard, glad that he agreed with them, and headed south, keeping the land always in view. Presently the current seized them again and they had little to do but watch the shore and see whether its character was changing. It remained the same all through the day. Something else did change, however, and it was a welcome novelty: as night came on, there was much less fog than there had been, scarcely any at all. After a while, it cleared away altogether, so that they saw the stars for the first time in many nights. This encouraged them, making them feel that they must be nearing a dryer, less frozen part of the earth. They were able to sleep through the dark, instead of having to row. There was a pleasant sense that all was well, from this safe resumption of habit.

When morning came, they were greatly comforted to see the land still with them. The contour was somewhat different from that of the day before. There were hills now, still snow-covered, but when they rowed nearer for closer inspection, it was seen that there were trees as well as snow on the hills. This was much more to their liking, and when they once more dropped Thor overboard, they hoped he would agree with them. But he proved hard to please and floated as before alongside the ship. A number of men were in favor of disregarding his wishes and going ashore despite him, but the Sea-King would not hear of it. He had the idol hauled aboard and gave orders to continue south along the coast. They must obey the wishes of the Gods, he admonished them, and besides they knew where this place was and could always return to it if they found nothing better. South they went again, keeping the snowy hills and trees in sight until night overtook them once more. This time there was no fog at all, so that they were able to discern the outline of the land against the starry sky, until their eyes grew tired and they fell asleep.

The following morning brought a great disappointment. When they awoke, there was no land in sight, of any kind. Immediately their spirits fell and they began to worry once more about the edge of the world and whether they were near it. They wanted to turn back to the wooded, snowy hills they had seen yesterday. But the Sea-King decided otherwise. There was a chance, he reasoned, that the land had not ended, but had curved away from them. It could not have curved to eastward, or they would have run into it. If it had curved at all, it was worth trying to find again, so he ordered the ship put about to westward. Late in the afternoon he was again proven right. Land lay due west of them.

It was low-lying ground this time, which was one reason why it hid so easily behind the horizon. When they had come near enough, they saw that it had a beach of white sand which gleamed even in the twilight. There were many inlets, too, while some distance further inland a thick growth of trees bespoke fertile soil. The belt of snow seemed to have been left far behind; they saw none. Good Lok had done ever so much more for them than they had hoped. As for Thor, if he opposed their wishes now, he would find it hard to keep their obedience. They dropped him dutifully over the side and waited for his response as he bobbed up and down, but their minds were made up, regardless of what he might say. One or two of them, however, paid him the compliment of praying silently that he would agree with them. To their immense satisfaction, he did. The tide was moving in, toward shore, and he let it bear him straight into one of the inlets. The ship followed where he floated, through that safe, pleasant harbor flanked by clean-looking sand-spits.

As they sailed deeper into the land, life suddenly became very different for the Sea-King, more so than for any of them. He had kept his word. "I will take command and bring you safe to port," he had said. Now it was done. Now he was released. No more need to banish his son from his thoughts. "Eric, Eric, I can think now of how to save you. Your father, Eric, is coming for you. Patience, my son, for a very little while."

He had been looking forward to saying those words, had been changing them this way and that for greater satisfaction, against the moment when they could be said. But they did not give him the expected relief and exultation. Another thought, strange and uninvited, but fully as strong as his wish to rescue his son, intruded itself and jealously claimed part of his interest.

We have little eyes in the back of our necks with which we see the unseen, and when they are open we have what we call a creepy feeling. He was conscious of it at that instant. Entirely without reason or cause, he knew that something or somebody was watching him from shore. It must be from shore, because everyone on the ship was looking away from him and toward land, noting its outlines in the growing darkness. The channel was narrow here, so the unseen watcher—if such it was—must be near enough to be seen. Yet the best effort of a pair of seaman's eyes failed to make out anything that would account for the impression. This sensation of being watched never left him, throughout all the time that they were to spend on this western edge of the world. He remembered later that this was the first time he had felt it.

In view of their misadventure with the Skraelings, it seemed wise to wait for daylight before stepping ashore. He decided they would come to anchor where they were, for the night. They lifted Thor out of the water with renewed respect for his judgment, gratefully placed food before him, then prepared to celebrate the successful ending of their quest.

A feast was in order. Since it was in the place which was to be their home, it must be a formal feast, at which they could be conscious of observing an event. The women broached the best of their provisions and cooked worthily. The ship became a guest-hall. Where the Sea-King sat at the helm was the High-Seat and he was their Hero, whom they had met to honor. They gave him a ringing cheer, such as he had not heard since the six Bonders acclaimed him their Sea-King in the wood near Thor's temple. It brought him back, by its very loudness, to what was going on about him.

Praise is handsome payment. He had looked forward to it, as the best part of his reward. But his son was to have been beside him when that great cheer was given, his little heart brimming with the triumph which he felt he had somehow helped to gain. Without Eric—

Two phrases that were hostile to each other fought for the attention of his inner ear. He heard and accepted both. They were "It cannot be" and "It is."

His companions were unaware of his feelings. It requires great effort to remember another man's grief. And their heartiness, given without stint, was a credit to them, since they, too, found something missing that they loved. They did not say aloud what it was. They could have, were it not that they were unwilling to think about it clearly lest they make themselves too sad.

They knew an artful way of tricking themselves into expressing what they shied away from but what they would feel better for stating. They called upon one of their number, a man with a fine, stirring voice, to make up a song.

The man understood what kind of song they meant. His companions saw him finger his axe and look toward the wood which was fading into night. You might have said he was going to sing about the axe and the wood and how the two together would make a temple or a house. But instead of being bold and vigorous, the song was sentimental. That really surprised

140

no one. All silently accepted it as what they had in mind. It told them they were homesick. The phrase "in Iceland" recurred regularly as a sort of refrain. Soon they were all waiting for it and murmuring it with the singer whenever it came around.

> I felled the trees in an Iceland wood,
> And built my home where the trees had stood,
>   In Iceland.
>
> Its beams were cedar, its roof was pine,
> Its floor was birch, and it was all mine,
>   In Iceland.
>
> I owned it all and it owned me too:
> We both were made out of things that grew
>   In Iceland.
>
> And now I'll build on a distant shore
> The self-same house that I built before
>   In Iceland.
>
> With beams of cedar, and roof of pine,
> And floor of birch, like that house of mine
>   In Iceland.
>
> I'll live in it when it all is done,
> And dream that I live in that other one,
>   In Iceland.

After that, they looked at one another, saw that all felt alike, and were on that account a little less ashamed. With a joint impulse, they flung their moodiness away, singing jollier songs and many of them. At last, realizing that an exacting day of exploration awaited them, they posted guards at both rails of the ship and tried to sleep. But the cries of strange birds that were also nesting for the night kept them long awake, reminding them in a roundabout way of Iceland, where the birds had cries that they knew, and where sleep therefore came easier and felt sweeter.

XVIII

WHEN dawn came, the land looked more wonderful than it had at their last fading glimpse of it at nightfall, and more wonderful still when the growing daylight sharpened its colors. But most wonderful of all was the sight which they themselves presented to certain eyes that were observing them.

From the cover of the near-by wood, four members of the Wampanoag tribe—three young men and a young woman—were watching. Amazed, breathless, fascinated, they peered through the foliage and discovered Iceland.

In one of the Sagas there is told the manner in which the Icelanders came ashore, but it was set down to be read by other Icelanders, who knew their countrymen's ways so well that many things did not have to be said; we shall never know them now, except by guess. It does not reveal how the newcomers seemed to the unaccustomed, excited eyes back of the trees. "During the night," says the Saga, stating only such facts as the home-folk might not know, "the tide had ebbed and the ship was aground in the middle of the channel. But they were so eager to get ashore that they could not wait for high water to come and help them beach the ship. They jumped over the sides and ran to the bank."

That gives a sympathetic notion of men who had been long at sea, who had left their homes and were now scrambling to find places for new ones. But the Wampanoags could not understand being long at sea, since they knew of no far-off ports across the horizon; and with limitless ground on which to pitch their tents, they could never have understood a man land-hungry enough to seize a little plot and call it his.

"It was fine weather," continues the Saga. "When they reached shore, they looked about. They saw that there was dew on the grass. They touched it with their fingers and tasted it, and it seemed that nothing had ever tasted as sweet to them as this dew." Thus the Saga describes these wandering farmers, who were overjoyed to find such splendid grazing for their cows.

But the Wampanoags had never seen a farmer, nor yet a cow. They were in fact unprepared, through centuries of habit, to believe anything but the wonderful and unworldly. This was no handicap to their thinking. It enabled them to find much more that was marvelous in their discovery than the Icelanders were finding in theirs. The Wampanoags could indulge in the luxury of astonishment, without having it spoiled by fear. Theirs was by far the more ancient nation of the two, tracing its ancestry through fox and beaver to the very beginning of things. They could not remember, nor had they ever heard of, a time when the world was different, so what could change it now? The only big fear is fear of change, and that did not exist. Anything that seemed new was only the old in disguise, holding neither peril nor discomfort, delightful to be examined and recognized.

What they marveled at mostly—taken for granted, of course, by the Saga—was that Icelanders have white skin. To men with copper-colored skin, or with brown or black skin for that matter, it always seemed, everywhere and invariably until they got used to it, that a man with white skin is dead. When copper-colored men—or brown or black men—die, the blood and color leave them. So the inference was clear: the white were the dead. That was nothing to be afraid of, however, for no wall of fear had been set up between dead and living. The dead had no hostility; if anything, they felt friendly remembrance of pleasant times passed together.

The armor and yellow hair of the strangers were a source of additional assurance. In the morning light, *they shone*. That had a special significance to the Wampanoags. Reasoning in terms of what they knew and believed, they decided that these pale, capering, shouting creatures must be the ancient dead, transformed into those spirits of light who daily bring the sunbeams from the sky. As they watched, they tried to make no

143

sound, by move or breath, which might alarm their bright visitants and make them fly away, but when the Sea-King joined the others, with Ingolf's ancient flashing helmet making him taller and more dazzling than any, the four Wampanoags could repress their excitement no longer and dashed back to tell the rest of the tribe the rapturous news.

The Saga does not tell us what was the first thing that was said there, in a European tongue, nor whether it was said by a Bonder, a Freeman or a Thrall, though we who live there now wish it had been recorded. Did someone shout: "Mine! Mine!" as they scrambled to take possession across the wet, clinging sands of the channel, or was it an exclamation of surprise and pleasure?

Apparently little time was lost in rollicking, after that first outburst. "When the high water returned," says the Saga, "it set the ship afloat. They rowed along the river until it opened into a lake. There they cast anchor, deeming it a safe place to keep the ship. Many salmon were in the water, the largest they had ever seen, and the ground was so fertile that they knew they need not build barns to hold winter fodder for the cattle. They decided to stay there."

The medieval chronicler, thus briefly recording their selection of a site for their new world, then states in a single, tiny sentence, their accomplishment of a vital, monumental deed. He says: "They built their houses there." That is all, and we are left to surmise much: how it was done, the eager planning, the back-breaking weeks and above all, what it meant to them to have homes at last. How much it must have meant is shown by the way Icelanders measured a house. It was their very own method and expressed their anxiety about the kind of life they would have in it. When it was all built, they paced off its length, three times. If, in these successive measurements, it seemed to grow longer, their fortune while they lived in it would grow ever greater. Probably the reverse was true, too, but the only records tell of houses whose length increased. They were a very hopeful people.

No trace of those houses remains, so they were built of wood, though stone was to be had near by. It was the custom in Iceland to build of wood and they meant to keep their Iceland customs. If they fit the place, good; if not, the worse for the place.

But the place had a mind of its own, or what was as good, a way of setting a man certain tasks which he must do if he wanted to live. The country they came from might claim their memories, but the country where they were claimed their work. There was always one more thing to do, at one particular instant, on one particular spot, on no account to be delayed; whereas the past remained where it was and when it was, changeless, patient, to be dealt with at one's leisure. Iceland had to wait upon present need, even if Iceland meant a little boy held captive, who must somehow be rescued.

"Somehow" is a desperate word. The Sea-King had no time to make his plan. There were too many pressing things to be done, and he was expected to give orders for his companions to carry out, as if they had made him Folk-King and Host-King too. Was there no one else who could take command? There was a little vanity in the question, and in the answer he gave himself: "No." It was an honor, of course, that they should so defer to him, a reward for having found him dependable, but it was a trap, too, for his wishes must be second to theirs. That was hard for a religious man to bear, for Wish was one of the oldest Gods, and the way you prayed to him was to tell him silently and fervently what you wanted; it was frustrating to have to do his Wishing on everyone's behalf but his own.

Most distressing was his inability to confide. To no one could he say: "I must go back to Iceland for my son." He had wrought too well, had found them too perfect a haven. They would never let even him imperil it. Son or not, no one who knew where they were would be allowed to return to Iceland.

He could not save Eric alone. He could not navigate a ship alone. In his first frenzy, when they stole his boy, he had thought he might, and imagined himself with one hand on the tiller and the other on the sail, disdaining sleep as he scudded before the wind toward Eric and vengeance. Now that it was actually to be done, such fancies were not enough. More than two hands were needed, to fight that westward-running current with oars as well as sail, and it would serve no end if he stepped ashore in Iceland, staggering like a drunken man for lack of sleep, to be slain before his son's eyes. He could not seek aid of anyone, and yet must. Who, then? Who, that was both some-one and no one? He laughed as he asked himself that meaning-less question, then realized that there was an answer.

Turker. What made him think of Turker? That Turker was a Thrall perhaps, and a Thrall was not really a man. It would be like both speaking and not speaking. Or it may have been the memory of Earl Haakon hiding under the pigsty with the slave Kark, for there, too, the price of aid was an offer of free-dom, which he had in mind to promise Turker. Would Turker betray him? Kark betrayed Haakon. Did all slaves carry knives against their masters? That group of his own slaves, whisper-ing by the roadside after the Priest's talk, stopping and bowing when he came by. Why? They were well treated. Turker was well treated. Hard to understand, unless you are a slave.

His Thrall always put him at a disadvantage when they were together. The mean, perfidious stratagem by which he had been captured came sharply back to memory whenever Turker looked at him. If only it had been done some other way—not by feigning interest in his little son! Here, for the first time, because he was thinking of making Turker an ally, he won-dered for an instant—oh, for the merest brief fraction of an instant—whether there was any way at all of enslaving a man that could make his slavery less bitter. At once he reproved himself for such an impious thought, remembering that a slave must not receive any sympathy, as if he were a man.

"Turker," he asked him suddenly, when next they were alone, "do you think about your son?"

"Yes," replied Turker, with no show of feeling.

"Would you like to see him again?"

"Yes."

"If you were free, you could go where you wished. Would you like me to free you?"

Turker made no sound, but his lips formed a silent "yes."

"Do you admit I have treated you well?—have given you good food and clothing?—have done everything you could ask for?" Turker made no answer, until his master added: "—ex-

146

cept, perhaps, that I have not set you free?" Then Turker answered, "Yes."

"Then you want your freedom, not to escape from me, but to see your son?" He thought he had tricked Turker into revealing the truth. If he hesitated in answering he should be mistrusted.

Turker answered immediately. "I am not free, and therefore I do not think like a free man. I think like a Thrall." With that he closed his lips tightly, refusing to make his meaning any clearer.

That left the matter where it was, with Turker's master knowing no more of his motives than before he had questioned him.

The Sea-King did nothing further about it for a few days, not wanting Turker to become suspicious and start looking for the purpose back of it until he was ready that he should. Meanwhile he concluded that his Thrall was homesick but not resentful. That was a mistake, but one that had to be made, because he needed Turker and must not think of reasons for doing without him.

His plan took fairly distinct form. He would suggest to Turker that the price of his freedom might be some sort of expedition to Iceland. Only "might be," not "would be," and it must be referred to in a vague, roundabout way, so that if Turker repeated it to anyone, it could be cried down as the exaggeration of a Thrall overly eager to be free. They would do nothing until the raid on the Orkneys was under way, which would be as soon as the men started thinking about women. At the nearest point to Iceland, he and Turker would make off in the ship's boat. Then a silent, unexpected landing by night, a stealthy approach to his homestead, a quick blow, and they would be off with Eric. After that—? All he could see was Turker going one way, and Eric and himself another, with all of Olaf's men and ships trying to find them. It was possible that Turker might put Olaf on the track, hoping for reward. Haakon and Kark again. No, he vowed it should not be like that. He would keep his part of the bargain, fairly and to the full, but if there were the least smell of treachery—"Slowly, slowly," he reproved himself, feeling his anger rising over a wrong that had not been done. "Until I take the first step, I need not lose my temper over the second and third."

When next he contrived to be alone with Turker, he again found himself beginning with the very subject that made him most uncomfortable. "Tell me about your son," he said. "What sort of a boy is he?"

"You saw him."

"I mean," said the Sea-King, feeling the old embarrassment, "what does he like to do?"

"To play at being like his father. The same as your son."

"They are about the same age, aren't they?"

"They are exactly the same age."

The Sea-King tried to get over his discomfiture by smiling as he said, "So are their fathers." As Turker did not return the smile, he pretended he had not meant to jest and continued seriously: "And both of us left them in the lands we came from. It is all the same, all of it."

"Not all," said Turker.

"Only that you are not free. But that," said the Sea-King, with a sly inflection of which he felt ashamed, "can be made the same, too." Now he waited, maintaining silence stubbornly. Turker would have to speak out. With one man wanting his freedom and another who could give it, there could be no fair dickering.

"There is a price, I see," said Turker, with disconcerting directness. "I will pay it. What must I do to see my son again?"

"Let us rather say," his master gently corrected him, "that we two have the same difficulty, which we might help each other to meet. I, too, would like to see my son. My problem is in fact greater than yours, for he is in Iceland."

"Ah!" cried Turker quickly. "Do you want me to fetch him for you?"

"No," replied the Sea-King, sensing a faint flavor of contempt, "I would not ask any man to save my son. That is for me to do. The most I would ask is help." Turker was about to shout that he would give it, but his master gave him no chance, for that would make it too definite, too difficult to deny. "We are speaking of what is unlikely to happen," he said. "Surely we two would never leave the others."

148

On that ill-concealed hint, he dropped the subject again and did not refer to it for a long time, though Turker hovered invitingly near. Before taking another step, he wanted to be sure that Turker was not repeating what had been said. He had not pledged him to secrecy, but silence would show he understood the need for it. When days passed, the absence of rumors assured him that Turker had kept his peace. But had the Sea-King suspected the reason, he would have drawn his sword and cut his Thrall's throat on the instant.

Despising his master's indirectness, Turker understood all the hints and guessed beyond them. He was being offered his freedom to help rescue Eric. What freedom? In this unknown land in the Western Ocean? He spat his contempt for so mean a bribe. After what he had suffered, he would have nothing less than to be free everywhere in the world, the free father of a free son. And *that*—That, only Olaf could give, and Olaf, too, asked a price. "Bring them back!" the Priest had whispered as they were pushing the ship toward the water. "All of them. Olaf must have them all!"

Thralls, being bought and sold, had a keen sense of price and value. Turker preferred Olaf's offer. The Icelanders would be given into Olaf's hands. All of them. Slavery or the adder-pit for every last one. "I shall see my son!" he vowed. "But my master shall not see his. Amen." He crossed himself to make the vow a holy one.

The moment of their next meeting was chosen by neither of them, but by this new-found land wherein they both were scheming. The Sea-King, faced by one of the duties which had now become harassing to him, decided that the country must be explored before winter, against possible enemies. He called the men together and said to them, "One third of you shall remain here to guard the houses and the women and children. The rest shall divide into two groups and explore in opposite directions. But go only so far as will let you return before dark, and let no man ever be alone."

The men thought this final order strange, not sharing his sense of being watched, but they would not think of questioning his wisdom. The Saga comments: "They followed his orders for several days," indicating that they followed their own whims soon after, to wherever the wild, natural beauty of the land beckoned and enticed. Those tired men, who had journeyed from so far away, must have found such magic in a sweet scent or a violet shadow that it seemed a gate to Paradise which they could not forbear to enter. To be sure, they should have followed their captain's orders. That they did not, very nearly brought a tragedy upon them. The blame lay in his own lessening fervor, which they were beginning to reflect. Half devotion to the Gods was getting half protection in return.

"One evening as they straggled back," the Saga continues, "they found that Turker was missing. They felt sad, because they had grown to like Turker. Each man blamed himself. Leif berated them angrily, bidding them follow him at once in search of his missing Thrall. But they had scarcely set out when they saw Turker returning. They welcomed him warmly, but he seemed not to notice them, being greatly excited. When they asked him where he had been, he answered them in Turkish and pointed in the direction whence he had come. Leif seized him by the shoulders and shook him and after a few moments he regained his wits and said, in the Norse tongue, 'I thought I had returned to my country.' 'Why did you think that?' Leif asked him. 'Because,' he replied, 'I found a vine with grapes growing on it.' Early the next morning he led them to where he said he had found the vine, and it was true. There were many such, covered with huge clusters of grapes of a bluish-purple color. Leif turned to his men and said, 'Now we will name this land to which Thor has led us. Iceland was falsely named to keep Harold Fairhair away, though it produces much that is green. Greenland, too, was named falsely, to lure my father's enemies, though it produces little but ice. But this land shall be truly named, since none shall know of its existence but the Gods and ourselves, and its name shall tell what it really does produce. Let it be called Wineland.' "

There was much enthusiasm over this. In fact, there was ever-growing approval of everything he did or said. He was firmly fixed in the leadership he was eager to abandon, as in a trap. Only Turker could rescue him from it, Turker whom he had so nearly lost. He hastened to make sure of Turker, in the presence of all.

"A man proves his right to be free," he said, as if he had always thought so, "by showing more spirit and cleverness than a Thrall need have. Now I give my word, for all of you to witness, that I shall set Turker free—" A pleased murmur began, which he cut short with the word "but," said with great emphasis, so that Turker would mark the condition he imposed. "*But*—it shall be in such time and place as will let the whole world know it has been done. That is, when we raid the Orkneys!" A two-fold cheer went up for that: sentimental because of Turker, and hearty because of the Orkney women.

The Thrall looked as grateful and surprised as he could. When they had congratulated him and left and he was alone with the Sea-King, he vowed he would do anything on earth to merit such generosity. When the detailed plan for Eric's rescue was at last laid before him, he feigned amazement at its astuteness, giving no hint that he had long since guessed it and had a better plan of his own. His fervor was unstinted, eager, reckless.

"I love Eric like my own Atyl!" he declared, kissing his master's hand. "I would try to save him in any case, free or not. I thank you for giving me the chance!"

"Hold your zeal in check!" the Sea-King had to caution him. "It may cause suspicion."

Turker expressed humble thanks for this reprimand, promising to keep watch upon himself as relentlessly as upon an enemy. He swore secrecy and loyalty by all the Gods of the Norsemen and by his own country's Gods, too, and even invoked the strange Gods of the Bulgarians that he had worshipped in his youth. The only Divinity by whom he did not swear was Christ, because Christianity was his present true belief, on whose mystical help he counted to get these Icelanders' heads cut off.

In his own hut that night, he felt dissatisfied with the trap he was setting. He would get the Sea-King back to Iceland and into Olaf's hands, right enough, but what of the others? If he failed to bring all of them, Theobrand might take it as a pretext to deny him his freedom. All through the night he turned the problem inside out and by morning he had solved it.

He went to his master with what sounded like an improvement of their plan, simple and obvious, and a much surer way to rescue Eric. Its only drawback was that the Sea-King would have to tell the crew about it, and might fall a little in their esteem, through seeming to put his desires before theirs.

"That is easily mended," said Turker. "I will tell it."

And that night he did. When they were all gathered about the fire, he suddenly stated it, making no attempt to lead up to it gradually, but as if he had just thought of it.

"Instead of raiding the Orkneys," he said, "why don't we return to Iceland and do our raiding there?"

From the shocked silence with which this proposal was received, the Sea-King feared it had done so much harm that there was no chance of their getting anywhere near Iceland. He was sorry he had let it be said.

But Turker was the better judge. He was also the better tactician. He waited patiently for the men to get over their first abhorrence of attacking their own land. Then, instead of trying to retract and laugh it off—as the Sea-King was preparing to do—he vehemently set to work to prove that the idea was an excellent one. The fact that he was a little man, the shortest of them all by a head, helped him. He sprang to his feet and paced about in the firelight, gesticulatingly excitedly, looking like one of those gnomes in whom they all believed, who climbed out of holes in the earth and got inside a man's head by saying what was true. Atyl the Great was a dwarf. And Turker was standing, while the rest remained seated. For once they looked up, and he down.

"It is no longer your land!" he cried. "Stop thinking that it is! You have not the least part of it now! It is in the hands of renegades, all of it, every inch that once you owned. It is not peopled any longer by countrymen of yours. All the men in it, the women, the very babies and dogs, have become your enemies, servants of Olaf, ready to help him track you down. You owe nothing to the land or the people in it—nothing except a revenge that will give the Skalds something to make a new song about.

"What a revenge I offer you! What could humble them more, these proud ones who never yet were raided?

"And Olaf! Their King, their darling, their all! What could enrage him more! He himself is coming to Iceland: perhaps he is already there. Olaf the All-Wise, the All-Knowing! He is searching for us at this moment, on every sea, in every land—everywhere but on his own threshold. We will make him the jest of the world, to be laughed at until he falls in a fit upon the ground, and the foam pours out of his mouth and the Divine Right out of his ears!"

All were intent on Turker now, fascinated by his little figure that quivered passionately in the firelight and the two sparks in his black eyes.

"And the prizes to be won!" His voice rose enthusiastically. "They are beyond what has ever been gained in any raid, as the voyage you have made is beyond any voyage.

"Iceland, which never paid tribute while you were part of it, shall pay it now to you, who have become sons of Wineland.

"There will be gold, to be taken from rogues that you know have it. Much of it was your own gold, which they have laid hands upon. You will know where to look for it.

"There will be slaves. Those men who have done you wrongs can be seized and brought back here to serve you, especially the Christian Priest. He, who thought to have you cajoling him, bribing him, seeking his favor, shall have his ham-strings cut, so that he has to crawl about on your floors like a dog, and you will call him by a dog's name and throw him bones and slops to feed upon.

"Our Sea-King will get his son, and his wife, too, if he wants her.

"You will all get women. There have been women taken before this, in many a raid, but not such women as these. They will be those who denied themselves to you because they despised you, or because their families were saving them for some Christian toad of Olaf's. They would not be your wives in Iceland. They shall be your concubines in Wineland.

"For myself, I wish only to be worthy of my freedom, to know I shall have earned it by helping you, who have been as brothers to me."

He paused. There was a short silence, and then such a ringing cheer burst forth as not even the Sea-King had been given.

The gathering broke up after that, the men talking excitedly of the new plan as they went to their various quarters. Turker

153

was at peace with his soul. He would fulfill the conditions the Priest had set. All that remained was to contrive how he would slip away from them when they landed in Iceland and tell Theobrand they were there.

The next morning the Sea-King awoke with a feeling of jubilation. Turker's plan had won everyone over. There were many swords now, to help in the rescue of Eric. It was as good as done.

He gave orders to provision the ship, which was a simple task in that bounteous region, and left his men to their own practiced knowledge of making sure it was seaworthy. Then at last he was free for a while, to do what had been crying to be done, since the night they came to anchor in the channel.

What he wanted, above all, was to follow his old habit of walking alone, within that near-by wood, bringing along no thought of people or things, so that he might sense the spirit of the place and find out what was watching him from those deep, cool shadows.

He had never told his men of the eyes that he knew were following him, because there was no danger from the hidden watcher. He had a deep reason for knowing it was so. *This had happened to him once before.* When? Where? He could not recall it, however much he strove to probe the dark corners of his memory. But elusive though it was and whenever it had been, it was familiar and associated not with peril but with ecstasy.

Toward the wood then he walked, with the growing light of morning, to haunt his haunter. Or, rather, he let the wood draw him. The nearer he came to it, the stronger grew the sense of familiarity, until it almost sang.

Then, suddenly, as he stepped at last inside the leafy enclosure, he recognized the delicious memory he had been pursuing.

Freya. Every bit of green and brown bespoke her presence. Here was the very place for her to dwell—where surely she must—with all his old dreams about her like a garment. How well, how truly this forest and this moment would befit her!— as aptly as did that far-off time and spot where once he thought

154

he met her. Here was that same untouched solitude, the same tranquillity, that same remoteness from everything but thought, that same sacred depth of Nature that changes a forest or grove or valley into a temple. And oh, that same great silence, made more silent still by an occasional tiny rustle of leaves, like the rustle of a woman's dress. He saw the green moss that was her velvet cloak, and the blue and yellow flowers that were her eyes and hair. Of course, of course, she lived here now, as once she lived, for all the same reasons, in the meadow near his home.

It was a strange fancy for a man to have twice, especially a man with the sad experience of a first mistake. Freya had turned into poor, pitiful Helga, a mockery of the dream that made him love her, but had he chanced upon her now, he would have clasped her again in his arms and kissed her again and called her Freya again. It was Freya and his own youth that were haunting him, hand in hand. Back, years back, they pulled him, through this magic wood into which they had lured him, to an earlier day before he had grown old, before he had a wife or son, before he was a Sea-King, the day in which he searched the meadow, whispering, "Freya, I love you!" and had not yet happened upon the fatal secret called "knowing better." He knew neither better nor worse now, for the spell of timelessness was on him. He knew nothing at all; he only believed. His lips formed the words "Freya, I love you!" without his having told them to do so, and as he thought he saw a shadowy figure flit just beyond the range of his sight, he said it again, of his own accord, "Freya, Freya, Freya, I love you!" Then he heard a faint little rustling sound. It was not the leaves this time; it was a woman's dress. He knew it for what it was and turned toward it.

At such a moment, Helga had stepped into his view, with her yellow hair looking like the beams Freya casts when she is the noonday sun. Now it was the Wampanoag girl whom he saw, with her black hair and bronze face looking as Freya looks when she is the sunset turning into night. Feathers were her ornaments instead of flowers, and shells instead of silver, and her dress was the brown of earth and bark. One thing, though, was the same in the Wineland forest as in the Iceland meadow: Freya's eyes, though changed from blue to black, still looked with love upon the man she had been watching.

The girl knew he had seen her, and stood her ground as he came toward her. When they were close together, the past fully enveloped him. All that had happened since that other time was undone, seemed never to have been. Then and now were one. His arms encircled her now, as they had then. He kissed her now, as then, and called her Freya's names: Giver of Love, Most Gently Born of the Gods, Wearer of the Flaming Necklace, Freya.

In that wood, on that shore, in those shadows, he could not have acted differently. All primeval places from which the Gods have not yet been driven are, in spirit and atmosphere, alike. A true believer feels haunted in anyone of them.

XIX

ERIC'S mother had not been married a week before the boy understood that his family had become his father's enemies. He realized this through little things they said softly to each other when they thought he was absorbed in his toys. And, from the way the neighbors looked at him, he could see that the hostility was general.

Before he could adjust himself to this attitude, another new experience was thrust upon him. He became a pupil in a school that was founded by his new father. He was seven years old, and he heard them say it was time they started shaping his life. His fellow-students were the sons of Bonders who had heard tales of what was happening in the rest of Christendom and foresaw a future in which a Priest would have more power than a warrior. It seemed to them that their sons might somehow become Priests, too, if only they could gain some of that lore which Theobrand possessed. They wanted them taught the cryptic arts of reading and writing, to which they attributed the magical properties they had always thought were in Runes, and Latin, too, which sounded, since they did not know its meaning, like an incantation.

Eric did not like the school. He wanted to be with his father. But no one knew that. The Sea-King had been a better teacher than Theobrand could ever be. He had taught Eric guile. "Be like the wind. When it is quiet, no one knows when it will blow." He was furious because the guest-house—*his* guest-house—was turned into a classroom, but no one knew that either. It was the first change in the place which Theobrand had made. When he lectured, he sat in the Sea-King's High-Seat.

The school was of a very ancient sort, whose form had come to them through Greece and Galilee. Its pupils were called Disciples and its teacher was called the Master. It was late in reaching Iceland because the rest of Europe was so far away.

On the Continent, for several centuries, old Priests had been teaching what knowledge there was to young Priests, so that by now they had it all. The rest of mankind, except for an occasional King, wallowed in a Dark Age, dependent on their Churchmen for such information as they chose to dispense. This gave rise to a belief, strange for such a religious day, that because Churchmen were then the only men able to read the Bible, no one else should ever be allowed to, but should only hear about it, from them, forever.

Theobrand taught his young Disciples what he himself had learned from his Bishop: a little Latin, a little Logic, a little Arithmetic, a little Geography and a great deal of Holy Writ. The Latin was not the classic tongue of Caesar, but the polluted speech of Medieval Rome; the Logic stemmed from Aristotle, but concerned itself only with the manner in which one should think about God; the Arithmetic dealt with simple practical facts, like the collection of taxes or how many cheeses would stock the larder of an Abbey; the Geography described a world that was flat and round, like a plate, and which lay between Up, where Heaven was, and Down, where Hell was.

157

Holy Writ was complete, detailed, massive, to be learned and never questioned. They were taught a new word, which came from Greece: "heresy."

They also had much to unlearn. Theobrand explained to them that the Gods of Asgard were really Devils. He did not say they had no existence. That would have been too much to attempt so soon. He first sought only to disparage them.

"They have been defeated by our God because He is bigger and stronger than they are. He is the *great* God, the Divinity; we name Him that because there is a root in our sacred Latin language which means God: 'Div.' But Odin and Thor and Frey are only little Gods, whom we therefore call 'Div-ells.' How marvelous, this miracle which God has wrought with words, by which we recognize these demons as Diabolos, the great Tempters of Holy Writ! Shun them! Throw Holy Water on them! Make the Sacred Sign at them! If anyone says to you that Troll-rocks, or death-mounds or temple-pillars can cure wounds, he lies and you must curse him, though he be your own father. They are but stones and earth and wood. Miraculous cures can be worked only by touching this Cross or the bones of dead Saints."

To the little boys who had to sit quietly while they listened and learned, the school became a woeful burden as soon as its novelty wore off. They were the first of many thousands of little boys, who from then onward through musty centuries would chant Latin verbs indoors, and never, never again be able to give all their time to imagining a rock into a ship or themselves into Sea-Kings. Nothing would be left of that earlier school, wherein they had romped their way to an earlier form of knowledge, but little glimpses they might catch as they stared wistfully out at it through windows.

It seemed to Eric, during one of the Latin lessons, that Theobrand was taking a sort of mean pleasure in making him say:

Sum es est
Sum es est
Sum es est

over and over, far oftener than the other boys, though he thought he was saying it the same way they did. Theobrand was not doing it through malice. It had occurred to him, while Eric recited, that his brooding little face was very much like his father's, the man into whose place Theobrand had stepped. At that moment he felt his first dim, passing dissatisfaction with what he had done with his life, but he hurriedly assumed it was dissatisfaction with Eric's Latin, and made him say it again:

> Sum es est
> Sum es est
> Sum es est

That brought him another quick, uneasy daydream about what he had done, followed by another furtive questioning of his own wisdom and another reluctance to know what was annoying him.

"No," he said. "There is still something wrong. Again."

> Sum es est
> Sum es est
> Sum es est

The truth was growing in Theobrand's soul and he could not hide it forever. It was revealed to him suddenly.

He woke up beside Helga one morning, about a month after they were married, and realized that he had had enough of her. He saw, with the clarity of sudden surfeit, that his desires had been of the flesh. To a Pagan, such as he once was, that objection would have been unthinkable, for Pagans liked fleshly pleasure and never pretended it was anything else. Not so this advocate of the spirit. He could not admit that the claims of the body had any validity. He had to hate what he had been liking.

"I have sinned," he muttered. "I have let a Demon get into me."

That was a terrible disaster to bring upon oneself. Demons were whatever was liked by the Heathen, whether it was appetites or Gods. They were small and furry, with sharp claws, and flew down your throat when your mouth opened to utter evil. After that, whenever you had a sinful thought, such as lust or rage, you could hear the Demon gurgling within you. Atone, and drive him out!

While he thus translated into religious terms his anger against himself for being a fool, he knew, under all his twisted thinking, exactly what had happened. He had built up a mighty hunger in his years in a hermit's cave; Helga had eased it, but he had paid too high a price.

He added up the items, as if casting an account. He was the husband of a fading woman whom no one else would marry. He had doubtless made her pregnant, so that his child would have Eric for a half-brother—an odious tie. She was a simpleton, now that he looked at her without desire, who had just enough guile to trap another simpleton, like himself. She had brought him almost no dowry. Hardest of all to bear, if he had only waited for the coming of Olaf, that grateful King would have given him any wife he chose, as a reward for converting the island: an Earl's daughter or Olaf's own foster-sister in Novgorod. Fool, fool, fool! And scoundrel, too, for leaving the path of virtue, which would have led straight to Heaven. Well, someone would pay for it!—or, as he said it to himself while he lay beside Helga that morning, atonement must be made for the great sin that had been committed.

Thinking over this need for atonement, he decided that the sin was as much hers as his—more!—and that a large part of the penance must be done by her. Since they had been so eager to have him in their family, then this was their joint sin, to be visited on every member of it. Yes, please God, upon that son of hers! He remembered Helga's words, immediately before the wedding: "This is your new father, Eric." He laughed, though he did not know why he found it amusing, and almost waked her as he said aloud: "Very well, Eric my son. My sins are your sins, too. It is my duty to see that you suffer for them!"

In the pursuance of this duty, he found a new enthusiasm. He exacted the fullest atonement from both mother and son. Life in the household became a round of fasting, praying and personal revilement. They were made to say, so often that the sounds ceased to have any meaning, "It is my fault. It is my fault. It is my fault." When they asked what it was they had done, he told them darkly that they were especially evil in thus denying their sin. When their heads ached and their stomachs were sick from being long without food, he said it was Beelzebub refusing to depart from within them, and decreed more fasting still, to starve the Fiend out. They prayed until their knees were sore, and if they uttered the slightest complaining word, they must pray yet once again.

To do him a kind of justice, he was even more severe with himself than with them. He outprayed them, outfasted them, and in addition beat himself with a hazel rod, wood being what the Cross was made from. However, the effect on him and on them was not the same. Aside from his greater physical strength, he had a support which was denied them. He was reliving, avidly, his old ascetic life in the Scilly Islands, where he had been protected from the world.

Poor, simple Helga could not understand what had happened to him. His sudden, venomous onslaught took her by surprise. He so bedeviled her that she rushed about hysterically to do his bidding, only pausing now and then to worry about her son. At such times Theobrand would tell her it was for the sake of Eric's soul and add ominously that she had better save her own. Convinced that everything he said was true, because she loved him, she would let herself be reassured and tell Eric to do as his dear, new father said.

Eric's very presence mocked him. "It is my punishment that I have another man's leavings," he thought morosely. Eric's father had possessed Helga when she had youth and freshness; it passed from her in giving birth to Eric; Eric had it now; it leered at him when he saw Eric. The vitality which the boy had because he was seven years old was a galling reminder of a younger Helga, now forever beyond reach. He felt that Eric was being purged of sin when that wicked young glow began to fade and holy pallor to take its place.

Theobrand set him difficult mental exercises in addition to his heavy school-work. He ordered him to memorize Scripture passages of monstrous length, though it took all of a day and well into the night, nor was Eric allowed to sleep or even nod until he could repeat it all, without error. Then, sobbing and wracked, he would fall asleep, exhausted, and his mentor was gratified that the sacred text had been absorbed by this erring little soul.

But the dreams that came to the agonized sleeper might have alarmed Theobrand had he known of them. They were dreams of the endless tales of Scripture that had been learned, but only and always of those that dealt with killing. How Cain killed Abel. How Samson killed the Philistines. How Judith killed Holofernes. How the Angel of Death killed the first-born of Egypt. And at last, as if it were in Scripture, too, how Eric killed Theobrand. The boy remembered that dream when he awoke, thinking it was one of the tales he had memorized. But it confused him. He was not sure whether the story of how Eric killed Theobrand was something that had been done or something he was required to do. A personage named Odin had somehow got into it. He was no longer sure who Odin was. The new things he was being taught were driving the old ones out of his head. And he didn't want to do great amounts of remembering. He wanted to play, and they wouldn't let him.

He tricked everybody and played after all. It was a game which he thought he had invented. He called it Hating. The part of it that was really of his own making was the way he found time for it, without seeming to neglect his tasks. He managed to play secretly at hating Theobrand, even while he did his heavy penances and studied his heavy lessons. To do it well he had to learn a new trick: thinking of two things at once, so that one of them would not take up the whole time. He started by thinking the two thoughts alternately, using his Latin as one of them:

> Sum
> Es
> Est
> > I will kill him
> Summus
> Estis
> Sunt
> > with a spear.

> Eram
> Eras
> Erat
>> I will turn the spear around
> Eramus
> Eratis
> Erant
>> in the wound.

This did not wholly please him, because there was always a little pause where the two thoughts met. That made him seem to be taking a little longer with his lesson than was usual, bringing extra penances from his relentless schoolmaster. He could have given up his secret game, but he was a stubborn little boy, and learned instead to do the whole thing faster. He accomplished this by thinking the two alternating thoughts as if they were really one long one, but increasing the speed. That left the pauses out and took this kind of form:

> Cum Caesar in Gallia Citoriore esset I will let
> the pigs ut supra demonstravimus eat his face.

With practice there ceased to be any loss of time at all, and Theobrand had no idea what Eric was doing. But disaster was sure to follow such mixed thinking, as it did.

Theobrand always made a point of sarcastically holding him up to the other boys as a model of scholarship, calling on him to recite before them all, and then pouncing on the mistakes which too little sleep and too much work made inevitable. The joke was not lost on the others, because of their Master's ironical tone, and was made more delicious by Eric's being the butt in his own house.

His evil moment came when he was called upon, as an example of his extra-curricular industry, to recite the story of the destruction of Sodom and Gomorrah. His vagrant thoughts of hatred and revenge, on which he was secretly feasting, had at last summoned forth distinct memories of Odin, from whom hatred and revenge spring; and when Theobrand's sardonic voice suddenly smote him, things ran together and he told the tale thus: "The Lord said unto Lot, Caw, Caw, Hugin and

163

Munin, go now and take nothing with you, Caw, Caw, Caw, and look not back, lest you die. Die, die, die, with a spear in your heart. I give you to Odin!"

His horrified teacher stared at him for a breathless, unbelieving instant. Then as the other boys gave a delighted scream of laughter, he snatched him clear of the floor with one of his great hands, and slapping him viciously with the other, whisked him from the room. He carried him, flailing him all the way, to the room where Helga sat beside her tapestry frame, making pious pictures. "Here is your son!" he shouted, shoving him toward her so violently that Eric stumbled and almost fell. "He must be punished, so that he never repeats what he has just done!"

Helga, turning pale, asked what happened.

"A Demon has entered him!" cried Theobrand. His voice nearly broke, so full of fierce joy was he in having caught Eric in a sin. "He has dared," he said, "to join God's name with that of a Heathen Devil!" He pointed sternly at Eric. "He is your son!" he cried. "Beat him!"

Helga covered her face, trembling, and sobbed, "No!"

"You must!" he insisted. "It is your duty!"

She kept her hands on her face and went on saying "No!" She was a timid, gentle thing, who had never hit anyone. He pulled her hands down and said, "You must!" with his face close to hers, repeating it as she continued to say "No." Her voice grew weaker along with her will and she obeyed him at last, striking Eric a faint little blow. But it was a blow, faint or not, and all three of them knew it and became silent.

Eric spoke first. He looked straight into Theobrand's face and said, "My father will kill you!" With that, he began to cry and ran out of the room.

Theobrand was after him instantly, not in anger but in hope. If Leif was really returning—! Olaf's fleet would be here soon! If Eric knew, for certain—!

He caught up with him near the outer doorway, where the boy was standing on a chair, trying to lift a huge spear from its bracket on the wall. He put his arms about Eric, almost caressing him, and set him back on the floor. "Don't be angry at me," he said. "I was only playing games with you."

164

"I hate you!" sobbed Eric, squirming.

"You mustn't," said Theobrand. "Hatred is evil. Tell me, is your father really coming back? Tell Theobrand."

"Yes!" said Eric stoutly.

"Why are you so sure?" asked Theobrand, stroking his head.

"Because he loves me!" cried Eric, weeping. "And he is going to save me from you!"

Theobrand felt a great glow of comfort. It did stand to reason that the Sea-King would try to get his son. Then, oh, what a trap could be set, with Eric as bait, and nothing needed but to watch him! He patted both his shoulders gently, as if he were a little cake, and all but kissed him.

XX

IN reaching the magic shores of Wineland the Good, the Vikings had done much more than fight their way across leagues of water. They had wandered through time, too—wandered *backward*—returning through many centuries to an earlier era. In Wineland, the Stone Age still lived.

We who live in the tail-end of the Iron-Age have maligned that Age of Stone, making slanderous jokes about it, by which we feel superior. We pretend that it has been so named because its men stunned their sweethearts with stone clubs and dragged them by the hair to their stone caves. Now why should any man do that, when a willing sweetheart under the stars is so much more satisfactory? There is a theory that women liked it, but it is held only by men. Say rather, it was the age in which stone was the strongest, most trustworthy, most lasting thing known, the closest that one could get to eternity. Beside it, all else was measured and judged. Of it, you made what you hoped would endure, those basic things that daily saved your life: weapons, stoves or idols. In the end, that ever-present, necessary stone shaped your very thinking, and no vow was ever so binding or sincere as: "I will love you until that great boulder is no more!"

Among the Stone Age's best gifts to the world were its women, one of whom was the Wampanoag girl who had fallen in love with the Sea-King. Her name was an Indian word which meant "the flower with the sad face." It fit her startlingly well and must have been bestowed when she was fully grown and her character defined. Flowers were always the prettiest things to which men could liken women, though it would be a greater compliment to call flowers women. Her face was indubitably sad, the sadness being of a great gentleness, such as comes from knowing that everything, however lovely, will grow, bloom and fade.

She and all her tribe chose to hold certain beliefs which made life more agreeable, without questioning too deeply whether they were valid. For one thing, they believed in money. The currency was a bead, carved from an oyster shell, and sufficient amounts of it could buy anything that was wanted. In this they differed very little from the nations of Europe, with this exception: when a Wampanoag was low in funds, it was perfectly legal for him to gather oyster shells and carve himself a fortune. Care, persistence and workmanship gave the beads form and polish and were what made the difference between shell and money; this was understood by all and was why they set a value upon it. Those who liked to be thought wealthy wore long strings of it on their persons; since anyone could indulge in such snobbery, it did no harm.

They had another belief, which often accompanies the need for money: they believed in the immortality of the soul. That made them happy, so no one disagreed or insisted that they prove it. Had they needed a proof, however, there was one at hand to which they could have pointed. It was offered by the flowers. These, too, were thought to have a future life, since no Paradise would be complete without them, and the Heaven to which dead flowers went was visible. It was the rainbow.

Love, the girl had heard, was an illusion, but a very nice one, well worth encouraging in oneself. If enjoyed without confusion, it would yield ecstasy. If allowed to run its course and vanish if it wished, it need leave no horrid trail behind, but only very sweet memories. When the Sea-King put his arms about her, she knew they loved one another and was ready to enjoy her happiness as it passed by, which even at that moment she was sure it would. It was no gift of prophecy which she had, only a willingness to see, without bitterness, what the earth was really like, during the seventeen years she had been looking at it. Having seen, she was better able to pretend it was otherwise. Sometimes she did pretend and sometimes not, whichever she found more pleasant, and the result was that she always seemed a little more flowerlike and a little more sad.

In keeping with her self-deception, she never admitted to herself that her golden-haired lover from the sea was a man. When her companions exclaimed that the Vikings were Spirits of Light, she had only to let herself be a little more religious than usual, to accept it most fervently. She had never read that Stone Age classic, the Old Testament, but she had as deep reasons as her sisters of Canaan for believing that "the Angels came to Earth and found that the daughters of men were fair." Her greatest test of faith was when he kissed her. Kissing was a custom unknown to her people, wherefore she had none of the emotional habits we associate with kisses, by which they upset us. It only seemed that a stranger's lips were forcing her own apart without her consent, and she found that repellent. But as there instantly flashed through her mind the kind of creature this might really be, she hurriedly stopped thinking and abandoned herself to her feelings. She let him go on kissing her because it seemed to please him, and it pleased her to let him be pleased. Then his words flowed over her. She did not understand them, but their tone swept her away from things as they are, to the way they ought to be.

They met many times, there, in his sacred grove, and each time he spoke and she listened. He needed to tell her what she had meant to him while he was searching for her. After that he had to tell her the new meaning she had for him, now that he had found her. And aside from all meanings and shadows of

167

meanings that he was trying to convey to her, he had the compulsion to speech that comes upon any traveler at the end of a long journey. She felt no urgency to say anything. She was more timid than he, or less vain, which made her shrink from saying her poor words to a celestial being.

He never doubted that his silent Freya understood. She did, at first, while he was speaking of how he loved her, for then he used the ancient tone, look and gestures that men revert to in moments of passion, wherever they have been civilized. She was less able to understand him when he began to tell her the adventures he had had while finding his way to her. He momentarily forgot her then and spoke to the air, telling his Norse tale in his Norse tongue, with a bitter little smile of memory. All she could tell from this was that he was thinking about the past and that it somehow distressed him. She reached for his hand. That made him remember her with a start, and he went on to tell the rest of the tale directly to her, to lay it at her feet, he thought. He began to stress his own part in what had happened: his devotion, his persistence, his desperate decisions; and then she understood him again, having heard the braves of her own tribe speak that way. She knew he was boasting. But that was after they had met several times. By then she loved him so much that it did not matter to her whether he was man or spirit or both or neither.

When, a few years later, Good Lok lost his divinity and became mere good luck, he could still be proud of the heavenly gift he had bestowed on his favorite son. The Sea-King had been given what most men do not even know they want: happiness so complete that they have to admit they are satisfied. He could not believe that any other man in love was ever quite that lucky. He knew many, who he felt would admit that their lot was *nearly* perfect, but it seemed they stopped there, dwelling perversely on tiny, remote possibilities of improvement. Some of them had a hypocritical way of complaining while yet making it seem that they were dissatisfied only on their loved one's account: "If only I could give her the riches of the world!" Sometimes it was the reverse, though it served the same purpose: "If only we were poor, the better to be each other's solace!" Or, sometimes, with more frank discontent:

168

"If only she understood me!"—more rarely: "If only I understood her!" There were other small, carping complaints, of which he was unaware, because the men who held them never spoke them and almost never thought them; they appeared dimly when love was at its highest tide and ready to recede: "If only she were the least bit taller, or shorter, or lighter, or darker, or more outspoken, or more timid, or more something or other!" Lok had freed the Sea-King of all these objections, thereby making him the very luckiest man in all the world, really in all of two worlds. He was the one lover whose sweetheart gave him nothing whatsoever to grumble about, nor even to avoid grumbling about. He found her perfect, their love perfect, the time and place for it perfect. To him was given what has been called a madman's dream: a perfect marriage. He had sought it all his life and found it in the only way he could: by crossing an unknown ocean and returning to a forgotten age. The greatest possible adventure had yielded the greatest possible reward.

They would have been unreasonable to expect such a high level of ecstasy to remain forever. They might have found it unbearable. Yet, when the first warning of a change came, they were deeply saddened; she, despite expecting it, he, because he knew but had forgotten.

It was the ship which reminded them of what lay ahead. They saw it one day, being rowed from its harbor back into the channel and anchored there with its dragon's head looking out to sea. Then the man remembered his duty and his son; the girl remembered how he had walked from ship to shore and knew he would now walk back again and return to the place in the sea where the sun rises.

The crew had it well stored with provisions now, and seaworthy. They momentarily expected their captain to give the order to set sail. But days passed and the ship still rode at anchor. There was no thought of questioning him, for he had become infallible to them. They were sure he had a reason for the delay. So he had, a desperate, hopeless reason, impossible to explain to them or to anyone, or, for that matter, to himself. He was waiting, one day more, one day more, hoping that something would intervene and knowing that nothing could. He made his anguish worse by swearing he would return; he knew that the very making of the vow proved it was hard to fulfill. How could he be sure? His Paradise had been so hard to find, so strangely found, so nearly not found at all. Evil things without number could happen, would happen, in the wild bloody places he must visit, to keep him ever from returning. There would be the voyage back to eastward, a fight if any other ship should see them, another fight perhaps in rescuing Eric— Merely thinking of those distant deeds and places made Wineland seem remote, as if he had already left it and was now far away, remembering. The old man with the nine daughters was calling him again. The white arms of the sea-maidens reached out toward him from the green water. He shrank back, deeper into the embrace he loved.

XXI

TURKER had not the reasons for patience that let the rest of the crew wait endlessly. Their homes were here, beyond the edge of the world; his was in the Styrian mountains. He had already forced too much patience upon himself; he suddenly found it intolerable to sit here for a single extra second of his life, waiting upon his master's whim. Master? He, Turker, was master now, because he was so desperately needed. He owned the Sea-King, not the other way around, and resented this strange new hesitancy, deeming it a sort of rebellion. He determined to run the cause to earth and speed them all upon the way he had planned: himself to his freedom, his companions to their death.

Now he began to watch his master, taking care he did not

seem to be doing so, and became aware of the frequent lonely walks and the day-long absences. These had drawn no one's attention up to then, since the Sea-King's lifelong habit of thinking out problems during a solitary stroll was well known: it was held to be one source of his infallibility. Turker alone refused to accept this easy explanation, his fixed purpose letting him take nothing for granted. He re-examined each detail, to be certain he was seeing clearly. He thus enabled himself to notice that when his master's steps neared the wood, they quickened, in a way that did not bespeak the tranquillity of thought. He noticed, too, that the walks began earlier each day and ended later. Finally he followed him.

Keeping a long, safe distance between them, he crawled stealthily from rock to bush, choosing to lose sight of his quarry rather than be seen by him. He did lose sight of him the first few times, so overly cautious was he, but his skill grew with practice, until one day, having clung to him until they were well within the woods, he saw at last, and understood.

He had only one, swift glimpse, through an opening in the underbrush. Then he put his head down and lay flat upon the ground, listening, but fearing to look again lest he be seen, though man and girl were so intent upon each other that he could have been bolder and yet safe. In that instant he had seen how lovely the girl was, and a wave of bitter envy swept through him. When he heard the Sea-King's tender, desperate avowals, heard him swear that he would come back, that nothing should keep them apart, he knew the oath would be kept if it were possible for a man to keep it. Throughout the entire day he remained thus, wretched because of the cold ground, listening, envying and silent.

Only when night was at hand and the lovers had gone did he venture to return to camp. His absence had caused no alarm, because of his previous safe return. When they saw him approaching, it was assumed that he had been exploring again according to his own odd notions and would presently astonish them with whatever he had found. Turker was glad to let them think that, fostering their mistake with a wink and a sly smile, and was thus able to go undisturbed about his own vindictive business.

171

In his hut, brooding over what he had learned, it was the girl's beauty that continued to torment him. He would not let himself believe that she had bestowed herself on the man he so deeply hated. But since he had been contradicted in this by his own eyes, he consoled himself by deciding she was not human. The Sea-King had so decided, too, with the difference that he had made her more than human, a Goddess; his Thrall turned her into something less: a Troll, an Al, a Lamia, enchanting their leader by unholy spells, to halt their voyage and Olaf's sacred vengeance. The way to offset the sorcery was to kill the sorceress.

When his free companions had first begun to accept him as an equal and thought he could be trusted with weapons, he had made himself a bow and some arrows. The bow was of a strange design. It was shorter than the kind known to the Norse and English and it curved differently from theirs, turning back upon itself at the ends like the horns of the wild eastern ox. It was really meant to be used on horseback and had been imported into his native land from Cathay and Khorassan, where small strong horses carried the swift-riding marksmen who in time would sweep across Europe. The Icelanders smiled when they saw the dwarfish weapon, but Turker liked the feel of it even without a horse to ride, since it lessened his homesickness a little. It seemed to him now that Fate had guided his hand in shaping it, for its small size would let it be wielded freely amid the low-lying branches of the forest.

The arrow for his purpose needed to be an unusual one. This was no human being he was going to hunt. He bethought himself of his amulet: his silver crucifix that had been a ring on Thor's finger. Unsuspected by the Heathen in whose midst he lived, he had prayed to it secretly, as fervently as once he had to river-spirits or the moon, that it would help him square accounts with his captors. Now, as he prayed to it once again by the firelight in his hut, it seemed to gleam with more than its customary brightness, and he had his answer. He melted it, shaped it to a needle-sharp point and tipped an arrow with it. Then he was satisfied. No witch's spell could ward off that. He could not sleep, thinking of what it could do. The magic arrow delighted him. All through the night he gloated over it, admiring it, balancing it, saying fresh prayers to make it more potent.

Part of his prayer was that when he went to the lovers' meeting-place, the girl should be there alone. If she were not, he was prepared to try again and yet again until all was as he wished it. He was newly supplied with patience, the combined patience of the hunter and the zealot. He would have gone to the wood in the middle of the night and waited, to be sure at least that the Sea-King slept, but for fear of wild beasts that the darkness might hide.

With the very earliest glimmer of dawn he was out and away to the wood, so carefully and quietly that none of the camp's guards saw or heard him. He carried his bow, with his silver-tipped arrow ready for its magic target and his other arrows for anything else.

When he reached the spot where he had lain and listened the day before, he lay and listened again. For a long time, or what seemed a long time, he heard only the sounds of birds and small creatures, bestirring themselves to meet the day. He forced himself to be motionless, so as not to disturb them and have their cries of alarm signal his presence. Presently their twittering grew louder and more excited, which told him that someone was approaching.

Fright seized him, at the thought that the man and girl might be together and this time perhaps find him. He had a terrified impulse to kill them both, and dreamed swiftly and wildly of seizing command of the ship and sailing it into Olaf's arms. He had sense enough to stifle this plan, born of panic, remembering that his bargain with the Priest was to bring the Icelanders to him, not kill them; and a hasty look through the shrubbery showed him that his prayer was granted: the girl was alone.

He was trembling, so violently that his shaking hand could scarcely find the silver-tipped arrow. He managed to draw it from the quiver, setting it to the bow as he rose to his feet. He stepped toward her, aiming. The twigs cracked as he pressed through them, and she turned toward the sound with a glad cry, expecting her lover.

She stopped short, not in fear but in astonishment, to find

173

herself looking at death. She knew it was that, by the face of the man who brought it.

He still shivered, uncontrollably, throughout his whole body, but she was so near he could not miss. He let the arrow fly and heard the thud as it hit her bosom. For a moment she remained standing. They looked at each other, both of them feeling more of surprise than anything else, at what had happened. Then she fell, without a cry.

Turker's trembling suddenly ceased. He felt eased, light, oddly happy. It was not at all like having furthered his revenge; it felt more as if he had satisfied his desire. Without casting another look at her he stole back to camp, as cautiously and secretly as he had left. No one saw or heard him or knew he had been away, but he almost wished they had. His heart was bounding with joy. If he had dared to make any sound at all, he would have sung.

His pleasure was the more intense because he was safe. No one could possibly know who had killed her, if indeed any but the Sea-King knew she had ever been alive. The arrow was not of necessity his: it was feathered from one of the birds that made their homes there, the same whose plumage adorned the girl's own dress. Nor was he in any danger from the sorceress herself. His sacred amulet was in her heart, making her powerless to take vengeance on him, unable to cast any spell whatever on anyone, or to forestall their journey back to Christendom. In his hut, he lay down for the sleep he had forgone, justified, free of fear, calm.

Nonetheless, when the Sea-King found the dead girl, he knew at once who had killed her. That knowledge, by thrusting itself in the way of his pain, helped him bear it.

It was the story of Haakon and Kark that made him sure. It sprang to the surface of his consciousness, shouting the slayer's name. Turker! He hates you because you own him! Nothing can change that!

It had been madness to think that master and slave could be truly side by side, for whatever purpose. As he knelt beside her, he again saw the white-clad group of Thralls, whispering in the darkness outside his house. Turker. He would kill him, more dreadfully than anyone was ever killed—presently, presently. Now he clasped her stiffening hand and allowed himself no thought but of her.

His grief was not merely that of a man for a dead sweetheart. She was much more than a woman. She was the last Goddess, the last proof of a once great Faith, as he was its last worshipper, and hers.

Some men think, and even say, that they love as no man ever did before. Of the Sea-King it might at least be said that he loved as no man ever did after him. The changing world forbade it. Gods and people were thenceforth to be separated from one another, as aloof as the sky and earth which are their separate homes. Their difference, rather than their sameness, was to be what mattered, so much so that there would have to be Priests to explain them to each other. As to any possibility of love between them, it would only be of a mystical, unearthly kind, inconceivable to people who had none but human experience.

As she lay there she was as pallid as himself, looking much more like any dead woman than the Goddess he knew her to be. He drew the arrow from her heart, to keep forever, then kissed her and said good-bye, though he knew she could no longer hear him. None of the Gods could hear him. They were all dead, as he had long known in his soul. The great battle of Ragnarok had been lost; it was being fought when he crossed the Ocean and the Thing was held in Iceland to drive Odin and his kin from their thrones. The dearest of that bright host had fled to Wineland to await him: with her gone, he could no longer deny that the great Doom had fallen. The good-bye which he said to her and to all of them was forever. The worlds of here and hereafter alike held no promise of a future meeting. Valhall and Asgard were in ruins, and all the Heroes' ghosts without a home.

He covered her with a mound of earth and stones. In it he placed his sword, within reach of her hand, as ancient custom demanded, so that she could defend herself against whatever there might be. It was near nightfall by the time he completed the mound. In the air above it, he made the sign of Thor's

175

Hammer, not with any hope that it still had power, but for the sake of those old times in which he could never again live.

Then this last of the Heroes wept. He had given his Goddess her due. Now he grieved for his dead sweetheart. He well knew she was that, too. It should not be supposed that he was in any sense mad. He was a man who had been deeply religious and deeply in love.

One last, long look at the mound, and he turned his back upon it, thereby making it part of the past, and started toward camp where his men awaited his order to sail. Leaving the grove of trees behind him, he entered the modern age.

XXII

THE news for which Iceland had been waiting arrived at last. A messenger came from Norway to tell them that Olaf's fleet would bring him there in triumph within a fortnight.

Immediately Theobrand's persecution of his wife and stepson ceased. He still would have enjoyed what he called saving their souls, but the need to prepare a fitting reception for the royal visitor claimed his whole attention. As Olaf's ambassador and herald, the Bonders looked to him to take the lead in the great welcome. Without any official decision, by vote or otherwise, it was taken for granted that the feast would be at his house, and that there Iceland would formally acknowledge Olaf's overlordship.

Theobrand had another, somewhat personal reason for giving special heed to the occasion. Bishop Sigurd, who had ordained him and to whom he was accountable, had moved the seat of his bishopric from the Scilly Islands to Norway, because of that country's importance as the new Christian center of the North. Sigurd was coming to Iceland with Olaf.

This being the first feast held at the house since he became its head, comparisons were sure to be made between the bounty of Helga's second husband and that of her first. That, even more than the need for properly greeting his King and Bishop, drove him to wild extravagance. He determined to surpass the feast given by his predecessor, though it ruined him. This policy brought exasperation with it, for every detail suggested the corresponding taste and judgment of the Sea-King, until it seemed to be really he who was the host. Furthermore, the profligacy of the preparations ran Theobrand deeply into debt, which he had to assume personally, as the estate was not his to mortgage, but Eric's. He was reasonably sure he would clear himself of this financial burden, custom requiring Olaf to make costly gifts of gold in return for hospitality, but he still worried about the unforeseen, for the reason that it can occur.

Having no taste to guide him, but only nervousness, he bought everything which he thought might somehow add to the magnificence. He had golden presents made for all his guests, taking care there should be more than enough, so that the very wastefulness would be commented upon. The handsome old tapestries were supplemented by others newly purchased from a Normandy trader. Similar additions were made to the family tableware and to the drinking-horns, gold and silver ornamentation being used whenever it was in the least degree fitting, and sometimes when it was not. The most expert wood-carver in Iceland was put to work making a High-Seat for Olaf; the scrollwork depicted his victory over Dala-Gudbrand, with Olaf himself—that is, an idealized notion of him, since the artist had never seen him—standing with his foot on fallen Thor, and at the top a Cross, carefully calculated to be neither higher nor lower than the top of Olaf's head, but exactly at the same level. A companion piece was made for Sigurd: a High-Seat of precisely the same dimensions, but with nothing carved on it but a large Cross, the contrast emphasizing the single-minded idealism of the Church; Sigurd's chair was really the handsomer of the two. There were magnificent, matched horses to carry Olaf and his party from the ships to the house, with saddles and bridles inlaid with silver, and Sicilian brocades for the hangings on all the beds. New straw was laid upon the floor, and outside the door near the road a huge table was placed, on which there would be food and drink for any and all, whether invited or not.

He was undecided what sort of clothes he should wear on such an occasion, weighing two effects against each other: the splendor of the King's representative or the austerity of the Priest. Vanity won. The hose and kirtle which he ordered were of scarlet, with a belt in whose buckle great crystals were set, and about his shoulders he hung a cloak of deep blue, edged with fur and clasped at his neck with a golden chain. He had his hair combed out and let it hang down to his shoulders, while about his forehead was a thin gold circlet. For all that, his deep-set eyes, peering out of his passion-torn face, made him look like what he was: a Priest in disguise.

When the preparations were complete and as he had ordered, he was still uneasy. He remembered how he had first come to this hall and had coveted it for his King and his God. Now it was theirs, with all the island, and he wondered whether they would be grateful. Of his reward in Heaven he was sure, and reasonably sure of his Bishop's praise. For Olaf's gratitude he had to depend on hope and logic. It would surely be so—Why should it not be?—After all, he had earned it—Olaf could not fail to appreciate—and the like. He had gay moments in which he saw himself honored and rewarded, and pompous moments in which he reminded himself that Church and Crown were partners and Olaf could not do without him.

Ransacking the storehouse for anything ornate he might have overlooked, he found Red Eric's old High-Seat, with the effigy of Lok on its pillars. He had it placed at the table, for himself to sit in. Lok was a Heathen Demon, but on the bare chance that he still had any power, it might as well work for a good Christian.

Helga was extremely pleased to be a hostess again. The grateful activities, of ordering the servants about and making sure that invitations were sent, were so precisely what she craved that she at once forgot her recent ordeal.

Eric was summoned to Theobrand's presence and sternly

178

ordered to try, "as well as his evil little heart would let him," to be a credit to his family in the presence of their King, and in the meantime to study his lessons and keep out of the way. Thereafter he had the forgotten experience of being left to himself.

At first he thought it was a trick, and kept his gaze fixed on his parchments, so that Theobrand could not leap at him suddenly from some hiding place and berate him. When he remained unmolested, he did not know for a while what to do with his freedom. By habit, he actually did go back to reading his lessons, especially those favorite Scriptural tales which dealt with murder. But he realized at last that he had a chance to play his old games, of which he had been so long deprived. Still not certain whether he was being watched, he made a false start in a direction which he did not mean to follow. Then, finding that he was indeed alone, he went to the rock which had once been a ship and played at being its master. But the crew was not there and neither was the fun. Next he tried defying the Trolls, but that, too, was pointless without the companion who used to praise his bravery. All the old games proved disappointing, for they were not as he remembered them. He was thrown back at length upon the new game he had invented: hating Theobrand. He returned to the house and tried to lift the big spear from its wall bracket. After a while he found he was able to do so by balancing it in the middle of its haft. But he could carry it only by using both hands. Wielding it as a weapon was altogether beyond his strength, so he put it back. At that point he decided to return to his studies, in case he was being spied upon. He was found, reading industriously, by servants who came to get him measured for new clothes. As their real purpose might be tale-bearing, he pretended to object to the interruption.

The nervous strain which the great coming event caused in this little family was felt also in many others. Each Bonder in Iceland was either hoping or worrying, depending upon his particular nature, and his household duly rejoiced or suffered. All topics of conversation except what Olaf might or might not do when he came were passed over quickly. Presently they spoke of nothing else and were impatient with anyone who tried to. There was too much at stake, too many details to fret about, too many attitudes to consider. What was the best way to make a good impression on a King?—more important, a good second impression?—a good lasting impression? What sort of manner did Olaf probably prefer? What sort of men? What sort of women? Not only all talk, but all thinking, concerned itself solely with what Olaf might like and want and the best way to get it for him before someone else did. Olaf, Olaf, Olaf. Iceland prepared to abandon everything it had been, and be remade according to Olaf's whims.

The Bishop received much less attention, almost none at all. It was said and recognized that Cross and Sword were equal in the new state of things, but the Sword was what they understood.

An uninterrupted watch was kept on a hilltop, for the earliest possible sighting of the royal fleet. As days went by without Olaf appearing, the tension grew. More days passed than had been counted on as likely, and yet he did not come. The waiting became unendurable. There were many theories about the delay, many disputes in which tempers were lost. Theobrand was asked, as an authority, what he thought was the reason. He explained, loftily and patiently, like a great teacher to inquiring children, that affairs of state often take more time than even a King expects and that loyal subjects must have faith that it is for the general good. When he was asked again, and yet again, he became less patient, then annoyed and furious, then screamed at his questioners that they had better stop harassing him or they would regret it. He took to going to the hilltop himself for a look at the sea.

During his first day of watching there, the very fact that he was doing it himself filled him with smug confidence, as if the trouble had been that others did not really know how to watch.

During his second day, he was suddenly seized with a hideous vision. He saw himself, clad in rags, back in his cave in the Scilly Islands. It vanished almost at once, but left him shaken. That humble estate, which had contented him in the days of his innocence, was a horror when seen from the eminence he had attained. Thinking it over in bed that night, he realized that it had occurred because of a preposterous fear that Olaf might not come to Iceland.

Therefore when he returned to the hill for his third day's watch, he was as grim and unyielding toward himself as to any of the others. He tolerated no doubts. Olaf would arrive, soon. Every distant sea-bird was mistaken for a mast appearing over the horizon.

But another day passed, and another, and another, and still Olaf did not come to Iceland.

Olaf never came to Iceland.

They waited yet more days, before they found out why. That was when, instead of the vast fleet with which they had expected Olaf to overwhelm their eyes, only one vessel arrived, and on it was not Olaf, but Sigurd the Bishop. It was late at night when his ship was beached, and none were there to greet him, since it was taken for granted that the royal fleet would enter the harbor by day and not risk the dangers of an unknown coast in the dark. But Sigurd had his own reasons for haste. With a few of his men he came ashore at once, stopping at the first house they reached to ask where Theobrand lived, and then was on his way in the direction indicated before news got around that strangers had landed.

Theobrand was awakened by the sound of someone pounding on his front door and a vaguely familiar voice calling him by name. He leaped out of his bed, thinking a messenger had come to tell him that the royal fleet was sighted, and wondering confusedly as he rubbed the sleep out of his eyes why it was therefore night instead of day. He was putting on his clothes, still not fully awake, when a servant came to tell him that Bishop Sigurd and his men were waiting to see him. This roused him to frantic action. He gave orders to light the fire and the torches, and dressed himself as fast as his nervous hands would permit, cursing this sudden arrival which had caught him unaware after all. Not daring to keep Olaf, as he thought, waiting, he completed his attire less neatly than he would have wished and ran to the guest-hall, clasping his cloak about his neck as he did.

The servants had obeyed his orders. Torches and fire were

burning as he burst into the hall, with an apology ready on his lips. He stopped short with it unsaid when he saw no one but Sigurd and a half-dozen warriors. True, that was all the servants had said were there, but he had not taken it literally and expected all the King's party.

He and Sigurd regarded one another in silence for a moment and then the Bishop burst into a roar of laughter which amazed his men, since they knew the dire things he had come to tell Theobrand.

"My Brand of God is blazing like the sunset!" he cried. "Wait!" he commanded as Theobrand knelt to kiss his ring. "Turn around a few times and let me enjoy this sight." Theobrand, confused by the strange order, obeyed it; then the Bishop held out the great jewel for him to kiss, saying as he did, "Don't begrudge me my laughter. This is very likely the last pleasant moment that will ever be granted to me—and to you, too, my poor brother whom I should have left in peace in your safe, damp cave." He indicated with a wave of his hand that his attendants were to leave.

"Has the King come with you?" asked Theobrand, when they were alone.

"Only in my thoughts," replied Sigurd.

"He is following?" asked Theobrand.

"No."

"He has been detained in Norway?"

"He has been detained indeed, but not in Norway."

"Why, where is he then?"

"In Heaven or Hell," said Sigurd, "according to the way his deeds are being measured." He waited, watching Theobrand try to make some sense of this, and tnen, seeing by his sudden pallor that he was making more sense of it than was bearable, he said, "There, the point of the sword is in your heart; the rest won't hurt so much." A jug of wine stood on the great dining-table, with its attendant drinking-horns encircling it. Sigurd filled two of them and handed one to Theobrand, saying, "A little wine for your stomach's sake. Your stomach will need to be strong, my brother."

"It already feels as if its bottom has dropped out," said

182

Theobrand piteously, and sat. They drained their horns, refilled them, and the Bishop continued:

"You need not be told that it is more than pleasure that brings me to this utmost island of the world, at night, without the King. Not that I am without delight in seeing my Brand of God again, and knowing that he has not had to wait for Heaven to get some of his rewards."

Theobrand understood the mild censure and wished he were otherwise arrayed, but he was too disturbed to dwell on that. He only said, "I see that something grave must have happened."

"So grave," said Sigurd, leaning forward to impress it on him, "that the only place in all the Northland wherein our faith still has a sure hold—is here."

"In Iceland?" queried Theobrand, astonished.

"In only one part of Iceland. And in only part of that part. I mean *here*, in this house, in this room, at this table, in these two chairs."

"But there were so many—have they all—?" Theobrand could neither grasp it nor say it.

"The Lord giveth," replied the Bishop, "and in this case it may be Odin who taketh away." He crossed himself, feeling he had blasphemed.

"Have they—all—gone back to Odin?" Theobrand faltered. "I do not see how that can be. They seemed so ready to take the Faith."

"Not all. Not yet. Perhaps they never will." Sigurd adopted a more serious manner, fearing that his perverse levity, which was a sort of anchor for his own sanity, might be bringing terror to his Priest. "It will all turn out as God wills. In the meantime we, being human, must work with what we know. At this moment I am sure only of ourselves." He put strength and courage into his voice, for his own benefit as much as Theobrand's. "And we two shall be sufficient, if our faith is great! There was a time when Peter was alone, and yet he was sufficient."

"Amen!" murmured Theobrand, without conviction.

"Our numbers do not matter. There might have been two million, or two thousand, or two hundred, on whom we could count. We happen to be two, so two it is. Two million trees shall flower once again, from these two humble seeds."

"Amen," said Theobrand again. "But is the case as desperate as that?"

"You shall judge. Perhaps I am too despondent. When first I heard the unhappy news, I thought of you, Brand of God, and how it was my fault that you have stormy days ahead. As it unfolds itself to me—who am none too good a prophet—you will have to swim against the stream that has carried you. For myself, I shall try to mend our fences here and there and other places, as long as my men are willing to ferry me about. I hope everywhere to leave blocks of granite behind me, such as yourself, standing until the wind shall change again.

"Here, then, is what has happened. Without it, we should have been too easily triumphant, and vain.

"In that eternally damned Heathen religion which both of us once followed, we were told of a great battle that would be fought on the last day, in which Odin and his fellow-Demons were to be defeated."

"Yes," said Theobrand, "the battle of Ragnarok."

"Well," said Sigurd, "that battle has been fought, but it is now called the Battle of Svold and the Demons have won it. However, the difference ends there, for it may well be the last day, for you and me at least."

Another long drink, for his own stomach's sake, and Bishop Sigurd told his Priest the story of the Battle of Svold, which was the most famous sea-battle of what we call olden times, in which Christians fought like Heathen and Heathen like Christians, showing that at bottom there was very little difference between them, except that one of them won and the other lost.

184

XXIII

THOUGH the Bishop had buried his Heathen youth better than had Theobrand, he could not help enjoying the story as he told it, relishing the blood and blows and trickery to a degree that would have called forth his pious rebuke, had he observed it in others. He seemed to forget that what he was relating might be a death-sentence to himself and his listener.

"If Olaf had left the future of his throne to God," he said, "all would have gone well with him and his throne, too, for God would have seen to it that the best possible King would always be sitting upon it. But Olaf would have it sat upon only by someone of his own blood, and to that end began looking about for a wife to breed him a son. The King of Denmark offered him his sister, but Olaf called her a Heathen bitch, and that set the Danes against him. The King of Sweden offered him his daughter, but Olaf said she was too ugly to rouse a love-lust in any but horses, which the Swedes are known to sacrifice before their idols, and that set the Swedes against him. Many Norsemen were already against him, under the leadership of Earl Eric, son of Haakon whom Olaf drove to his death under the pigsty. The Earl and the two Kings put their three fleets together, the better to fight him, and their three heads together, the better to trick him.

"Just before he sailed, he was indeed wed, to a Christian maid named Thyre, but she tried to kill him with a bodkin on their wedding night, and it turned out that her Christianity was a fraud and she was the daughter of a slain Bonder, trying to avenge her father. Olaf had her head cut off, and sailed for

Iceland. I think an Iceland woman might have been his Queen, if he had ever got here.

"King Olaf's fleet was the greatest that ever sailed the Ocean. It filled the whole harbor of Nidaros, the ships lying so close together that a man could walk from shore to shore with no trouble beyond climbing over the rails. The largest but two was The Crane, the largest but one was The Little Serpent, and the largest of all was The Long Serpent, which rose like a mountain amid hills. If Olaf has done nothing else for Norway, he has left it the sight of that fleet, which will be described from father to son as long as men have eyes and the memory of what they saw with them, in Nidaros harbor.

"Now that there is no longer any King Olaf to hear us, or to have our words told him by spies, we may say without endangering our poor skins that this fleet was largely the child of his vanity. He had it in his mind to be the greatest King who ever lived on earth, rivaling Charlemagne and Constantine, whose example it seems had filled his heart not only with God, but alas, with envy, too. But besides serving his vanity, he had a clear and crafty purpose in building that mighty fleet, over and above the avowed aim of celebrating his entry into Iceland. This island was to have been the third jewel he would add to the crown of Norway, not the first. He meant, after setting sail, to alter his course suddenly, head for the Skagerrak and fall by surprise upon the Danes and Swedes in turn. The name by which he wanted to be known was Olaf, King of All the North by the Grace of God. I fear that the word 'Olaf' was the part of it he valued most.

"His three biggest ships, and the pride he took in them, were what wrecked his plan. The Crane, The Little Serpent and The Long Serpent were the undoing of Olaf as the tower of Babel was of its builders. They sailed last in the immense line, for the greater fear such a culmination would evoke in the beholder. The fleet sailed in a straight line down the coast, but these three, needing deeper water, had to take a longer way, around the Island of Svold, counting on their greater number of oarsmen to help them catch up with the others further on. It was on this roundabout course that Olaf's enemies reckoned, knowing the Northern waters as well as he did. They lay in wait for him in a cove that he would have to pass, ready to pounce upon his three ships with their three fleets.

"I was on my own ship, which was among those that went on straight ahead. A day later, when we began wondering why the Crane and the two Serpents had not rejoined us, we turned back to look for them and learned what had happened. Here is what was told to me, by a man we picked out of the water.

"While the Earl and the two Kings kept watch on a high point of land, a horseman came galloping to them from the other side of Svold and told them they had made a mistake and their prey had escaped them. Olaf's entire fleet had sailed by, he said, with hundreds of ships so huge that he could not tell which were the three they sought, but they were among them certainly and had evidently found it possible after all to steer safely through the inner waters. When the two Kings heard that, they turned on Earl Eric, accusing him of treachery, for the plan was his that they had followed, as he was the one who had seen the three great ships and was sure they needed the deeper water.

" 'We see now,' said King Svein Fork-Beard the Dane, 'that Earl Eric fears Olaf, and does not dare avenge his father's death.'

"The Swedish King, whose name is Olaf, too—Fat Olaf, his men call him, to mark him from the other—added his taunt. 'It shall be sung in every country in the world,' he said, 'that Haakon's son made us sit here with all our host, like frogs in a pond, because he feared he might meet his father's fate.'

"Earl Eric became enraged at this and answered them: 'The Danes and Swedes are very brave because no enemy is near. I suggest that we draw lots now, while you are still so full of heroism, to see who attacks The Long Serpent, for when you see it you will not be so eager.' They did as he proposed, more in scorn than any other way, and it was determined that the Dane should attack first, the Swede second, and Earl Eric third, if indeed by then The Long Serpent was still afloat.

"Just as they settled this, an immense ship came into sight, larger than any they had ever seen and larger than any the messenger had seen on the other side of the island. Instantly the two Kings admitted that Earl Eric had spoken the truth, and asked his pardon for their affront.

" 'The Long Serpent is even greater and grander than I thought it would be,' said Svein.

" 'It is worthy to be the bearer of our great enemy,' said Fat Olaf.

"They wanted to begin the attack, but Earl Eric laughed at them. 'The ship you see is The Crane,' he said. They doubted his word and were ready to believe he was the coward they had thought him, and that he was merely finding a new excuse for avoiding battle.

"But a moment later they saw an even larger ship following the first. It was only The Little Serpent, yet they made their same mistake once more, and again Eric laughed at them scornfully.

"Then fright suddenly seized them and it was the Earl's turn to taunt them, for a third ship appeared around the point, far larger than the first two combined, so immense that long after the prow had glided into view they were still waiting to see the stern. It was magnificent in its design, and so covered with ornament that the gleam of the sun upon it dazzled them, so that they found it hard to continue looking at it, while its reflection set the waves aglow and made it seem that another great golden ship were swimming below it. At its stem and stern were the mighty head and tail of the Giant snake that gave this greatest of ships its name.

" 'Now,' said Earl Eric, 'you are seeing The Long Serpent.'

"Their three fleets were so hidden by the headland that The Crane and The Little Serpent saw them before King Olaf could. The first two ships stopped rowing and waited for their King. He called across the water to ask why they waited. They shouted to him that their enemies were facing them in great force and urged him to put about and row full speed for safety.

"To that, King Olaf answered, 'Lower the sails and put out the oars to stop the ship. I will die before I will run. Tie our three ships together, side by side. We fight.' This Olaf was a man, my brother, such as we have seldom seen. All things that were loved and admired by the Heathen he did better than any, and did it against the Heathen.

"His orders were obeyed. The ships were lashed together, with The Long Serpent in the middle. At first the splicing was done so that its stern extended beyond the other two, but Olaf would not have it so. 'I will be first in battle, not last,' he said. The commander of the stem, Ulf Red-Beard, grumbled at this, saying there was a difference between courage and folly and that they could fight better if the three stems were side by side. Olaf heard this and said angrily, 'I did not know I had a coward aboard,' and aimed an arrow at Ulf. But Ulf was as brave as any man, and replied, 'Aim at your enemies! Before this day is ended, you will not think you have too many men of your own.' Olaf did not shoot the arrow.

"Olaf took his place on the highest deck. He wore a gilded helmet and carried a gilded shield, and over his mail he wore a kirtle of red silk. He wanted to be recognized by the enemy, so that the hardest fighting would come in his direction. Like his great fleet, this was no mere vanity: his example made each of his men a Berserk. They bit their shields and shouted to let the fight begin.

" 'Whose standard is that which floats above the nearest fleet?' Olaf asked. 'It is the Danish King, Svein,' was the answer. 'We will tie his forked beard in a knot,' said Olaf. Then he asked whose was the second fleet that waited some distance behind. 'That is Fat Olaf, the Swede,' a man told him. 'He shall eat a supper of fish tonight,' said Olaf. But when he asked about the third fleet and was told it was commanded by Haakon's son Eric, he made no jibe, but said, 'They will give us our hardest fight, for they are Norsemen.'

"The war-horns blew, the war-cry rose from both sides, and the battle of Svold began. It happened as Olaf had said it would. First Svein attacked, with sixty Danish ships, but his great numbers did not win for him. The three ships of Olaf stood higher out of the water than any the Danes had and showered arrows and darts upon them, which they did their best to return, but their best was not good enough. So much blood poured over the Danish decks and down their sides that it is said they looked as if they had been newly painted red. At last the Danes had their fill of this vultures' feast and withdrew, leaving their allies to carry on the fight while they bound their wounds and got fresh men from shore. But such of their arrows as had found their marks had done great harm, for Olaf could less well afford his losses than his many foes could theirs.

"Olaf was right, too, in his guess about how the fight with the Swedes would turn out, though he found it harder to prove. Fat Olaf and his men used grappling-hooks and tried to board the Norse ships, and it cost hard fighting and many deaths to beat them off. It was swords and axes this time, and those who were strong and clever enough to split a man into two even halves had a chance to show their skill. A great surprise was the courage of Fat Olaf. He was intent on fighting it out, sword against sword, with his namesake, and cut a path to him that brought them face to face. Then the two Olafs met, in what everyone agreed was the fiercest fight of all, and they showed such hatred of each other and such recklessness in satisfying it, that for a while the rest of the battle ceased, while all watched these two. Fat Olaf was in his berserk fury, and screamed that there should be only one Olaf, so that neither would need be called fat. His best weapon was that same mass of flesh that made him rage so; he hurled himself at his foeman and pressed him back against the rail by his very bulk. He had his sword to Olaf's ribs, and everyone thought to see it rammed home, when Olaf struck him a blow with his mailed elbow that sent him staggering back like a butchered ox. Olaf followed him before he could regain his balance, picked him up, fat and all, as if plucking a flower from a meadow, and tossed him over the rail back into his own ship, onto which he fell with such a crash that all thought it would sink. This so encouraged the Norsemen and so disheartened the Swedes, that the decks of the three Norse ships were soon cleared and the invaders sent scurrying after their Danish friends.

"It was Olaf's misfortune that his guess was also right about what would happen when they fought Earl Eric and his Norsemen. The Earl's ship was named The Beard, because it had a cluster of iron spikes projecting from its prow which indeed resembled a great black beard. These spikes had points, for ramming, and sharp edges, too, which could cut through ropes and rigging when driven against another vessel. When, as had been agreed upon, he entered the fight after the defeat of the

190

Danes and the Swedes, his first deed was to drive The Beard between The Long Serpent and The Little Serpent, cutting the ropes by which the two ships were held together and setting the smaller one adrift. The Earl then steered The Beard around to the other side of The Long Serpent and cut The Crane loose from it in the same manner. The two smaller vessels were at once surrounded by dozens of enemy ships from all three fleets, and were boarded, this time successfully, for it was no longer possible for men to jump down to their aid from the higher deck of The Long Serpent. It is said that King Olaf's warriors on The Long Serpent grew so furious that they tried to leap across the water to their comrades' aid, as if their very rage could carry them like wings. Many were drowned in this manner, being carried to the bottom by the weight of their mail and by their weapons, of which they would not let go.

"Then The Long Serpent and the men on it who yet remained alive were all that King Olaf had left to keep him on his throne. But these were a mighty force, for Olaf said to them, 'We need a hundred times as many men as we have, to win this fight. So each of us must become the equal of a hundred.' They heeded what he said and very nearly did it. Among the best was Einar Shield-Cleaver, the great bowman. As The Beard turned toward The Long Serpent, he shot at Earl Eric, who was sheltered by his men behind a wall of shields, keeping such a stream of arrows in the air that the Earl dared not step forth, but was a prisoner where he crouched. He had, aboard with him, a group of Laplanders, famous for their marksmanship, though none of them was the equal to Einar. They stood with their mouths open, marveling at his skill, until the Earl screamed at them, 'Stop gaping at that bowman, and shoot him!' Then they shot a cloud of arrows at Einar, one of which struck his huge bow as he was drawing it, and it split with a loud report like the ice cracking in the harbor when Winter ends. King Olaf heard the sound and asked, 'What was that which broke just now?' 'Your hold on Norway,' Einar answered.

"Then the Earl grappled The Beard and twenty other ships to The Long Serpent, and his men began climbing up the sides in such great numbers that, though many of them were slain, many others managed to reach the deck, and Olaf had too few

191

men left for them to be in all the places where they were needed, while those few were so exhausted that they could scarcely lift their swords to strike.

"All that remained at last of all The Long Serpent's crew were Olaf and half a dozen of his men. Earl Eric and his Norsemen closed in upon them, and though the defenders fought with greater bravery than ever was seen, even in this battle, they were driven back, step by step. One by one, King Olaf's last warriors were killed, each of them taking many lives before he gave his own. Kolbiorn the Skald died singing a mocking song about how many of them he had killed:

> " 'I empty my veins,
> And so do fifty Danes.
>
> My death-wound bleeds,
> And so do twenty Swedes.
>
> I end my course,
> And so do seven Norse.'

"And then only Olaf was left, with nothing to protect him any longer but his own sword and shield. He still aroused such terror that no one dared come near him. So Earl Eric formed a ring around him, of Danes, Swedes and his own traitor Norsemen. But Olaf made a rush, cut through them as if they were grass, and ran to the prow. Then he climbed, as he had once climbed up the Smalsarhorn, up the side of the great gilded serpent's head that formed the ship's stern. There he stood, high above the battle, for all the ships and all the men to see.

" 'Come down and fight!' screamed Earl Eric, and his men repeated it, yelping like wolves.

" 'No,' answered Olaf, 'I still am King, and it is I who call the tune. If you want to fight, you must come up here.' He was the only calm man of them all.

"Eric ordered his bowman to take aim at the King. 'Come down!' he ordered him again. 'There is a certain snug corner that I have been saving for you—a deep pit, under a pigsty!'

" 'I know a deeper place than that,' replied Olaf, and as the

192

arrows flew up toward him, he put his shield above his head and leaped into the water.

"They saw where the shield lay floating, and surrounded it with small boats. But when they snatched the shield from the waves, Olaf was not under it. They did not know, nor were they able to find out, whether he was drowned, or whether he swam under water a great distance and escaped. He was great in many ways, and swimming was one of them.

"And there the matter stands. Alive or dead, Olaf has left an uneasy world in his wake. He has lost Norway, and Iceland, too, if he ever had it, and whatever else he meant to lay his hands upon. Haakon's son has it now, and he has said he will change everything to what it was before, as if Olaf had never lived.

"But that he will not achieve. There is one thing he cannot undo, and from that you and I must take heart. Men have tasted what is new; the old will never again satisfy them."

XXIV

THE Bishop could stay in Iceland only a few days. He said, "God be with you!" to Theobrand; then, hoping he would prove stanch, sailed to other ports and other Priests, and presently to other Kings.

Theobrand's only comfort lay in that wish that God would be with him, for he now found himself in the deepest spiritual crisis of his life. His tragedy was that when he had become a Priest he had not ceased to be a man. Now that it was no longer possible for him to be both, they warred desperately within him, to see which would at last kill the other.

Whatever he was as a man, he was an honest Priest, and as such he fervently wanted to live up to his Bishop's adjuration and be a rock of the Faith. For that, he knew he would doubt-less get his throat cut, since the Bonders were already leaping back into Odin's lap. Neither persuasion nor reasoning would move them now. His best argument always had been Olaf's armed might, as theirs was now Earl Eric's. If he met them, it could only be in battle, for which he must rally such true be-lievers as he could find—But there he stopped. None but slaves would be his allies.

He still was Heathen enough to face death in a good sword-fight, but not Christian enough to trust a slave. He misjudged them, as the Sea-King had, as any master must misjudge a slave. It was beyond the reach of his mind to know that this time they would have been true. They would have fought. They might have won, and held the island for Christ. As he counted his several chances upon his beads, he could see only that he would be alone and betrayed, hunted through swamp and forest as Olaf once had been, as Olaf had later hunted Haakon, as Haakon's son would hunt him now.

One course lay open, but he did not want to see it, and marked off all the others first. "I might try this stratagem—or this—or this—" he mused, knowing that none of them would work, and then, trapped by his own logic, let himself come to it. "I might once more be a holy hermit, somewhere far away and unknown, amid simple fisherfolk. They would value my wisdom and bring food to my cave—"

Ah, no. He could not go back to that. He had sometimes thought wistfully of it, but he knew he had come too far, had changed too much and been bitten too deeply by success, ever again to be the simple soul he was. If he were now to sit in a damp, chilly cleft in a rock, he would have no holy thoughts there, but would listen always for echoes from across the Ocean, waiting crazily for a second miracle and a second Olaf. He looked about at the grandeur of the Sea-King's hall. Then his beads slipped through his fingers to the floor, and his tears followed them. With hands clasped—downward, for he could not face the sky—he prayed. It was his last prayer, and in it he made a choice of the way he would take. It was none of the ways he had examined in his beads, but another still: to be such a man as he really was, as honestly as he could.

His God was no mere concept to him, but very real, seated on a real throne on a real golden floor above the sky; so he tried earnestly to explain the choice he was making and why, and where he thought the blame lay.

"Lord, I can be Your Priest no longer. I have failed You. In my cave, I meant to serve You, and the glory of Your presence was as sunlight in my dark retreat. But You caused me to leave my cave and learn what life could be outside it. I have tasted fine food and drink, and I wear this splendid cloak about my shoulders and this golden circlet on my head. Forgive me, Lord, and pity me: I can never again do without these things, for the hermit of the cave is dead and the King's ambassador is sitting in his skin. Here will I stay, as long as I am able, come what will. Good-bye, dear Lord. Amen."

He exhaled deeply, and all of him that had been sanctified seemed to float away on his breath, leaving its human husk behind. He felt curiously empty, needing something to fill the unaccustomed gap within him. There was nothing at hand for this but wine. Bishop Sigurd had suggested, in kindness, that he take a little of it. That little soon grew into a great deal.

But there was no more help for the man than for the Priest. His personal woes pressed in upon him. He needed some way to get rid of his debts and, if possible, his family. His prestige was gone beyond regaining. The Bonders would not trust him, even if he offered to join them. They had too much old hatred for him; his head would be carried to Earl Eric as a proof of their new loyalty. Nothing was left but his solitary magnificence and his wine. For many days after the Bishop left, Theobrand did not stir out of doors. He ordered the fire and the torches replenished and sat in the great guest-hall, dressed in his finery, imagining as he grew drunker that Olaf still lived.

Despite himself, he had an ally: Helga. She broke in upon one of his sodden dreams and offered him her help. Her eyes were swollen from weeping over what had happened at Svold and how it hurt Theobrand's fortunes; but she had put her grief behind her and roused herself, out of and above her habitual meekness, to the point where she wanted to do battle. She tried to awaken him to action, to the fighting spirit she had first seen and admired in him, when he outfaced the Bonders at her husband's feast.

"You must stand against them all!" she exhorted. "You must preach the Word!" She was back in that night, forgetting what had happened since.

Theobrand turned his reddened eyes toward her and almost groaned. He ached with tiredness, from being pulled in many directions, by King, Bishop, Bonders, God and himself. Now she had come, too, to help pluck him apart. "The battle is lost," he said sullenly. "I can do nothing alone. Let me be in peace."

"What are their numbers," she cried, "against the fire of your speech? You will make them see the truth! You will shame them!"

As he looked at her, through the drunken haze with which he was surrounding himself, he began to hate her afresh and see plots where there were none. "You are eager to get me killed," he said, narrowing his eyes slyly.

She put that down to his drunkenness and tried to encourage him, declaring that she would stand beside him and if they died it would be together.

Theobrand shook his head stubbornly. "I shall die soon enough," he said, "with or without you. When your husband hears the news of Svold, he will come back."

"You are my husband."

"That is easily remedied," Theobrand sneered. "You cast off husbands as a snake does its skin."

"I love you," she answered, holding back her tears.

This irritated him. It was true and she was putting him unbearably in the wrong. To meet that he made himself more sarcastic and churlish. "You will make his homecoming very pleasant. You will hand over to him everything he once owned —his house, his hall, his farm, his son, and the trinkets and ornaments I have added as well, if he is willing to pay for them. You have been a faithful guardian for him. He may even be glad to have you back, with his other possessions. You seem very desirable, to a man who has been without women a long time."

196

She began shrinking back into her meek self. "I know you are tired of me," she said sadly.

"*Tired* of you? If I had never met you, I might have married Olaf's foster-sister."

"But Olaf is dead!"

"I know it!" he screamed. "And you take pleasure in reminding me of it!"

"That is not true," she protested weakly.

"Don't speak to me of truth!" he shouted, with his rage now in full sail. "I know the truth! I've preached it and I've heard it and I know it at sight. Every move you make is to remind me of what I want to forget—of what I might have been, but for you. You are filled with triumph, now that you have made me no better than yourself. What a fine, sly trick you and your father played on me! You foresaw that Olaf meant me to rule Iceland, and that I would have my choice of women, from among the noble, the beautiful—yes, and the young! You schemed and plotted and called me your guest, and made haste to tie me to you!"

To this mixture of partial truth and enraged distortion, Helga could only oppose the single truth on which she leaned, "But I love you," and could not understand why he did not see the immense difference that made.

"Do not think," he rushed on, "that you were the first woman I had seen, or could get. There were many, who used to come to my cave—beautiful women—more beautiful than you ever were!—They would place their hands in mine for comfort and ask my counsel, though never once did my soul yield to my body. I was strong then, before I knew you, before you destroyed me! I was a man of God!"

"But you still are!" cried Helga, bewildered. "And you must speak for God, now!"

"Speak for God, speak for God, speak for God," he jeered, mimicking her tone. "Why must I speak for God?"

"Someone must. In a moment like this—in such an hour of trial—if even a single voice is raised—"

"Why not your own, since you are so zealous?"

"Who would listen to me? I am no one."

"You are too modest. Have you forgotten?—you are a Saint!" He roared with laughter at that great joke of his.

"You once did call me that," said Helga gravely, "and because you said it, and because I love you, I promise you that if your lips are silenced, I will speak. I will say the splendid things you have said to me. I will carry them in my heart. I will remember. But while you are able—you, who have a gift of words—"

Theobrand turned from her with a contemptuous grunt and began drinking again. He drank a huge draught, much more than he wanted, because he knew she would be distressed to see him befuddling himself now. It was a relief to hide his face behind the big, two-handled cup and not have to meet her hateful, righteous eyes. He wished he had succeeded in keeping his rage at a high pitch. He would like to have thrown the wine in her face. There was no way of getting around to it now.

Helga saw his fingers tighten around the cup as he refilled it, and his look of hate gave her some sort of idea of what he was thinking. Then his face was hidden again by the cup as he tilted back his head to drain it. When he took it away, she was gone.

Before Helga fell in love with Theobrand, she had never felt very deeply about anything. That was fortunate for her, in such rapidly changing times, for she was thus able to throw away one idea and receive another with little discomfort. But when this man, whom she thought truth itself, had called her a Saint, her heart seized upon it. Absurd though it had seemed to him as he said it, to her it became a simple, sacred fact, to be believed humbly and without vanity, and of which she must always be worthy. Even now, as she left him swilling in the guest-hall, she had the memory of that exalted moment when, though he meant it for deceit, he had brought a purpose into her life.

XXV

THE news of the Battle of Svold spread quickly. Even while the Bishop had been telling it to Theobrand, the Bishop's men were telling it to Theobrand's house-servants, and the survivors of the battle were telling it to whoever had picked them out of the water. The victors boasted of it, their Skalds sang of it and their swords carved it on any Christian who refused to believe that God had let it happen.

Soon there was only one place where it was not known. That was on the ship which was bringing the Sea-King and his men back to Iceland. They alone, who never had accepted Olaf's rule, thought he still ruled.

As they put out from Wineland, it was the rowers who, facing the shore as they bent to the oars, were the last to see what they were leaving. The Sea-King, in his High-Seat in the stern, saw only water and horizon. He had, however, no reason to look back. What concerned him lay ahead, both in space and time,

He had a strange amount of courage for a man whose Gods had just died. There was very little left to him, by which many live. No more mystery. No more illusion. Only reality and the sudden chilling need to face it.

Perhaps he would have ended his life with his era, had he not possessed an unusual safeguard against that kind of despair. This was the ancient prophecy in which his Gods had predicted their own end.

For a religion which never preached humility, that was very humble. It was also very helpful. Through warning him that the new would one day surely slay the old, he was saved from being under an empty sky. In time, a soul as practical as his might even accept the strange, conquering God. For the moment, he was enabled to consider what he must do next, with no allies but other men, as had been done before there were Gods of any kind.

There was comfort in still having tasks. The tiller felt very real to his touch, and it was he and the crew—*and nothing else*—who were holding the ship to its course. And besides steering, there were two things which must be done, no matter who or what dwelt above the clouds. He must rescue his son and kill Turker.

Revenge in particular would be a grateful duty. There was no longer any reason to hold back from it. At last he had his grievance, to justify the trick that had stolen Turker's freedom. He could look his Thrall in the face now, without flinching, and plan how to kill him. Custom demanded that a murderer be slain by the nearest in kinship to the dead: surely by himself, who was in truth her husband. In Iceland the law said that murder could be paid for in gold, it being held that gold and blood were equal. But what gold could a Thrall have? And what vast amounts of it would there need to be, to pay for such blood as hers? By all the reckoning he knew, a life must pay here for a life.

These two aims, of rescue and revenge, served him in place of his old beliefs, as a source of fresh energy. They gave him an almost gleeful abandon, not unlike that he had felt as a boy, when he only played at being rescuer or avenger. He was able to set his men an example of endurance in the fight against the westward current that had been their friend. His voice was the loudest in their songs, he stayed awake longer and strove harder than any and evoked tremendous efforts with tales of the famous deeds of old times.

Through one of these tales he made certain that he was right in suspecting Turker of the murder, not merely seeking a victim on whom to vent the bitterness of his loss. It was the story of the five sons of Ragnar Lodbrok and the revenge they took on their father's slayer. Although the revenge was for the murder of a father instead of a wife, by sons instead of by a husband, upon an English King instead of upon a Turkish Thrall, it was revenge nonetheless and took many patient years to achieve, requiring the sons, among other tasks, to gain their victim's trust by founding the city of London. Their revenge at last was so complete that all five were satisfied. Their father had been slain for possession of a handsomely carved throne-chair, so now they bound their captive and made him judge a wood-carving contest among them; the one he declared the winner carved the blood-eagle on his back.

The Sea-King told this with his gaze fixed throughout upon Turker, to see whether he would turn pale or his forehead begin to sweat, never looking away from him for so much as a single word. When he had finished, the pallor and sweat were both seen, and Turker knew it, and though he explained that they were due to the excitement of the story and the vivid way it was told, his master knew the real cause, and Turker grew nervous, wondering whether he did. It was the first time the advantage of their positions had been reversed.

The whole of Turker's scheme, to deliver them all into Olaf's hands, did not suggest itself. The deepest plot a Thrall's mind seemed capable of forming was for an attempt on his master's life. So the Sea-King slept with his hand on a dagger, and then only at such times as he was sure Turker was already asleep.

He could not kill Turker aboard ship. That was not through fear of anything his men might say or think: they would accept anything their leader did. It was because of a promise, which had to be made good. He had told Turker he would free him.

"I give my word," he had said, "for all of you to witness—it shall be in such time and place as will let all the world know it—" He must keep his word, even though he must also kill Turker. Both had somehow to be done.

The problem did not trouble him. There was even a certain pleasure in thinking of fanciful ways it might be solved, and another pleasure in tormenting Turker in the meantime.

One morning, when they had been three or four days at sea, he told the crew he thought they were passing over the very spot where the great father of serpents, Ormungunder, lay on the bottom of the sea. He seized Turker by the collar, dragged him to the rail and made him look into the depths, shouting at him as he did, "Look! See where Thor flung the monster, long ago! There he lies, still hoping that men will be sacrificed to him, as once they were!" Turker was frightened, thinking he was about to be just such a sacrifice. Yet he dared not struggle, being unsure how much the Sea-King knew, and could not let it be seen that he had a reason to be afraid. His master held him thus for a moment, then released him, roaring with laughter all the while.

Soon afterward the Sea-King asked the crew's advice, about what he should do to Theobrand if he caught him. "This Priest has done me great wrongs," he said. "He has told my son that what I taught him was false, and turned my wife into a Christian under my roof." Then, turning to Turker, he said, "You, Turker, are—like the Priest—a foreigner to Iceland. What revenge can you suggest, that he would find most harrowing?"

Confused and upset, Turker replied uneasily, "A quick death might be the best," and then gave the weak reason that the avenger might be surprised by his victim's friends if he were too long about it. His companion's faces showed him that he was sounding too much like a Thrall again, so he hastily changed his answer. "Revenge itself," he said, "may not be as worth having as we suppose. What does it do, after all, but waste one's own time and effort?" Then he realized that he was sounding too much like a Christian, so he gave a loud laugh and pretended it had been a huge joke, to repay the one that had been played on him with Ormungunder. He proposed that when they landed they should all keep together, and make their first undertaking the rescue of Eric and the capture of Theobrand, who could be tortured at their leisure when they were back on the ship, and thus enliven the voyage back to Wineland.

This delighted the crew and restored their enthusiasm. Besides being a reward to their Sea-King for all he had done for them, it was so attractive that they would not consider any other course. Someone started chanting a bit of doggerel, in which they all joined, and by its rhythm they were able to row much more easily:

> The blood-eagle flaps his wings,
> And flies to the East
> To kill a Priest.

> Row to the East,
> Row to the Priest,
> To the East,
> To the Priest,
> To the vultures' feast,
> Row, row.

They were in such high spirits that the Sea-King did not tell them that the great Doom had fallen upon Odin and Thor and their kin. They would find it out for themselves when the time came. Until then, let them keep their glee, since it was getting them to Iceland the faster. He knew what they did not: that they could get revenge and treasure and women and honor and all else they valued, whether they did it in the name of the old Gods, or the new, or none. Those rewards awaited them in Iceland, and they were steering and rowing there through an ocean that was only an ocean, not a Giant who was plotting against them. He found a new pleasure and pride in pitting his mind and muscles against something that had none.

His men went on singing their song. So did he, with just as much fervor, but he had his own secret words to it:

> The blood-eagle flies to shore,
> To settle a score,
> For me, not Thor.

It was just at sunset, one day, that they at last caught sight of Iceland. It was very far away, a mere break in the horizon line, but they had seen it too often to be mistaken. There had been many trips before in which they had returned to it, though they had then been Icelanders coming home, not Winelanders come to raid.

They could not possibly be seen from shore, for their ship was too small and too far out at sea. If there were any lookouts —which, they reasoned, there would be if Olaf had not yet arrived—they would be scanning the East for him, not the West, whence no one ever came.

Following their time-honored raiding tactics, they waited beyond range of vision until dark, then raised their sail and pulled strongly for shore. If Olaf's fleet were in, it would be

203

in the harbor, so they headed instead for a cove about a mile to the west of it. Every inch of the coast was so familiar to them that the darkness was no hindrance, and they were able to reckon that they would beach their vessel a little after midnight.

That would leave them about five hours before people would be up and aware, in which time they must do what they had come for. So as not to waste any of it ashore in useless talk, the Sea-King now laid down the plan that they would follow when they landed.

"The instant we touch ground," he said, speaking softly (for voice can travel a great distance over water), "you are to pull the ship clear, but only so far as will let you push it quickly back, in case there should be need. The ten of you who pull the oars nearest the stern will stay behind to guard the ship. The rest will come with me. We will remain together as Turker suggested, going from place to place in force, to my house first. Such captives as we take are to be gagged and have their hands bound, and the six of you who pull the oars nearest the stem have the task of goading them to the ship with your sword-points. Of those we do not capture, none are to be left alive to give an alarm, and as we have agreed that we shall be among foes, old feelings need not stand in the way."

Then he read them Turker's death-warrant. He had it ready now, worked out to his liking.

"When we reach my house," he said, "I shall redeem a promise. With Theobrand and whoever is with him as witnesses, before we make them slaves or cut their throats, I shall set Turker free."

He quickly stopped the cheer they were about to give, lest it be heard ashore, and added silently, to himself, "And then shall Turker die!"

Such a death would pay for that other, in the Wineland forest. The Thrall must die bitterly, while he was first tasting his freedom and dreaming how to use it.

Turker's heart beat high. His master was planning something, but what it was he did not care. He had duped them all. They would stay together, like silly sheep, and he would run ahead of them in the darkness, to Theobrand. When they got there, a hundred Christian spears would await them in the shadows.

To shore they sped, Master and Thrall scheming to outwit each other, not knowing that Olaf had outwitted them both by drowning in the waters off the coast of Svold.

When they landed, the men at once went forward with the plan they had been given. They pulled the ship aground, just so far that its stern still floated, and the ten rear oarsmen stood guard about it. The rest set out, along the familiar ways they had never thought to walk again. The darkness was complete, without moon or stars, but their drawn swords were ready for whoever might chance to meet them.

The Sea-King wondered, as they went toward his house, how Theobrand would act when they caught him, whether as coward or martyr. Would he plead for his life and offer to renounce his faith, he who was so ruthless with other men's faiths?—or would he face them with brave contempt, believing what he believed, sure that he was on the winning side?

Turker had no trouble slipping away. The others had no reason to suspect he would, when he had his freedom to gain by staying with them. He almost laughed at them.

He stood still, letting them walk past him in the darkness. Then he left the path and ran toward the house by another way, so they should not hear his footsteps. He knew the country-side as his master never did. He knew where Thralls hid to avoid punishment, and where they kept their stolen bits of gold and silver with which some day to buy their freedom. He knew where a Thrall had buried a Freeman's body, and where he hid the knife he killed him with. The rocks and thickets were his secret friends. They knew him and helped him on his way.

As he raced toward Theobrand, his thoughts raced, too. His son, his home, his country—he was going to get them all back. They came nearer with each step.

When he reached the road outside the gate, he saw that a light was shining out from under the door of the guest-hall. Good. They were awake. No need to pull Theobrand out of bed and waste time making him understand. He climbed over the gate and hastened along the path to the door. He was full of his coming triumph. "They are here, all of them!" he would say to Theobrand. "Now, man of God, I claim the reward you promised!" He raised his hand to the great iron knocker and rapped boldly with it, as befit one who would soon be free.

The door did not open immediately and he fretted with every precious second. While he waited, he wondered why there were no guards. His heart sank with sudden fear that the Winelanders might have somehow got here before him and left no one alive. But then the door opened.

As he stepped inside, he did not see anyone and wondered who could have opened the door for him. It seemed to have been done by an invisible hand. He whirled about, thinking the person must be behind him. Still he saw no one. Then a voice, coming strangely from below, said, "Turker!"

He looked down, and saw Eric.

Old habits seized upon him. "Eric!" he said. "Why are you up so late?"

"There was no one to put me to bed."

"Where is your mother?"

"At my grandfather's house."

"Didn't she take you with her?"

"Yes, but I came back."

"Where are the servants?"

"They ran away."

"And left you here alone?"

"Oh no," said Eric gravely, "they left me with *him*." He pointed.

Turker looked, and saw for the first time that someone was sitting in a chair in the middle of the great hall. He hurried to him.

Turker had expected many men. He found only one, and that one was dead. The magnificent decorations, old and new, glittered and gleamed by the light of the fire and the many torches in their stanchions. In the very center of it all, in Red Eric's old High-Seat with the effigies of Lok on its pillars, sat Theobrand the Priest in his blue and scarlet clothes, with the fur cloak about his shoulders and the golden circlet about his

206

forehead. That he had not fallen or slumped was because he was pinned to the chair by the great spear which had hung in the bracket near the outer door. He must have been very drunk, and his slayer very persistent, for the heavy spear to have been forced through that far.

As Turker looked at him, unable or unwilling to realize what this meant to him, he heard Eric speaking.

"I gave him to Odin," said Eric proudly.

"You?" asked Turker, brought to his senses by horror.

"Yes," said Eric, and seemed to be waiting for praise.

Turker seized him by his little shoulders and shook him. "Why have you done this?" he cried. "I never harmed you! Why? Why?"

Eric did not understand this. "I gave him to Odin!" he repeated stoutly.

"There is no Odin!" Turker screamed at him frantically. "Christ has killed him! Only Christ lives! Christ and Olaf! Where is Olaf? Where is the King? He is waiting for me! I must see him!"

"You can't!" Eric answered, and began to cry because this was the first time Turker had ever been rough with him. "You know you can't!"

Turker heard the crunching sound of many feet coming up the path from the gate. *Running* feet. How quickly they had got here! They must have found that he was missing, and hurried after him. They knew. He could never trick them again.

Here was his last minute on earth, unless he could get Christian help. Summoning all the will he had left, he made himself speak gently to Eric.

"Why can't I see Olaf?" he asked.

"Because Odin has him, too," said Eric. "I thought everyone knew that."

It was true. Turker could see it was, by the boy's earnest little face, and his last spark of hope faded. He made an uncertain step forward, to bolt the door, but desisted. It swung open and the Sea-King came in, his men back of him.

All Turker wanted now was to make sure he would leave this life, in which everyone had cheated him, and reach a Heaven which he hoped would be more honest.

"Help!" he shouted, knowing there would be no answer.
"Help! The Heathen have come back!"

Then he faced them all, crossed himself and waited, as the
Sea-King came toward him with drawn sword, to free him.

XXVI

He will return, he will return,
   King Olaf is not dead,
The Heathen temple he will burn,
   And cleave the Heathen head,
And they who say they saw him drown,
   Their lie will have to own,
When Olaf wears again his crown,
   And sits upon his throne.

So sang the Thralls. They had been counting on Olaf to do
many strange and wonderful things for them against their
masters, far more than he really meant to do. They had prayed:
"Thy Kingdom come, on earth!" and thought Olaf would bring
it about. Now they wept, hid their daggers and their crucifixes,
believed and sang.

The women sorrowed, too. During Olaf's short reign, they
had acquired a deep piety which would not be shaken. They
also were Thralls, though without the name, and so received
no Christian sympathy for their more ancient bondage. But
they had heard that men were going to reckon all other men as
their brothers, from which it might be hoped they would
reckon all women as their sisters.

The men, feeling safe and superior as they crept back into
their familiar Heathenism, laughed at their wives for singing

208

the Thralls' song. Certain that the old ways were eternal because a battle had been won, they made up a little song of their own which mocked the other:

> If Olaf did not die,
> If they who say so, lie,
> Then tell me, Christian, why
>   Does he not come back to his Kingdom?

Helga's father, old Jatmund Jatmundson, sang it one morning, a week or so after the Winelanders had returned to Iceland. He was seated on his horse, riding to the Sea-King's house, and singing mainly because he hoped the song would please. There was no music in his heart, for his daughter was back in his lap. "It is unlikely that Fate will be kind to me a third time," he had said to his sons, "yet I can do no worse than fail."

That third time broke the charm, as followers of Lok know it often does. The trouble was that Jatmund, for all his shiftiness, could not match his swiftly changing times, nor had he the capacity to believe that one of the things that had changed was his daughter. To him she was still the meek, obedient, female child of his household, who at worst had an occasional flare-up of temper. She had scarcely ever taken a step without his say-so, and it was inconceivable that she could jump, for her own reasons, into a new epoch.

No sooner had he set out for the Sea-King's house, than her suspicion, which was one of her new and unsuspected traits, was awakened, and without too much effort and a minimum of guile, she got the truth out of her brother Gorm. Instantly, with raging clarity, she foresaw how her father would try to cajole the Sea-King: by belittling Theobrand, mocking his weakness, and scoffing at all that had happened as the whim of an empty-headed girl. She dashed away from her astonished brother, leaped onto a horse and galloped after her father, determined that no such mockery should be made of her dearest memories, no matter what lie she must tell to offset it.

The Sea-King was coming out through his front gate, holding Eric by the hand, when he heard Jatmund singing and recognized him. He smiled, a bit grimly, having heard what Jatmund had done in his absence and how he did it.

"You sang a different song a while ago," he said, as the old man greeted him.

"I was wrong and hasty," said Jatmund, dismounting.

"Perhaps you are again."

"Not unless Olaf rises from the waves and all his warriors with him."

"And if I told you that Olaf lives?"

Jatmund was startled by the suggestion, and not unready to believe it. The Sea-King was a great Hero now, the man who had stood almost alone on the side of the Aesir and made a mighty voyage in their behalf. His words, however strange, should be heeded.

"Is Olaf still alive? Do you know it, for a fact?"

"Olaf is more alive than those who killed him. That is a riddle, such as Odin used to ask. You, who once more believe in Odin, should guess the meaning."

"You are not a Christian, are you?" asked Jatmund quickly, then lowered his voice, though only Eric was near. "If you have news that others have not, then perhaps you and I could be the first—"

"I am not a Christian. I am not sure what I am. Whatever it may be, it is not something I put off and on like a shirt." Looking at him directly, he asked, "Surely you have come here to ask me something more than where to aim your prayers?"

"Yes," said Jatmund, seeing he could not get to it gracefully. "Helga. After all, she is Eric's mother."

"That is true. She may see him when she likes, and he may visit her. I shall not prevent it." He turned away abruptly, taking Eric with him, and started toward the harbor, where the ship was about to leave for Wineland to bring back those who had been left there.

Jatmund found himself following them, bargaining ignominiously. "If I may tell her you forgive her—"

"There is no need. I bear her no ill will."

"You are right!" exclaimed Jatmund. "What is past, is past. What if she did think she loved the Priest? She always was light-minded—and he is dead—"

210

"She loved him and he is dead. I do not think she is light-minded now."

"Then may I tell her that you will see her?"

The Sea-King stopped walking. "You may tell her that I understand her sorrow. Tell her, too, that if her life becomes too wretched in her father's house, she may always find shelter from the rain under my roof." He waited silently, until it became clear he wanted the visit to end.

Jatmund took the hint and turned to remount his horse. But even as his foot touched the stirrup, Helga came riding into view, not at the slow, reluctant canter with which Jatmund had come, but galloping furiously, like a Death-Maiden from Odin's hall, with her yellow hair streaming behind her and her eyes blazing with such anger as they had never seen in her or thought she was capable of having. She reined up her horse when she was close upon them, and while her father silently cursed her brothers for not keeping their mouths shut, she ignored him and addressed herself to the Sea-King.

"I did not tell my father to come to you!" she cried. "You owe me nothing and I want nothing of you!"

Jatmund saw the little he had achieved about to be undone. He tried to calm her and get her away. "You need not have come, my dear," he said, forcing his lips into a paternal smile. "We have just had a friendly talk about your future. I have been entrusted with certain messages to you, and on the way home—" He took hold of her horse's rein, as if to lead her away.

Helga turned upon him swiftly and brought her riding-whip down upon his hand, so that he snatched it away, more with astonishment than pain. "My future is in other hands than yours!" she said sharply.

Her father turned toward the Sea-King and tried to laugh. "She means her God," he said. "One would think the Battle of Svold had never been fought—that her Priest was still alive—"

"There will be other battles, and other Priests," Helga replied. "Do you think that Olaf's God was drowned with him? This is no wooden idol which you are mocking, that can have its gold and silver stripped off and be chopped up for fire-wood. A light has shone upon the world and will shine again."

"You have become something of a Priest yourself," her

ture and relics of the Norsemen, fully illustrated and divided into categories.

John Beveridge, in *The Olaf Sagas* (on page 100), weighs the question of whether the tale of Leif Ericsson's voyage was a later interpolation in one of the Sagas, and the degree of our credulity to which it is entitled. On this point, the "Viking Tower" at Newport was, according to Henry W. Longfellow, known in his youth as "the old mill"; and a Runic stone has been found as far west as Minnesota which experts have pronounced both a hoax and authentic.

H. G. Wells: *Crux Ansata* summarizes Church policy, including the period of Charlemagne's reign and that following.

Encyclopedia Britannica: article on "Celibacy" discusses the early right of Priests to marry, and when and why it was revoked.

Henry Goddard Leach: *A Pageant of Old Scandinavia* (Princeton University Press) presents scenes from Norse life via selections from its literature, and from descriptions in the literature of other, contemporary nations.

H.M.